ENTER THE BARDO

PEMA WANGCHUK

BLUEROSE PUBLISHERS
India | U.K.

Copyright © Pema Wangchuk 2024

All rights reserved by author. No part of this publication may be reproduced, stored in a retrieval system or transmitted in any form or by any means, electronic, mechanical, photocopying, recording or otherwise, without the prior permission of the author. Although every precaution has been taken to verify the accuracy of the information contained herein, the publisher assume no responsibility for any errors or omissions. No liability is assumed for damages that may result from the use of information contained within.

BlueRose Publishers takes no responsibility for any damages, losses, or liabilities that may arise from the use or misuse of the information, products, or services provided in this publication.

For permissions requests or inquiries regarding this publication, please contact:

BLUEROSE PUBLISHERS
www.BlueRoseONE.com
info@bluerosepublishers.com
+91 8882 898 898
+4407342408967

ISBN: 978-93-5989-220-7

Cover Design: Norden Wangchuk Lepcha
Typesetting: Namrata Saini

First Edition: November 2024

ACKNOWLEDGEMENTS

I still remember my first sincere stint as a writer where I was called upon by a dear friend to write for his humble website Rock the Hills...The site dealt with everything musical and the readers were consistently greeted by an assortment of weekly articles,a compendium if you will, relating to bands and music from the world over...It was the first humble effort to further the goal of reading and writing on a digital platform...Rock Street Journal , the then monthly rock magazine with it's musings on gigs,events and bands from India as well as the world was 'struggling against the tide' because of some unfortunate event(the ones who know will know)...therefore the website kind of filled the void that was much needed at that time, at least for the reading population...An effort to restore the past glory of the site also atrophied (the scrawls and parchments collecting digital dust),probably wilting due to humanity succumbing to it's twin vulnerabilities...that is acute torpor and laziness...

Therefore at the outset,I'd like to thank all the readers who ensured the success of the website...The readers who reached out and urged me to scribble more...It was during that time that the first seed,the idea of writing something more substantial was sown and I kept hacking away at the keys after that...Big thank you to all the caretakers and monks of the monasteries all over Sikkim for giving a detailed tour and shedding light on various Thangkhas and murals...It was divine education...A big thank you to Anum Norden #Shakalaka, for his 'paintmanship' (if there's such a word) for his bold usage of colours and flamboyant artistry straddling the entire real estate of the book cover...Any artist worth his salt shall agree to his craftsmanship...Another special mention must be Dr.Brian Weiss, celebrated psychiatrist,a graduate of Columbia and Yale Medical School whose works like Many Lives Many Masters & Only Love is Real inspired and added a new dimension to my craft...Also Graham Coleman whose English translation of The Tibetan Book of the Dead added to the research... A special mention to the folks and blokes at BlueRose Publishing viz, Misses Rashika, Shruti, Janvi,Mansi,Jasleen,Shreya(the in-house editor) and Mr.Sameer for their words of guidance and help through the wilderness of publishing and beyond...

They say writing is a cathartic experience and it has been true for me as well...Without sounding biblical,the experience was also a fleeting sojourn for me into the purgatorial realm,wherein during the exercise,various demons and dark energies in the purgatory were faced,slayed and excorcised...Not to lay emphasis on the phrase that 'Life imitates Art',but some measure of experience maketh your writings as espoused by the Late great Nepali litterateur Indra Bahadur Rai in Aaja Ramita Cha...

To my family,my creators my parents who ensured not only the best education for me but also instilled values that maketh a man(to complete the proverbial line)...A big thank you to my brother Agya Tseten (Zlatan) for gifting me brotherhood and friendship,two valuable gifts inherent in us throughout the ages and time before our birth...To my club Denzong Dragons FC,the entity that keeps me sane, and the dedicated fanatics who have ensured the club's existence and success (p.s. we need to do more)...To the Chokra Boys,my equals,my betters (Batch of 2003,geographically scattered the world over) for teaching me love and sincere competition and for always being there...You boys have shown and proved that the most important thing in life is showing up no matter what...something which should be humanity's credo...

Thank you to my mentor and teacher, Sir Prabin for guiding me constantly...Although our discussions are more on shoes(now I can discern a Balmoral from a Blucher), Vinyls, Turntables, State of Affairs than books, but I believe any knowledge is important and valuable and through other things I've learned more about life and writing...Monk is Shoes,Jazz and Liquor (correct me if I'm wrong Sir)...

Sir I hope there is reduced 'school boyish awkwardness', now that I've, through practice, tried to 'purge' the writings of such sacrilege...

Finally I would like to thank every reader in whose minds the words of my craft shall echo and in the process expand your old rusty cranium (haha)...Time for you to Enter the Bardo...

To my Amla & Apala for being my source of

Strength, morals and power,

To Sonamla, to whom I owe a debt past telling, now

more than ever,

And always to the beauty, divinity and enigma of my

Kinnae...Guru Padmasambhava...

Although there are references to places and monasteries mentioned in the book, they are just incidental to the plot and not real...However the existence of some hallowed societies and practices is real...This is purely a work of fiction, far removed from reality and the narrative tries to blur the line between the two...A suspension of disbelief, if you will...

'...I somehow feel a sense of excitement when I think about the experience of death...At the same time though, sometimes I do wonder whether or not I will really be able to fully utilize my own preparatory practices when the actual moment of death comes...'

Commentary by His Holiness, the XIV Dalai Lama,
On The Tibetan Book of the Dead,
By Graham Coleman...

PROLOGUE

The deserted monastery's vast space was dimly lit by twin street lights on opposite ends. Whistling winds stole into the temple premises akin to an ancient vengeful spirit,hell bent on expending demonic terror and carnage in it's wake...

Dawn was approaching. . . *'I have to finish the task soon before day breaks'*, thought the killer panting and heaving towards a tiny moving frame a few yards ahead, that flitted and inched away every time the killer got close. Its gazelle-like meandering moves confused the predator.

'I don't know why?' thought the little boy as he evaded a sudden lunge from the dark figure behind him. His tiny multiple steps combined with the least traction that his new pair of shoes provided did little help. A big gash on his head now squirted blood as he ran for his life.

Shortly before, Tuolku Tenzing Wangchuk, the newly recognized monk, had completed his evening prayers and was socializing with his peers and seniors in the Gompa. Suddenly, he was called to perform impromptu rituals outside the monastery.

Young Tenzing despite being a five year old since recognition, had been in a boot camp for the past two years as an unwilling initiate into the arcane world of Buddhism and its philosophy, its teaching of the dharma and mysticism. Being the recognised Boddhisattva, his task was now cut out for him. *It was an onerous privilege.* Tasked with serving all sentient beings, to teach them the way of compassion and enlightenment.

He cherished the invaluable knowledge passed down by the ancients, considering it precious and sacred. He was being groomed for a life of spiritual responsibility, tasked with propagating the teachings of dharma to end suffering and the cycle of rebirth, ultimately striving for Buddhahood—*the ultimate aim.* He therefore, had to be schooled first. And thus, his life here in the monastery. It was a rare privilege, something that wasn't lost on this innocent sacred child, who felt a deep-seated pride in his sacred calling. A pride though devoid of any worldly conceit.

Having to leave his family, his friends and his old life behind at the tender age of three, Tenzing had readied himself for a life dedicated to the dharma. Tenzing had been uprooted from his domestic milieu at a tender age and the perennially chanted refrain, *'I take refuge in the*

Buddha, Dharma and the Sangha' had been his ultimate credo. Still life in its infancy, Tenzing had strange miraculous visitations and inexplicable bursts of coherent babble relating to something, some incidents, random as it may seem, but as randomly linked to his previous life. In time, his parents, bewildered by their son's incoherent ramblings and baby babbling, detected an uncanny essence in the strains and syllables. Their Buddhist intuition led them to seek the counsel of a head monk in the nearby monastery. The head abbot had contacted the Nechung oracle, the institution handling such matters. The news of the initiation itself had garnered such fare and fandom for Tenzing and his family that they were overnight celebrities in their village.

A series of tests had followed, and he had come out successful. He had been recognised as a higher lama of the Kagyu lineage. . .

Thus, the normal life of a child had now been consigned to a devoted regime of study and practice of Buddhism and its teachings. The routine at the monastery had been a strenuous one. From early morning meditation, learning the art of the recitation of mantras while interpreting them to their sincere meanings, to contemplating life and trying to answer about its purpose at such a tender age seemed difficult for the three-year-old.

But, having overcome the initial inertia associated with such exercises, Tenzing breezed through such a quotidian practice. Extempore nocturnal retreats to adjacent holy caves and Chortens, and even occasionally at the local charnel grounds, he observed, were the most difficult of all exercises. His youthful and inexperienced mind absorbed the totality of these retreats, formed by the tutelage of his chamberlain and young entrants, his contemporaries, and his pals. All of his fears and anxieties had been tried, and he had shown to be an honest and wise Dharma learner.

Tenzing ambled outside the gates sporting his brand new Tsomba gifted by the monastery. His desire to keep admiring the ornate stitches on his boots was evident from his actions of lifting his robe every time he took a step forward. Even a teeny glance in such mild illumination satisfied him.

'Tenzing', his young cohort, had called him outside the Gompa after the prayer sessions. Realizing it would be another one of those meditative retreats, the young Rinpoche had prepared himself well. *'It must be one of those retreats*, he thought as he tried to run his mind through the things he might be expected to do.

In his playful gait and relishing his new Tibetan boots gifted to him by the monastery the day before, young Tenzing reached the center of the space outside the Gompa.

'Tulku Tenzing', a tired, albeit clear voice from behind the darkness, called him. The figure inched slowly closer towards the newly selected incarnate. From the shadows, the figure emerged and came into full view.

Though surprised by this unexpected visitation, Tenzing's hands folded automatically. 'Tashi Delek la,' he greeted. His body bent double into a deep, reverential bow.

Tenzing smiled at the figure. A little conversation ensued between the two and the young Tulku was quick to sense that something was amiss. *I'm pretty sure it isn't about the retreat,* ' the young Tulku was quick to know.

'I think I better go and catch some sleep, ' Tenzing said and turned quickly to begin his dash for the monastery.

'Without warning, a huge blow was directed at him and thundered on the little boy's head. Tenzing felt a stabbing pain radiating from within his skull. Yet his legs out of their own independent volition kept him going. The assailant lunged after him, the movements encumbered by age and the heavy sagging robes.

In an instant, holding his head, the young Tulku made a dash towards the Gompa with the killer in tow speeding behind him.

The child's surprised burst in speed had caught the killer off guard and the heavy robe and the chase after had given the child the kinetic edge. But the killer was nearing him.

'Not so fast' the killer breathed menacingly and used all the might to clutch at the flailing robes of the young Tulku in determined desperation.

'A few inches away from the monastery and I'll have made it,' the young child thought in his tired despair and distress.

'I am almost there. ' Two huge hands pincered and engulfed the tiny body from behind and the momentum turned the figure's lunge into a tackle so rough, their bodies skidded across the gravel, the rough stones lacerating their skins.

Each inch that he was dragged along took him further and further away from the monastery, from his friends. . . his family. . . and indeed his very life. . .

****

The cobbled path leading to the Zurphu monastery scraped vigorously as a dark wooded figure dragged the limpid body of a small child and headed towards the temple. The mangled bunch of the monastic robes of the Tulku provided little friction. The strength of the killer prevailed. Heavy swirling fog descended on them as the killer laboured with the load towards the main temple. The tall figure stopped at the door and heaved a sigh.

As the first light of dawn approached, the killer's rugged hands rummaged through the monastic civara or robe. Retrieving a bunch of keys with a temple seal from the waistband of the inner garments, the trembling fingers examined the cold metallic shapes, damp with moisture. A sigh of relief escaped the killer's lips as the temple seal on the keys sparkled faintly. *'Yes, the shine and illumination of our purpose shall improve as the dayprogresses,'* the killer thought with a faint smile. It had taken a few tiring but precision-laced minutes to retrieve the keys from the main vault of the temple premises. The plan had unfolded like clockwork - a surreptitious task guided by the machinations of Karma, working in their favor. "The foundation of our battle has been laid," the killer sighed. The last part of the act was tricky but well executed - opening the common dormitory and completing the crucial task of bringing the new Tulku, the newly incarnated child lama, into the rear end of the monastery. *'But it had to be done.*

Heaven has no place for idle souls,' the killer thought, recalling the teachings of the Gyanla, the teacher...

Kneeling beside the lifeless body of a small child on the cold gravel, the killer held the boy's hands in silent prayer and contemplation. "You had to be released, dear Tulku," they whispered. A silent, excited yelp escaped the killer, piercing the stillness of the quiet dawn. The corpse of an eight-year-old lay on the ground - the job had been easy and quick. The gash had inflicted enough trauma to end the young Tulku's life swiftly. A sudden push on the forehead from the front and an equal opposing force from the back had resulted in a murderous click, severing the child's spinal cord and hastening the death.

It had been a full three hours after the job and the bruised contusions speckled on the child's neck... The killer sat there by the steps of the temple cradling the Tulku's corpse. The moments laboured by... Involuntarily, the rugged hands trembled on the 108 beaded Buddha pearls or mala and started to murmur prayer chants... A soft rhythmic invocation... *'I Silently and devoutly contemplate on the 108 afflictions or kleshas... These kleshas are diverse and different. A true by-product of the living... An assortment of pointless negative accretions right from birth'...* The killer reflected on the teachings of the one true teacher. . . *'consisting of destructive human emotions including the 3 poisons of ignorance, attachment and aversion'.* . . A faint beatific smile broke on the killer's face. . . *'And yet it has been accomplished,' the killer* thought taking pride and contentment in the feat. The realisation began to dawn on the killer. . . *'The time is indeed propitious'.* . .

"Proud of me...Gyan la will be," mused the killer, adjusting the shredded and worn-out monastic attire after retrieving the keys. Changing or buying a new robe had never been a concern, for as a true disciple and student of Buddhism's Tri-ratnas - the Dharma, Buddha, and the Sangha - the killer was free from worldly materialistic trappings. Wants and desires were deemed futile in the great scheme of things, as an attachment only perpetuated the cyclic trappings of Samsara. The invocation of such thoughts was an excited reflex, a testament to the teachings of Gyan la that had suppressed the darkest recesses of the killer's past, bringing complete faith and repose in the teacher.

The task at hand was clear - to bring true deliverance to the body and send it to its true abode. The killer reflected on the meticulous dogmas shared by Gyan la, learning about the ideas of cause and effect, of action and reaction, and of sincere labor bearing fruit - all of which had come true for both the killer and the teacher.

Slung over the killer's left shoulder, the lifeless body accompanied the killer as it inserted a key into the temple lock, turning it with a slight torque. The wooden doors swung open, revealing a sanctum adorned with radiant Buddhist art. The walls, adorned with gold, crimson, and turquoise, contrasted the dense black and grey monochrome of the nightly world outside.

In a trance-like state, the killer plodded inside the Gompa room with purpose, the body still balanced on the shoulder. As they moved, the hundreds of lighted butter lamps fluttered, casting strange black shadows on the walls teeming with deities, patterns, silhouettes, and profiles. The vast array of paintings elevated the refulgence of the room.

Coming to a stop in front of a specific mural, the killer paused. It depicted a fierce-looking demon garlanded with skulls, holding a wheel within which layers of other colorful paintings were embedded. The wheel, divided into six distinct radii, formed separate compartments, each adorned with different paintings.

'Yes, this is the one, that will deliver me from the cyclic existence, and grant me enlightenment and Buddhahood,' the killer surmised and with a singular push forced the door shut from inside. . .

'Now the real work begins,' sighed the killer for the dawn was inching closer and the task at hand was as important as the murder that had just been committed. .

ENTER THE BARDO.

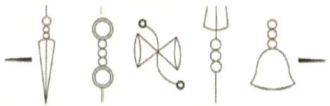

The tender lights of predawn fell on the century-old Zurphu monastery, inevitably highlighting the ornate Buddhist sculptures and art on its facade. The intricate pattern of paintings and sculpting was replete with such artistry throughout the monastery. The prayer flags fluttered in the winds that blew in from the North. . . The cool breeze that was redolent of any morning was slowly getting subdued by the oncoming warm light. . .

Built-in the mid-1700s, the Zurphu Monastery is one of the oldest and certainly the largest in the state. . . Representing the Karma Kagyu school of Tibetan Buddhism, the monastery serves as the main seat of the Kagyu lineage and the abode of its most important head,His Holiness the Karmapa. . . Originally built in the 16th century by the 12th Karmapa Lama-which later remained in ruins-it was rebuilt by the 16th Karmapa after fleeing Tibet with much patronage from the Demazong Royal family. . . Apart from the sacred relics of the previous Karmapa installed in it from a sacred monastery in Tibet, the Gompa is also home to a seat called the Dharmachakra Centre or the wheel of Dharma which contains the valuable teachings of Lord Buddha on attainment of Nirvana or liberation. . .

His bespoke tiny cell, reflected tasteful monastic frugality. Sacred Thangkas adorned the walls, and the niches below the windows, which overlooked both sides of the monastery, were bursting with heavy tomes on Buddhism and ancient Lamaistic writings. The only incongruous presence was that of a Telerama TV. But even this contraption was so old and worn that it had begun to blend itself into that medieval arrangement of things.

Over the years, Lama Tashi had devoured these books. Through reading, meditation, and sheer force of will, he had accumulated an encyclopedic knowledge of Buddhism. However, his inquisitive mind had made forays into other bodies of knowledge too. Literature and science weren't the only objects of his enquiring mind. His catholic and ecumenical outlook spilled over into the profane domains of humour - paperbacks, fiction lite, and even comics. His youthful appearance belied the eighty-one years of his existence. His countenance radiated a serene calmness that could only be attributed to the rigours of his learning and meditative habits honed through countless hours of contemplative practice.

He had joined the monastery as a novice and quickly risen through the ranks to become a Lama and now a Khenpo or leader of the monastery. Though much water had flowed through the Teesta and the Rangit since his parents brought him to the monastery in his infancy, his recollection of those days was still vivid and unfading. He remembered sadly watching his parents walk by after depositing him there. The receding figures that he watched longingly through the windows of his cell were still etched in his memory, and sometimes in his more wistful moments, he ran them again and again through his ageing mind.

To others in the Monastery, he was a strict disciplinarian matched equally by his kindness. They deferred immensely to his enormous erudition. Each day he started with an hour of meditation, which he followed up with rituals paying obeisance to the Buddhist pantheon of gods that adorned the Gompa's pedestal. "Om Mane Padma Hun. . ." he vocalized involuntarily as he adjusted his robes.

He slipped his feet into the ankle-length Somba and descended silently down the weaving stairs of the Gompa. The high whitewashed walls on either side bore intricate paintings illustrative of the complexities of Buddhist philosophy. He remembered how even as a six-year-old child, he had tried to make sense of the myriad illustrations - from those that spoke of the cycle of birth and death to Guru Padmasambhava's projection of the wrathful ones and the demonic slayings, to the poignant tales of the Milarepa. Slowly, as he went through rites of initiation and teachings under the feet of the monastic masters, these fantastic shapes began to make sense, and he understood the subtle nuances of the wise and profound messages that they were designed to impart.

The stairs took him past the dormitories of the junior monks, some aged even four or three years. At times he peered in to catch the monks sleeping serenely inside. Careful not to wake them up, he opened the main door and shut it quietly behind him. He then trod lightly on the pebbled stretch that led to the main temple premises. His age caught up with him, and that exertion through almost 70 meters of the winding pathway made his heart beat heavily inside his chest.

He rummaged through the folds of his robes to find the bunch of keys strung around his waist. He selected the one with the Temple Seal and inserted it into the keyhole. After a couple of clockwise clicks, the huge doors swung open, the creaking of its ancient hinges breaking the silence of the morning.

"Kuencho Khenno," screamed Lama Tashi as he stood transfixed in horror at the sight that greeted his eyes. Quickly, he turned around and heaved back to the monastery with an agility uncharacteristic of his age. He had to reach the others as quickly as possible and raise the alarm.

ENTER THE BARDO.

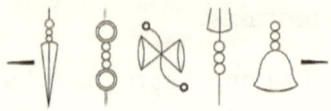

"Tomorrow, would you still love me if I am not able to do it at all?" He asked, peering deep into her eyes, which shone with the radiant hues of her cosmetic contact lenses. 'Air optix,' he guessed. He ran his fingers through the silken strands of her well-conditioned hair, making ringlets out of them. In such moments of tenderness, he wanted to elicit an honest response from her.

"...some things can be changed, but some others are unchangeable...," she replied with a tinge of regret in her voice. Her gaze was fixed on the statue of St. Francis, which glistened in the light of a waning Kolkata moon. The evening prayer service had just begun inside a quaint parish church on Park Street when he entered its holy precincts for the first time. They were welcomed by a chorus of dissonant gospel songs, which segued into a feverish collective falsetto after. The effect on him had been electrifying. Not entirely religious or spiritual, but a different sensation had flown through his entire being.

Was it her presence? Was it the presence of God? He had never been able to find out...

The screeching sounds of a heavy metal riff that emanated from the tiny speakers of the smartphone woke the man up with a start. He shot up from his bed and awoke instead to an angry, heavy metal riff that haemorrhaged from his cell phone, which resonated heavily around his room. 'What a rude awakening'? He half chuckled to himself as he shuffled himself out of his deep morning slumber and out of bed to respond to a Megadeth ringtone. Still lumbering in a somnolent heap, he answered, 'yeah!' with a deep, groggy morning voice, only to find that the call had ended just in time. . .

In spite of the cobwebs inside his mind, in spite of the throbbing grogginess of his morning head, the man could muster a reply. The silence was then oddly disturbed by the sound of the cartridge on the tonearm ratcheting on the frayed ends of the vinyl on the turntable. It had finished spinning some Baroque-era Bach and Vivaldi. The phone rang up again. This time, the man sensed a higher urgency. . .

He fumbled among the sheets for the phone that had now begun to blink with the impatience of something that was used to being picked up and cajoled at the shortest notice. But just as he put it across his ears, the call died. He tried pushing some random buttons to coax a response. Finally, frustrated, he threw it away. Thankfully, it landed with a reassuring thump somewhere. 'It's the bean bag,' he told himself as he tried to go back to sleep. But soon he found that it was impossible to sleep. He slipped out of bed to find the phone. Indeed, it was ensconced nicely within the leatherette folds of the beanie. He put it on to read the time.

At 4:00 AM, the LED screamed. Who could be calling me at this time? He wondered.

He felt around for the bed switch and put it on. He forgot that he had replaced the CFL with a high-watt LED. The menacing brightness of the new bulb stung the man's eyes. Whatever little vestige of sleep had remained was now completely vaporized by this luminous intrusion. His modest apartment suddenly felt naked, every portion of it revealed in its prosaic starkness. Finding this room hadn't been easy. But once he procured it after much haggling with the property dealer first and then the landlord, he set about turning it into his true abode.

Though sparsely furnished, the pad was home to the many old-fashioned items that he squirreled away after lurking around in forums and striking bargain deals. A radiogram, two turntables, the innards of some exotic class A amplifiers, tubes and sundry cables, a pair of huge horn speakers, and a Nakamichi deck were some of the audiophile detritus that he had managed to collect over the years. For the man loved tinkering with these vintage gadgets. . . Taking out a vinyl from the cover,giving the grooves on it the softest cleaning touch and spinning. . . All for that pure analog experience. . . Besides this aging hardware, his shelf was packed tight with cassettes, CDs, and vinyl records. The only piece of electronic incongruity in that retro heaven was a Panasonic TSC 60KSB landline phone.

Also conspicuous by its absence was the television, which he never watched. When he was not listening to his music, he was reading his books. And for that, he had to thank his teacher. 'Gyanla, ' the man let out a soft whisper, an incantation more so. That realization made him offer a quick prayer for that noble being who had not only gifted him the divine erudition but saved him as well in the process.

The cool morning breeze began to waft in from the half-open window, and the man's thoughts lent themselves to a distant memory.

A young boy, the victim of an intentional action, lay on the hard bed in the dank, sunless room of a government detox center. He opened his eyes to see a sea of faces peering down on him. His nostrils reeked with the stench of vomit. Vomit clogged his throat and spilled over from the sides of his mouth. Fortunately, they had brought him on time, and the doctor on duty had managed to induce the regurgitation that had probably saved him.

That sense of relief, however, was not shared by the sick boy. "You should have let me be," he groaned. As he slowly came around, his life and the emptiness that he was trying to escape from enveloped him like a dark ocean. He retched up again. Noxious fluids clogged his nostrils and his throat. This was a far cry from the bright lights and the illuminations that he was hoping his death wish would grant him. The reality of living was more hellish than the death that he had been denied.

'But I will not give up,' he thought. *'The effects of ill-fate are still there running under my veins,'* the boy struggled to free himself. The center's employees could do little to pacify the sick child. Fists rained on them. The boy kicked them and clawed at every instance. Every day was a challenge for them. "This is the worst case we've seen to date," said one of the attendants. "We should just give up on him. Let him fend for himself," said another, wiping his bloodied nose. All hope was gone...He definitely heard them...Yes he definitely did...

Clasping both his legs and kneeling down in the prayer hall that day, the man wanted to heal. The power of good indeed prevailed and suddenly one day, a being came into his field of view. He wasn't one of the uniformed hospital personnel busying themselves to save him. Slowly, as his eyes adjusted, he could make out the wrinkled visage of an elderly monk murmuring the syllables of what could have been a prayer. The man pulled up a chair and sat beside him.

"What do you want?" he asked.

"You," he replied.

"I want you to be free from this mess, this suffering," he intoned as if repeating his prayer to himself.

"So you want to save me?" the boy sneered.

"Isn't it too late for that?"

"No, it's never too late for anything."

The quiet determination of that elderly monk won over. He designed a regimen that combined the old and the new. Medical science and religion became the twin agents of his rehabilitation. But first, he had to be restrained. The monk chained him to his bed and left him to the elements. The agony of his cold turkey was acute.

"Remember, if you come out of this, you will emerge stronger. You will see things with clarity that your circumstances have denied you up until now. Just don't give up." The boy knew the words to be true; being chained to a metallic pole near the monk's bedside, he found out that the days and nights were indeed long and lonely initially. His body, now adjusting to an unaccustomed environment, shivered continuously, throwing spasms uncontrollably. But deep down, amidst all the suffering and pain, an iota of human resilience had taken birth, and the boy was determined to fight his situation and come out victorious.

'Sometimes the only way out is through the fire. . .' And he did.

As the days passed by, a new vitality surged through his veins. His demons had been exorcised. The elderly monk, having gifted him his corporeal body, now set about working on his soul. The man was an eager vessel for that kind of filling. He began to read and read and read. He discovered a whole new world in the pages, and he had barely scratched the surface.

"I never knew it was possible, Gyanla," the man said one day to his teacher. The teacher understood the question but didn't answer. And as his knowledge about the precepts grew, so did the bond between the teacher and the student.

Finally, he told his master, "I am fine now, Gyanla."

The winter chill had set in. Warmth had fled the land. Biting cold winds from the north blew in gusts, stinging their faces and billowing their robes. Gyanla looked deep into his eyes. It was as if, through these windows, he could peer into his very soul.

It had been three years since he had taken the man under his wing. Those years had been rigorous and hard. The learning had been relentless. The most arcane and esoteric branches of Buddhist philosophy, with all their recondite profundity, had been opened up to him.

His visit to the de-addiction center hadn't been a random affair. It was something that the constant churning of the wheels of karma had thrown up. With a sense of relief, unburdened by expectations, the master let the protege fly out of that hermetic coop. He could, after all, summon him when he needed to. The training, at least for now, was complete. The man plonked himself on the bean bag. The waning moon's rays fell on his lithe body and onto his tattoo. For him, it had never been about individual expression or fashion. The tattoos had been about salvation. The man now straddling an arm's length of artificial pigmentation was once against the artform and although his choices in the past were questionable and warranted such marks, yet he didn't give in.

'This is what individuality is all about, said one of his cohorts in an effort to coax him to ink himself. The man did not understand. '...this is change—an ultimate form of expression,' said the other. It still didn't register. And although sometimes his inebriated state naturally tugged on at his testosterone and tattoo parlors baited them with their late-night shifts, mostly feeding on such drunken vulnerabilities, the man did not give in.

Then one day things took a nasty turn. His life was now heading towards a *'life-sucking abyss'* with no one at its wheel. He was alone, morose and depressed. He wanted a way to end all this. *'Maybe there's plenty of hope in the next*, he thought. His determination was resolute. His idea was heating up inside him... *'...faster than a junkie's spoon...?'* Then he did it. Unfortunately for him, he failed. The sea of eyes peering down on him that day seemed like otherworldly beings to him. In his desperate time, he felt a great justice had been denied to him. Among all this chaos, salvation had arrived in the form of a frail old monk who stayed by his side from then on. The new life had filled him with hope and promises. And as soon as he had started to reside in the capital, the first thing he had thought of getting himself was inked. He had read about the history of tattoos and where they were headed. From the terracotta ruins to the Egyptian pharaohs, the culture of inking oneself had survived the sands of time. But for him, it hadn't been about fashionable statements or even individual expression; it had been about salvation. His victories over his demons and exorcism. Evolutionary, he thought, echoing the Darwinian thought about tattoos. Though the art world threw a plethora of choices at him, the man was patient and zeroed in on an image of Vajra's sphere on his forearm. And the sphere had been symbolic of his belief in his firmness of character and awakening. 'This is going to hurt, the artist said before embarking on the inking on the man's arm. The man looked the other way.

The constant buzzing of the needle as it tapped in and out of his forearm, dislodging pigment into his skin, had been like a ritual both satisfying and cruel. Each time the needle forayed into his dermis, he was as close as possible to exhuming his demons from the past in the hope of finding the message bearers of a counterfeit nirvana. And when it had ended, it had all been satisfying. Now, when the man walked outside, he often found it ironic when he was met with suspicious eyes. *'The stigma attached is real,'* the man thought and chuckled to himself, thinking how the word itself had undergone metamorphosis to mean a mark of social disgrace when it originally meant the constant marking by a needle on the skin. But the irony was not lost on the man because, everywhere, humans were constantly making other adjustments to change themselves, sometimes just to feel good, to live long and healthy... The man rattled some names in his mind, *'like surgeries, drugs, CRISPR and even using common cosmetics to change themselves in an effort to standout... 'a form of individualexpression,'* the man scoffed.

It had been five years since Karma Wangden had moved to the capital. Working as the Maintenance Manager at Namgyal Institute of Tibetology, he finally managed to settle down to an organized life—something that was alien to him before. The NIT was established in 1930 with a mission to curate and propagate Tibetan Buddhist history, culture, and identity. It is a repository of ancient, priceless texts. The old parchments and writings have been stored with the utmost care, and the curator takes great technical care to preserve these sacred vellums for generations to come. Some of the artifacts that it houses can be found nowhere else in the world.

ENTER THE BARDO.

While Karma settled down to a life of officious routine, the mundane monotony of pushing files and pens sometimes pushed him to the edge. Sometimes, he wanted something racy and fantastic that would provide him with more than the metaphorical *'shot in the arm'*—an escape from this routine...a momentary foray into the absurd from this *'temporal existence of a lie.'* And sometimes, in his weaker moments, he was revisited by episodes from his past. The memory of the chemicals that remain buried in the depths of his being came close to being exhumed again.In those moments, he remembered Gyanla and the fortitude that he had imparted to karma.

"No, I must not let my master down," he repeated to himself as he tried to chase the demons of his past. '...*The chemical harbingers of doom, the message bearers of a counterfeit Nirvana, had to be slain...*' The man kept reiterating the words...Perhaps someone would paint a tapestry of his struggles and adorn the walls of a monastery, he thought.

A chill blast shook him out of his reverie. A car honked somewhere. The dull heaviness of sleep slowly began to bear down on him. Suddenly, the old KSB Panasonic phone in the corner of the room started to ring. Karma tried to ignore it, but the urgency in the room was unmissable. He fought through the torpor of sleep that was now descending on him, wave after wave. The ringing persisted. He finally picked up the phone. The call dis-engaged with a beep, and Karma Wangden sighed, having missed another call. But he didn't realize that the call had been forwarded to his answering machine. A deep breath from the other side of the line was frighteningly audible. Then a baritone voice canned inside an answering machine intoned, "Karma, we need your help. Something terrible and unspeakable has befallen us. Hurry to me!" The phone went dead, followed by the ominous sound of a dial tone in the distance...

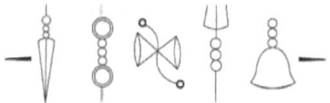

'. . . Seated with pride and a wrathful smirk, dispelling all negativities,

The precious Lotus-born Guru of Oddiyana, encompassing all three ages,

Wrathful power dispelling and subduing demons,

I invoke you Pema Junyi to destroy all outer, inner and secret obstacles,

And lead us to divine fruition. . . ,

Amid the dense foliage surrounding the gompa, a sinister figure lurked in the western woods, perfectly concealed by the dark vegetation. Facing the Zurphu Monastery, the ominous figure released an evil sigh, fingers rhythmically playing with the *Thenga* while chanting the Vajra Guru mantra. Just moments ago, the figure had witnessed an aged lama retracing his steps from the main temple premises.

'Everything is unfolding as prophesied,' the killer thought with a malicious grin. "My supreme teacher and I won't stand for inaction; we must act swiftly." The hooded figure inched closer to the tree line, observing the terrified temple monks rushing into the main gompa.

Satisfied with the chaos left behind, the figure turned back and headed towards a parked vehicle on the main highway. After adjusting the robe, the figure ignited the engine and drove northward, seamlessly blending into the dull light filtering through the forest canopy. Controlling the vehicle with precision, the killer reflected on their gruesome deed—taking the life of a young boy just minutes ago. "The first one was always the toughest," the killer mused, "but now I've completed all four assignments. The teacher will be proud. "

A slight grin exposed the cross-stitch on an old facial gash on the killer's left cheek. The morning sun had just touched the asphalt on the highway when the vintage ambassador car revved ferociously and sped away into the capital, leaving behind a trail of mystery and terror.

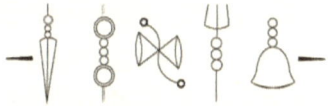

The long, winding road snaking its way into the heart of the capital town proves to be tedious at both points of egress and entry. Traffic jams clog the arterial highway 31A. As the road snakes into the city, various smaller roads, lanes, footpaths and staircases link it to the numerous suburban habitations. Almost all the other areas in and around the capital link up to the main highway; the suburban roads thus morph seamlessly between these two points, facilitating convenient movements. It also becomes the main entry point through a check-post in the east to the capital for tourists and people coming from other states to take in the bountiful beauties the state has to offer through tourism or light commerce. The MG marg, or road, has become a ubiquitous landmark, pervading the streets of cities in India. The homage paid to India's Father of the Nation stands in the form of a 10-foot bronze statue of him holding a stick in a familiar 'disobedient' stance.

Although the state became a part of the Indian Union in 1975, the sacrifices and his beliefs in *Ahimsa* were surprisingly not lost on the denizens of Sikkim, and the transference of patriotism was well absorbed, with his credos of non-violence resonating deeply in the hearts of all the denizens. Gandhi is revered and respected throughout the nation. The marg, a modest stretch of tiled promenade pathway, is the showpiece of the town and a haven for tourists all year. Flanked by a mix of commercial enterprises and restaurants on both sides, the pathway itself proves to be a pedestrian's paradise, saving the visitors from the violence of the roaring traffic and the malaise of modernity and physics that affects the rest of the capital. The state emerged as one of the top tourist destinations, with achievements extolled by myriad online portals. It has indeed become one of the most sought-after places to provide much-needed relaxation and panoramic comfort to thousands of jaded travelers. The route also serves as a daily place for transit for the students of different schools and colleges and also for the many government employees who have to travel up north to their offices, often battling and snaking through never-ending traffic jams. After 15 years of becoming a part of the Indian Union, the state definitely transformed into a developed tourist destination, with visitors from various parts of the world entering and enjoying the God-blessed land of plenty. Urbanization definitely increased, and with commerce doubling and trebling every year, more footfalls and influxes have been witnessed.

'Where honesty and sincerity become the fabric that stitches society, prosperity follows, and where prosperity follows and thrives, more bodies will want in on the wealth, and where wealth forsakes wisdom, more bodies will want in on the loot...'

In his government-sanctioned Bolero vehicle, the newly cadred and appointed IPS officer, Yangtso Brahma, waited patiently at the Gurudwara in the suburbs as the long, winding line of vehicles in front of him slowly cleared. He drummed his fingers on the dashboard, sometimes giving way to a staccato rhythm, perpetrated by an impatient mind. He knew it was his responsibility to regulate and investigate any illegal activities that might arise during the tourist season, even though crime rates in Sikkim were relatively low compared to other states in the country.

While his colleagues in different regions grappled with serious terror threats and religious unrest, Yangtso's challenges were relatively less severe, and that was a blessing for a fresh imcumbent—*or a curse*. Yangtso breathed a sigh. Despite the place being almost a crime-free state, Yangtso was a stern and relentless enforcer who vowed never to go easy on offenders and criminals.

Yangtso, a medium-built man in his thirties, stood at 5'8" with a closely cropped hairdo that accentuated his broad facial structure, giving him the appearance of a young wrestler prepared for a quick grapple on the mats. His high school physique, honed by years of strenuous training at the local grounds and gym, endowed him with the agility and physical prowess necessary for his demanding job.

He walked with long and authoritative strides, keeping a significant gap between his legs, and his speech was measured and authoritative, befitting his status as an enforcer of the law.

"Sir, phone," said Alex, the driver, carefully handing over the wireless device. The cacophony of traffic outside drowned out the faint crackle of the wireless within the vehicle.

"This is Brahma; come in, over," the officer spoke into the receiver.

"Yangtso, you need to report immediately to your precinct." The trembling voice on the other end relayed the urgent message.

"I'll be on it, over," the officer responded, passing the receiver back to the driver and taking a deep breath. After collecting himself, he instructed Alex, "Straight to Zurphu monastery." Yangtso's expression contorted into a frown. "There's been a murder of a young and recently recognized Tulku..."Alex knew it was serious because his boss said, 'Again...?' A question born from disbelief rather...

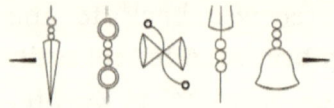

"Khenpo Tashi...your tea is served" the attendant mumbled as he placed the mug of freshly prepared buttered beverage in front of the Master. Khenpo wasn't in any mood for the tea. His eyes wore a squalid and vacant stare. His ageing body seemed to have grown smaller inside the cavernous folds of his monastic robes. His deep-set eyes were fixed on the concrete floor.

The Khenpo had never witnessed such a horrifying scene in his entire life. For a man devoted to learning and practicing Buddhism since his early days and exercising the knowledge, this was too much of a macabre event for him. His life was dedicated to the Dharma and its practice. From Buddha's 8-fold paths, and the principles of non-attachments to the non-violent edicts of the religion, his life was consigned to the preaching and practicing of the edicts for the benefit of all sentient beings. *'I take refuge in the Buddha, Dharma and the Sangha'*. Lama Tashi's mind couldn't fathom and comprehend what had just happened inside one of the country's oldest hallowed monasteries. He just sat crouched in his chair rhythmically playing with his beads. . . The movement more of muscle memory than an exercise in piety. His entire body now loose and shaken succumbed to the effects of gravity resembling a mass of old muscle hanging from the chair. . . An event so unprecedented and gory had occurred in the confines of this 100-year-old monastery which had left the Khenpo shocked and speechless. . .

'Whatwas happening in these hallowed halls of ancient virtue, ' ?he mused as his hands mechanically felt through the beads of his rosary, searching for answers.

He glanced at the simmering cup of tea on the table and picked it up but as soon as its creamy saltiness met his tongue, a wave of nausea welled from the depths of his bowels and he retched. That convulsion almost made him lose his bearings. A few young lamas came to his aid and helped him to his feet. A yellow slimy rivulet flowed along the cobble stones which some novice was quick to wipe off with a wet rag.

The other monks helped Lama Tashi find his steps again after he threw up a lime-yellow fluid on the ground lined with embedded stone slabs leading to the monastery. . .

The Khenpo now having regained a measure of his composure, sought out the monk who was next to him and asked . . . "Did you get through to Karma"?

"Have you been able to contact Karma?", another frantic query followed...Stanzin, a middle-aged monk from Leh Ladakh, shook his head indicating failure but motioned with his hand, signaling continued attempts to connect. The Khenpo tried to forget and erase the gruesome scene that was etched in his old mind after having witnessed it just a few minutes ago. However, he couldn't shake the thought from his mind. His thoughts wandered into an expanse and space where he bravely faced the gut-wrenching images and incidents that had just occurred and tried to confront them.

Never before in his life had he witnessed such horror. It was too much for this holy man of meditation, whose life thus far had embodied the non-violent virtues of the eightfold path propounded by the Buddha. It was a life lived according to the credo - "I take refuge in the Buddha, Dharma and the Sangha". Such a mind for which rectitude had become second nature couldn't fathom or comprehend the meaningless of such macabre violence.

'What was happening in these hallowed halls of ancient virtue,' the Khenpo again echoed his earlier thought.

The turn of events indeed had simply been unprecedented in the annals of this hundred-year-old monastery.

The place had been one of the many bastions of faith and worship, catering to the pilgrims and the sick and needy...

Just like an unbridled thought racing in its whim, the horrible image came back to plague the Khenpo's mind. He tried to walk the cobblestoned quadrangle quickly as if expecting that physical exertion to help expunge the grisly image that kept playing in his brain.

'The passing away of time is inevitable; the scourge of it even gnashes at mighty kingdoms and civilizations; whatever monolithic concrete and beautiful edifices stand, it eventually consigns its fate to time and ends up being ground to bones and dust; it devours everything and nothing remains in existence for long for everything is temporary and everything is nothing... "Time inevitably erases everything. No edifice of manly vanity however beautiful can withstand its ravages. Bones are ground to dust. Everything becomes nothing," he contemplated.

The impermanence of things, the letting go of worldly desires and attachments, harmony amongst beings and at the core of it all, non-violence, these were the principles along which he had led his life so far.

Lama Tashi silently reflected on such dogma that the philosophy encompassed and taught. teachings about impermanence and letting go of attachments and material desires...To free oneself from *Samsara, to* shun the pleasures of life, and to learn and practice the art of non-violence. Yes, non-violence was the most important edict that was at the core of Buddhism, and the lessons of compassion, tolerance, and conflict resolution ensured a peaceful existence in the community, not only for the monks but also for countless other believers living in complete harmony. *So how could anyone commit such a thing, then?* thought Lama Tashi. The senselessness of the morning's carnage was in complete contrast to these ideals of probity that had been the bedrock of his existence thus far.

Once again, those horrifying images came back to haunt him. The limp, lifeless body with its gaping mouth that seemed to have fossilised a cry of mortal terror. And strewn around it the messages.

No sooner had the image materialized in his head like a nightmare, then another terrifying thought engulfed him, and he froze at the mere recollection of it. He mentally recreated the image of the monastery and pieced together the scattered papers around the lifeless body. *Yes, the message...*

'Yes, scrawled on pieces of paper were the words...'

'...illusions...that...created...words...God...'The messages lit themselves in the Khenpo's mind with incoherent sporadic bursts...and before he could construct something meaningful out of it... the image of the body of the young innocent Tulku haunted him more...

The little seven-year-old boy whom the lamas according to their time-tested precepts and prescriptions had identified as the reincarnation of a high Rinpoche now lay murdered in cold blood.

What kind of a monster would inflict such unspeakable violence on such a cherubic child? What purpose was he trying to serve, what vile agenda was he trying to bring to fruition?

And this child, a Tulku from the Kagyu sect wasn't the only one. He was the fourth victim.

The plague that snuffed the life out of the three reincarnates from the other sects had now visited them too. There was no knowing to what terrible lengths it would go in its murderous zeal.

ENTER THE BARDO.

"Wherever you are. . . Karma . . . you have to come here fast." the Lama mumbled and walked

towards the commotion that was building up outside the Gompa.

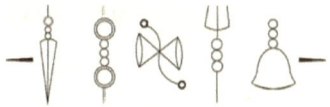

A long beep emanated from the wireless telephone after the message played. The sound was cut.

Through the stillness of the dawn's silence, amplifying the urgency accompanying the caller's voice and the message he relayed. *'Gyanla'...?* Karma Wangden let the name out. The word more of a surprise than a realization.

Karma sat bolt upright in his bed. His sleepiness disengaging rapidly.

'What must have occurred for Gyan-La to call me at this hour'? and the hurried way in which he spoke displayed a demeanor tantamount to nervousness, Karma recalled.

The early morning call from Gyanla woke Karma with a start. It wasn't usual for the teacher to disturb him like this. Something was definitely amiss. He needed to get there fast, he thought.

Emergency calls weren't new for him. But because it was his teacher who was at the other end of the line, the urgency was on another level.

Whatever it was, Karma knew that the Khenpo needed his help and fast. It was a clarion call.

Emergency that the monk had thrown toward him, a call for help like a call for a light inside a dense and dark tunnel. Above all, it was a call from his old friend and guide, and Karma Wangden knew better than to ignore it.

Without wasting much time, he jumped out of bed and into his clothes from his collection in the wardrobe. A tight-fitting shirt thrown over his little body quickly hid the ink tattooed on his left shoulder... The pale light of the bedside lamp shone on it as he threw a shirt over it. The other ink on his body was a sketch of circles and lines. A genius and an artistic maze of self-expression, geometrically straddling and aligning his body. *'It tells a story'*. The story embedded within the contours of the ink that expressed the demise and rise of the bearer. . .

Having a fit, muscular build, the t-shirt and the drain-piped denims came as a natural choice. Karma's sartorial taste veered towards the modish.

ENTER THE BARDO.

The 20 eyelet Good Year Welted Nevermind boots from their core collection was something Karma Wangden had always wanted. The shaft and the upper portion had an assortment of stylistic Gypsy imagery that screamed impermanence. The welt stitch straddled the sole of the boots. But the badge of honor that the boots possessed was the patina effect that Karma Wangden grew to admire and pleasure as the boots aged. '*Someday I hope I land an Indie boot from Alden...*' Karma Wangden sighed... 'in Shell Cordovan',he said it out aloud in a hope to manifest...Karma picked up his keys and gave his black and disheveled hair a little Mohawk touch with a tiny smear of the nitro-wax.

A lambskin leather bomber jacket completed the look.

Casting one last look at his disheveled room and ruing the fact that his schedule never allowed him to give it the tiding up that it sorely needed. Karma Wangden shut the mortise-tenon lock on his door with a familiar click and bounded down the stairs.

Outside, dawn was descending upon the capital. A few were out for their morning jogs.

The athletes limbered along the length of the stadium grounds, loosening their joints and trying to shake off the lingering winter sleepiness. The last remnants of darkness slowly succumbed to the ever-inching light of dawn. The streets and the corners of the capital slowly witnessed some physical movements that grew with each passing second.

The still of the morning air was disrupted by the mechanical din from the reverberations emanating from Karma's machine as it ripped through the road in menacing urgency.

The athletes had just begun their morning session inside the stadium when their routine suddenly got interrupted by a loud, menacing roar of Karma Wangden's Ducati Titanium Diavel from behind, with the rider navigating the monstrous 900 cc high torque wheels with ease. . . It's ergonomically designed cowling, coupled with a custom Yoshimura exhaust, helped the rider glide with great speed,whizzing past everyone with heightened urgency.

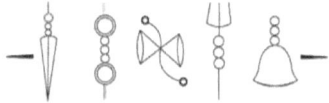

It was rare for Zurphu monastery's tranquility to experience a setback so early in the day. The typically serene and quiet holy setting had suddenly been invaded by a swarm of curious minds. At such early hours, the usually serene and meditative environs of the Zurphu monastery were a hive of activity. The monks shaken out of their pious equanimity congregated on the square in groups, animatedly speculating about the sudden turn of events. Some locals sensing the unusual, gathered outside the fences, curious and eager for a morsel of information. Everyone tried to make sense of the goings on there. The befuddled monks gathered and cast ever-inquisitive stares, accompanied by several villagers from the Gompa's neighborhood, attempting to uncover the true explanation behind the monastery's bewilderment. Their casual inquiries were interspersed with interrogational murmurs to one another, yielding no solid replies.

The state with its fair number of mobile hospitals on wheels catered to emergency health crises. The medical mobile vans outfitted with cutting-edge medical technology, allowed for immediate care and assistance. These outperformed even the gurneys stationed in various metros in the country.

The paramedics sat idle behind the monastery, with just a few medical personnel entering and departing the main temple, where the body had been discovered by the Khenpo, Lama Tashi. The turmoil, whispering, and overall disruption on the temple grounds early in the morning drew a lot of unwarranted attention to the hallowed site. The faint overtones of melismatic sirens in the distance, which intensified increasingly after each second, created perceptible tension and heightened curiosity. The staccato of the sirens was followed by a cavalcade of police cars racing through the last 150 m into the Gompa grounds, answering, however partially, 1 or 2 inquisitive minds.

IPS Yangtso Brahma alighted the vehicle and walked with his sure steady gait while looking around at an audience of unknowing faces—hundreds of sets of eyes—welcoming the officer with questions and queries of their own. With gimlet eyes and a steely gaze, he scoured the sea of eyes before him.

'A sudden unnatural physical movement, a tendency to preclude a direct gaze, a nervous

anxious tic', wished Brahma, hoping for such physical betrayals. The Police Academy had taught him to home in on such signs...that it was plausible for the perpetrator to mingle with the crowd immediately after an event.

Discovering nothing, he strode away directly to the epicentre of activity...The mobile ambulance unit with its flashing lights and wailing sirens and inside which they had lain the body of the slain child monk on a gurney. The officer slowed his walk after reaching the place where the paramedic van was parked, behind the monastery. As he neared the gurney, he caught a glimpse of the body inside the van, neatly covered with a light green hospital sheet. 'Lobzang', Yangtso Brahma cried out to one of the accompanying inspectors. 'Make sure everyone in the temple premises is secured and interrogated properly, including the monks and especially the head of the temple. '

'If you home in on anything that strikes your attention; make a note and report back immediately, barked the IPS officer, to everyone's bewilderment at the sudden change in the officer's rather genial tone.

'Lus, huncha sir,' Lobzang nodded and ordered three other constables to follow him.

ENTER THE BARDO.

The remaining 6-7 home guards, constables, and armed personnel nervously waited for their orders, forming an arc around the officer.

As Inspector Lobzang and the others walked away from the van towards the temple premises, Brahma ordered him to also summon the senior lama of Zurphu monastery while they were at it.

Taking a bow as a sign of direct assent to the orders, Lobzang disappeared into the main temple with the other three constables in tow.

With slight trepidation and muttering imprecations under his breath, Yangtso Brahma opened the door and entered the paramedic van from behind, slowly lifting himself up and into it.

The little space inside the paramedic vehicle was jammed with medical paraphernalia and contraptions...The air too was fragrant, with vaporized chemical residues billowing all around. The coroner, a hirsute medium-height guy with a chubby appearance and a fat belly, glanced up from his report to see the intruder. When he saw a higher-ranking police officer enter the vehicle, he swiftly stepped over to the gurney where the body was stored and handed the officer the report.

Yangtso Brahma immediately spotted the coroner altering his meticulously observed inquests and casually removed them from him.

After a lengthy pause, the coroner sought to curb the tension and break the ice, "Everything is in the report, sir." Brahma skimmed over the report.

"The time of death, the cause," added the coroner with supreme confidence.

'Does it also say the identity of the killer? replied Brahma rather rudely, to which the coroner stood silently.

The officer lifted the sheet completely, exposing the rigor mortis body of a little child lying dead and inanimate like some subject under a petri dish awaiting scientific observation. Brahma covered his nose and mouth with his hand upon seeing the child's body before him.

"You washed it?" The officer asked the coroner after carefully observing the body. His tone implied more of an assertion than a question.

The coroner nodded, catching a faint whiff of medical ablutions in the air, which served as a hint for the officer's observation.

"Yes, sir, the victim was struck by a large item at close range, but the blunt force trauma did not kill him," said the coroner quickly.

"The markings on the side of the neck and the medical report indicate that he died as a result of a spinal shock."

The coroner paused and after weighing his words carefully added with some degree of finality-

'The killer twisted the head'. Yangtso Brahma alighted the gurney and slowed his usual gait to a stroll...The officer realised that there was something sinister connecting these crimes...

Taking a stroll alone outside, Brahma thought, *'A definitive pattern emerges...The MO undoubtedly remains the same. '*

ENTER THE BARDO.

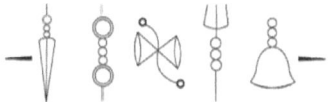

The Diavel tore into the Gompa premises, skidding into the pebbled path and spraying a granular mist of aggregates and dust into the air. The breakneck speed allowed the machine to easily cover half a kilometer from the main gate. It careened into one of the temple's grass paths, adorned with beautiful seasonal flowers, but Karma countered the torque with ease before skidding to a stop in front of the monastery.

Karma Wangden got off the bike and surveyed the surroundings.

The monastery was a hotbed of activity. But what caught Karma's eye was the sight of the police cavalcade parked randomly at the temple's flank. It was as if their occupants had just jumped out and run off in a tearing hurry, freezing the automobiles in their tracks. Static and yet they seemed to be going somewhere.

Earlier, he had seen them snaking in through the bends as he sped to overtake them just when the lights of dawn were on the dark tops of the capital hills, when Karma spotted the tiny dots of the vehicles moving towards Zurphu monastery on the opposite hill. He had switched to full throttle to get there as soon as possible.

'Official urgency was no match for the haste that devotion inspired' Karma Wangden scoffed. But credit to them that they had not lagged very far behind.

Karma held his helmet in the crook of his arm and ran up the stairs. Athletic agility rose to meet the demands of an emergency. Soon he would be face-to-face with his beloved and revered Teacher,his Gyan-la. And he would know everything.

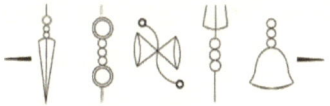

A brokenhearted Lama Tashi sat in one of the chairs in the monastery's visiting room. His physical and mental dissociation from the frenzied movements that had begun within the room following the pandemonium of murder in the monastery. With a single door enabling escape and admission, the enormous and wide space was swiftly losing ground to a swarm of monks. The Khenpo, stunned and agitated by the visions in his thoughts, cut a lonely figure as if lost and roaming in an unknown land. When he saw a man in a dark attire hurrying up the temple stairs towards him, the transformation in his wretched face was all but evident. *'It's him'*, he sighed.

'Finally, he's here,' Lama Tashi heaved a sigh of relief and turned and looked patiently towards the door, anticipating the moment and eagerly awaiting the eventual return of his protégé to him.

Karma Wangden took a first turn right on alighting the initial steps in a hurry, made a quick jog for 10s, and then entered a room full of monks, rookies who had started with their training, and being invigilated by a senior lama of 50-55 years.

'Gyan La?' asked Karma to the instructor in a soft, respectful, hushed tone, his words barely making a sound.

The instructor pointed right to the only door open on the far side of the corridor. Karma thanked him and briskly walked towards the door, his hands instinctively touching the murals on his way in.

As he approached the Khenpo, Karma breathed slowly, his every step marked with anxiousness and need. Karma inched slower and closer to the Khenpo and knelt before him, offering entire reverence to his old friend, guide, and guardian angel, as if they were old friends meeting for the first time.

Karma felt an enormous sense of compassion and care for Lama Tashi as he stared at his weak physique. The scholarly charm and warmth of a knowledgeable man had now faded into a whirlpool of sorrow, guilt, and terror that was slowly but steadily consuming him. Karma carefully approached him, and as he got near, he bent low in front of Lama Tashi to pay his respects by touching the Lama's forehead with his, as is customary in Buddhist tradition. Lama Tashi slowly reacted to the familiar presence in front of him. His furrowed brows and welled-up eyes began to tear through the watery veil, thus beginning to make sense of a being in front of him. A figure began to take shape, and he knew at that very instant that all his prayers would be answered. Tugging and pulling at his denim sleeve, Karma Wangden wiped the tears from his master's face with a soft touch.

"What is it, Khenpo?" Karma asked as he bent down in front of him. It had indeed been years since Karma had been away from the Khenpo, and the elapsed time showed in the body of the lama. The skin once taut and strong had succumbed to the frailties of age and now gave way to a soft, stretchy bulk of flab loosening with each passing year. The hefty grandeur and strength of youth, now a distant memory.

"My son," Lama Tashi spoke as he straightened himself against Karma's weight. "Something unprecedented and unfortunate has occurred in the temple, in this home of the Gods, in this peace-loving region, and it is going to destroy and break everything. Whatever lessons and knowledge that we've learned and imparted for centuries stand threatened. This very edifice," Lama Tashi signaled to the monastery, "the bastion of faith, learning, and practice, will be ground to dust." The Khenpo paused for a second. "The sacrosanct teachings, the wisdom of ages, the truth will be lost forever. The fruits obtained by our leaders from years of sincere meditation and practice will all go sour unless we stop this man who calls himself 'the messenger.'"

Karma listened with intent to every word the teacher was saying. Yet, he couldn't understand anything. "Lessons, knowledge, destroy. . . the messenger. . ." He was out of his wits' end.

"But having you here gives me hope that we can still tide over this together, Karma," Lama Tashi said as he hugged him. A semblance of hope returned to his beady eyes. "You are here, Karma; you must solve this and bring everything back to balance again. Just don't breathe a word about this to anyone." Karma nodded and looked at the old man reassuringly.

"Not even to them," Lama Tashi added in a whisper and pointed Karma to the oncoming policemen across the room.

ENTER THE BARDO.

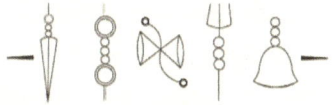

Officer Yangtso Brahma's gait suddenly resembled an angry bull on a parade. . . His general demeanor flustered, his gaze scathing. The academy had taught Brahma to be a tough officer. A strenuous regimen of mental and physical courses had sculpted a geeky individual into the instrument of a lawful enforcer. His friends during their sojourn at the academy often joked about how Brahma had literally done a Kafka. The obvious by-product of such a pedagogical exercise was toughness in character, with a pedantic eye for the tiniest of details. And Brahma developed and sharpened that edge over the years. He scoffed at the state of affairs in front of him currently. '*At my crime scene,*' the officer hissed. Every spatial element of the crime scene was impure. Every object is now devoid of any answers to the officer.' Sol, he barked an order to the junior, who was timidly in anticipation of such a resultant outburst. 'Now I don't know who, but it's evident the place has been tampered with. The junior officer nodded in assent. 'Now you are familiar with the fact that in the realm of criminal investigation, whatever the conditions existing at the time and immediately following a crime, the direct surroundings blanketing the scene should never be contaminated by anyone.' The officer nodded again. Brahma then spoke into Sol's ears and issued a command. . . Sol left the room hurriedly. The officer squatted in front of the pantheon of gods on the pedestal and rued the useless presence of policing instruments strewn on the floor around him. In there, the room uselessly hosted an inanimate bunch of yellow barricade tape, finger print brushes, and a host of other policing paraphernalia, which to Brahma currently seemed like a cesspool of waste and human error. The officer stood up and walked out of the room and summoned the other law enforcers and authorities and commanded them. . . They swiftly positioned themselves, preparing to seal off the crime scene.

Inside the gurney once again, Brahma let out an angry sigh. He was infuriated at the protocols being ignored, a frown zigzagging his forehead at regular intervals. His hardened frown the obvious result of his mental state currently.

"How can they do this?" Brahma wondered as he moped meditatively inside the gurney, his body overcoming the torpor of mind preceding an investigation. "Breaking all the rules of investigation and then calling us for our help?"

snarled the officer. Although bearing a calm and peaceful disposition, his implacable and steely determination to nab and punish the perpetrator of any felony was unrelenting. He silently eyed the corpse in front of him in the hope of extracting vital clues that would solve the case. Clues were the hints, the lifeblood, crucial in any police investigation. They were like pieces of a jigsaw puzzle that would render the mystery of any crime futile and defog the mysteries. But the clues had been tampered with before they cordoned off the area. True, the police were the first ones to arrive at the scene, but what surprised him was that they were led inside the paramedic's gurney first instead of the crime scene. Sol, the junior officer, neared the gurney. Brahma alighted and towered before Sol. 'Sir, your doubts have been answered and. . . 'a pause 'and what,' barked Brahma. 'You were correct, sir.' Yangtso Brahma's frown thickened.

Brahma now exhaled, and in a hint of comfort, the officer pursed his lips. He plonked himself atop the police vehicle and took out a jaundiced-looking old pouch with Cohiba cigarillo scrawled on the cover. He lit it up and took a long drag. The fresh injection of raw Secaderos nicotine into his bloodstream made him forget the dull, careless affairs of the morning. The officer, Yangtso Brahma, was distraught and furious after learning about the affairs as soon as he reached the monastery this morning. The investigation protocols had been swept aside and the space tampered with. But now a semblance of normalcy crept in him. . . Because, with a slight trepidation a few moments ago, his junior officer Sol confirmed his doubt. Sol had been instructed to question the coroner. And Brahma had just found out that the main temple room where the body had been originally found had been touched, contaminated, and cleansed of all clues. The officer had been shocked to find out that the body of a murdered child had been stripped naked and washed by someone without his knowledge or consent.

'Sir, the coroner maybe, then, 'Sol interjected Brahma's thoughts. . . ' Brahma eyed Sol for an instant and dismissed the obvious easy theory but held on to it weakly: "Maybe,"the officer muttered.

"Definitely not by one of us," sighed Yangtso Brahma. He alighted the vehicle, and taking a small stroll outside the gurney, he stared at the lungtah flags high atop the hills surrounding the Zurphu monastery and silently thought, 'But by someone who had the temple keys...by someone who didn't want us to see the body in its original form.' The officer walked a few steps forward and added a final voice to his thoughts: "But definitely by someone who could be in charge here."

The department-issued Motorola walkie-talkie assumed a static tone as Alex readied it for a message.

"Yes, come in," the device relayed. Another short static, and an officer answered, "Yes, sir, over." The inspector's tone echoed around the van.

"I want you to silently exit the room, officer. . . Over," the command hushed. The static continued.

"And meet me outside. . . fast. "

"Yes, sir, over," the inspector in charge replied, and he started exiting the temple guest room along with the other three constables.

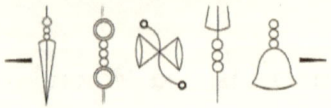

Lama Tashi leaned in from his chair and dragged his old body towards Karma Wangden. Each slow movement of the body forward was marked by a great amount of effort and work.

"Here, Gyan-la," Karma quickly moved in towards the Khenpo and kneeled before him, anticipating an attempt at speech but, more importantly, the reason for him being there.

"A great evil has befallen us, Karma," the Khenpo slowly started, with every attempt to erase the image from his mind.

Karma Wangden, still anticipating the real reason for him being there, peered intently into the old monk's eyes, trying to elicit the real cause more quickly.

"Never has an incident like this occurred in a place of worship like this," Lama Tashi continued. Drawing a few deep breaths, the Khenpo drew his gaze directly into Karma's eyes and said, "Karma, I want you to keep an open mind when I say things to you today." The student nodded... "Trust me and have faith in me and my judgments, and we shall overcome this inhuman tragedy that has struck us." Karma looked at him with intense focus, not knowing how to react to his Gyan-la's words. He had been called here for a service, but he was at a cul-de-sac inside his mind as far as he was concerned...Karma Wangden didn't have any option but to feign a response...He nodded...

"The events over the past few days that have occurred elsewhere in the monasteries throughout the state, and here too, will act as a catalyst...," Lama Tashi paused and continued, "...and further other unfortunate events as well,..." The senior Abbot stared blankly at the floor for some time before he resumed, "I fear this murder and the similar events that have occurred in the past few weeks have a ravenous appetite to set in motion the evil wheels of the monster's machine." The veteran monk had been certainly distraught by the events that had taken place at his place of worship and couldn't summon the mental acumen to string them into sensible words to his protege. But he had to, no matter how and what and fast because he had complete faith in his young protégé...Fate had conspired in bringing them together and the monk knew that he would be able to stop the rampant evil that was running amuck in his holy abode...

"Karma," the Khenpo resumed, "An ancient dark force has reared itself and is threatening to shake the very pillars of our philosophy. The Abbot looked up at the holy murals sprawled across the entirety of the room and held his gaze on the paintings..."...It was of Heruka, the fierce protective Vajrayana deity...Lama Tashi resumed, "These incidents are vehemently trying to upend and question the very practices and texts of our beliefs..."

Though for good measure the Abbot had managed to enlighten Karma on the events that had transpired, the student still couldn't understand wholly what the Khenpo was telling him. It was evident that something terrible had happened and that the Gyan-La needed his assistance. Yet, because the incident had terrified him fully, the Gyan-la was just taking an immense time to divulge all the details to him. He just prayed that the old monk not conflate the matter anymore...Without egging the Khenpo for a quick explanation, he instead braced himself for a patient response.

"Karma, a man's journey that he makes must not be understood in terms of singularity but in the sense of how many has he covered." Karma leaned in closer and shook his head, slowly affirming the Khenpo's words.

"The universe's simple cause and effect principles,the man's volitional action , alone determine the kind of path he takes into the afterlife..." Karma shook his head, a great many theological examples entered his head... "What he becomes is decided by the man's deeds or actions in this lifetime." Lama Tashi drew a sporadic breath every time he delivered a line to Karma. The truth—the real incident—was as bewildering and confusing as the state of mind he was in.

Karma Wangden couldn't fight the great amount of palpable tension in the air. His body language and general demeanor suggested that. Karma touched Khenpo's forehead with his and urged him to continue.

"I discovered a Tulku's strangled and battered body inside the main temple shrine." The Abbot blurted out...

Karma suddenly was startled and looked back at the Khenpo, more shocked than surprised, and held the stare for a couple of minutes longer, half urging the Khenpo for an explanation and the other half still shocked at the news. The Khenpo continued, "in my entire lifetime as a monk until now, I have never seen or experienced such a barbaric act. The very warmth and life of this holy place seemed to have been stolen after that."

"What Khenpo?" Karma stood erect. 'A murder here inside the gompa'.? It was now starting to make sense to Karma Wangden as to why he was summoned here...

Like everyone Karma Wangden was well aware of the heinous murders that had previously rocked the Capital's top monasteries...It was the fourth murder that had been committed, and the modus operandi of the crime—strangulation and battery—suggested the killer or perpetrator to be the same. The public outcry and the faith holders' cry for justice had gone all out against the administration and more so against the police force...The religious zealotry had upped the ante against the establishment and called the Police establishment inefficient... "So what is the police doing,?" a local media had questioned a Police Officer then, "Whatever needs to be done to catch the perpetrator, but for now, let us do the job without any interference, please...the officer answered with fiery clarity..." You mean to sit at your job doing nothing," a journalist had fired back from the crowd...It had been a media frenzy in the capital after that, as hundreds of domestic and international media houses lodged themselves at various monasteries where the murder had taken place. First, it was the Du-Zhong, one of the oldest of the monasteries in the state. Then it had been En-Zhong, the Zhongkhang, and then the Zurphu monastery.

The capital was converted into a 'newsy-noisy' town overnight as hundreds of capsuled media vans with their rooftop dishes pointed skywards snaked and jostled throughout the capital making a beeline towards the scene, trying to get that extra media bite about the incidents. The entire region and the world, in general, was transfixed in front of their televisions for updates on such events. Karma Wangden was one of them. But he knew little about the fact that the next crime would be committed here at the Zurphu monastery. He paused for a second and inched closer to his teacher. Trying to contribute some obvious sense of help to his master...

"So why shouldn't we tell the police about this?" Karma replied instantly. "They might be able to help us."

"No," interjected Lama Tashi loudly, surprising Karma, the echo of his reply occupying every silence in the room with great resonance.

"This is something that concerns us and not them," the Khenpo continued, renewed energy now entering his vocal cords."Karma Wangden didn't understand... "The most they can do is launch an investigation, but I doubt they have the stomach to digest that which they can't understand and see." The student tried to keep pace with the teacher... "Once the realm of realism ceases, the other one begins, where the line between reality and fantasy is blurred. Where reality in esotericism enters and takes place, adding a new dimension to events around you." The Abbot Lama Tashi reiterated, '...a new dimension to events around you...' Still, it made no sense to Karma Wangden. "Reality, fantasy, dimensions. . . "

"And Karma, I want you to help me in nabbing this murderer of the gifted souls. . . and that too fast..."

"What, Gyan-la?" Karma said, horrified. The media had been feeding him enough news about the recent murders that had taken place in the capital. An unprecedented series of murders had been committed, and the victims had been all recognized child Tulkus of different Buddhist sects. First, it had been Gelug, then Nyingma, Shakya, and then finally the Kagyu sect.

"It is only right that we tell the police about this," Karma continued with the same heightened shock and surprise. "They might be able to stave off this; they have more expertise and manpower." Karma again knelt before his Gyan-la stared into his ageing eyes and said, "The police are better equipped for this. And how could we possibly do this and solve this all on our own?"

Lama Tashi let out a long sigh and looked out of the window at an audience of people trying to engage and inquire about the events unfolding inside. A big crowd had already gathered outside the Zurphu monastery gate and was accompanied by the usual murmurs and the likes of an informal gathering.

He got up from his chair and trudged slowly towards the window, summoning Karma to follow suit after him. Karma Wangden gently, albeit in a firm manner, held his old and feeble hands and escorted Lama Tashi to the window.

The Khenpo, not knowing how to react to Karma's bewilderment, didn't know how to break the main news that he had yet to tell him. His apprehensions about withholding news from him would surely drive Karma irate. But he also knew that gradual dissemination was need of the hour, lest confusion ensues.

Resting his hands on the window sill with Karma flanking him on his left side, Lama Tashi followed up his explanations with deep and long breaths, not knowing how Karma would react eventually.

"I discovered the Tulku's body inside the temple and"...a pause, "removed it from there," Lama Tashi said, a long silence hanging in the air after that.

"What, Gyan-la?" Karma shrieked. "You did what?" Lama Tashi slowly continued, "When I discovered the body inside, I also saw some messages which were there, hundreds of paper pamphlets, similar ones found earlier in the other murders, which carried the same texts..."

It was true that the former murderers of the same nature had hundreds of pamphlets strewn around the corpses of murdered children. All of them conveyed a message. The law enforcement officials, including Officer Yangtso Brahma and his team of the entire State Police, had done well to stave off curious minds from the case, lest they interfere with the investigation. Brahma knew better than to allow for tampering again...

The Khenpo took some moment to breathe and resumed, "These messages, the texts were all in their original form in letter and spirit...It was more of a warning, an ominous threat than a message." The Khenpo drew a long breath and continued, "I will show you what I've witnessed, and you'll know what it is all about..."

"Yes, I want to know that," Karma retorted, looking a bit flustered when doing so.

"You know that there are some abstract and esoteric parts in Buddhist texts, texts that every devout Buddhist should first understand and then preach and practice." Lama Tashi peered into the young eyes of Karma and delivered his final statement about the incident with clarity and focus.

"Karma, I found out through the messages and the environment in which the body was found that the killer means for us to repent for our sins through the 'intermediate stage' in the afterlife."

"What sins are you talking about, Gyan-la? I cannot understand." He paused and took a quick breath, "And what do you mean the intermediate stage?"

Lama Tashi stared silently into the crowd for a few seconds and then replied, "We are men of God, the bearers of the ultimate message, the source of hope and belief for millions of people all over the world. We do the Lord's bidding day in and day out. No matter what religion or ideology we share, the truth always remains, and that is people from all walks of life will eventually look towards us as the bridge between their prayers and God." Lama Tashi looked intently at the crowd below and continued, "The chaos, the confusion, and the mass hysteria that surround people and their everyday lives are evident and inevitable. Their only solace and comfort about their existence lies in a single word." Karma Wangden knew it was always the WORD... "That word, Karma, my son, is faith. Faith can make a man rule and conquer the world; it can give a humble poet the required pain that he needs to push his pen towards beautiful sonnets; it can give a helpless woman strength to endure hardships; it can help a child to look at the world and make him think that everything is possible. But most importantly, it can renew a hardened agnostic's belief in God." The Khenpo slowly returned to his chair, with Karma in tow behind him, and looked earnestly into the young man's eyes and resumed, "However, it is an undeniable fact that although we act as a link between the people's prayers and hopes and Him, we are still mortals, and as mortals, we are encumbered by our selfish desires and interests, thus sometimes failing in fulfilling our Godly duties with perfection."

Karma Wangden listened intently with rapt attention to whatever the Khenpo was saying, even noticing a chilling warning overtone in his oratory.

"We give in way too easily to some pleasures of life that we forget that we are ultimately the messengers of God and His teachings. And when the cauldron of our negative karma and deeds is full, the sins of our institution become all pervasive and transparent, and the very word that gave us life from day one, that faith, keeps eroding gradually and turns to dust before our own eyes. "

The Khenpo slowly removed the mala from his wrist and started chanting inaudibly. He knew he had to convince Karma Wangden about something so abstract that it was nearly impossible for any layman to comprehend.

"The killer, my son," Lama Tashi resumed, "is trying to make us suffer for our actions and deeds." Lama Tashi continued, "And most importantly, he wants to do that in this life of ours and the intermediate stage as well."

Lama Tashi held Karma's hand with some brute force, surprising the young boy, and whispered the two Buddhist words for the first time in years, "The Bardo Thodol..."

Karma in turn held his master's hand tightly and looked shell-shocked into his master's eyes. "The intermediate stage!" Karma thought, now crystal clear as to what the Khenpo had been trying to convey the entire time. "The Intermediate stage. . . the in-between. . . the period between death and rebirth, in Buddhist philosophy." Although Karma had a fair share of knowledge about the stage in theory, he had never, of course, experienced them, as he was still alive. But something told him that the Khenpo's fear was legitimate, and he tried to understand them fully. *'The intermediate stage, The Bardo Thodol,'* thought Karma Wangden and sat transfixed on the floor beneath him.

ENTER THE BARDO.

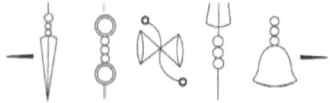

The murky mists of the October sky bathed Chorten Monastery in white, engulfing the confines of the monastery with its mildew-covered material. It converted the once-pristine facade of the edifice into a damp, dotted world of fungal hyphae. Relentless blasts of fog swathed the surroundings in their damp, eerie embrace. Outside in its expansive courtyard, a dark, hooded figure, playing with the thenga, elusively cut across the expanse of the monastery with a slow, purposeful gait as sure as the encroaching mists. The killer lifted the robes, sagging in the dirt, and peered at the watch, ignorantly shackled on the left wrist.

The courtyard pattered with the feet of the novice monks, recently ordained and undergoing training for a lifelong career of practicing the faith and preaching. They skipped and ran to the changing rooms as their monastic lessons progressed for the day. Their latent and unspoken dream was still trying to attain Buddhahood and enlightenment in this life or the next. The air was noisy with their chattering.

There was an atmosphere of play and purpose. Anticipating no visitors early this morning, the figure was surprised at the presence of tourists walking and praying, some of them still in somnolence and some engaged in 'soul searching' in the Gompa premises. They paced the quadrangle, being obvious curious 'shoppers' of temporary salvation and scenery.

The killer despised their presence. From the very core of his being, he revolted against the reasons that he imagined brought these here.

'They think they've understood us? . . . if only they understood their faiths better. . .' Their presence in the pristine sanctum repulsed the killer. The killer paced forward, *'an instant gratification. . . instant enlightenment. . . fast in this lifetime. . . futile. . . a big pretense.'* The killer stopped in its tracks, looked behind the edifice, and thought, *'When it comes down to sacrifices and choices, everyone's status is at stake. Their beliefs crumble when reality hits them. Sacrifices and action form the core of philosophy.'*

'They want a quick salvation, as if such were possible through a half-lifetime of piety.' The figure rapidly played with the beads of the rosary. *'They are mistaken, and what is worse, their impatience is corrupting the very essence of our searching.'*

The rhythm on the beads slowed. A beatific smile cut across the killer's face. . . *'But I have initiated the action that will put an end to such chicanery. Such an insidious charade. The highest expression of faith is deed, and that sacrificial deed has been done. This anointing with blood will set things right by re-aligning the cosmos of our beliefs. '*

'Yes, that's what my teacher told me and promised, and I have immense faith in him,' the killer said aloud.

'It's 5:00 a. m. ,' thought the killer. "I have now completed and initiated something so unprecedented at the behest of my Gyan-la—something that I'm proud of and that will surely help us reach the annals of immortality. . ."The figure neared the myriad tiny prayer wheels with the engravings of *'Om Mane Padme Hun'* calligraphically drawn and stacked in a religious array outside the Chorten Gompa. Touching the forehead with the first part of the pillar from among the four corners of the edifice, the figure slowly started the routine Quoras, the customary perambulations of the prayer wheels in a clockwise direction. The hard and scarred right hand shook vigorously as it lifted from underneath the robe and initiated an action on the first prayer wheel, sending the diminutive and stout yet pious cylindrical object into a tizzy.

With every rotating motion of the wheels, the killer was reminiscent of and thankful for the day that he had met the true Supreme Teacher.

'The heavens must've torn asunder when they sent you to me, Gyan la?' The lonely figure completed the first side of the four squares. *"And to be under your constant care and guidance all along. You have really helped me look at this world in a different way."*

With a steady and swift motion, as if signaling urgency, the dark-hooded figure completed the remaining two physical rotations of the squares. Panting and heaving with every heavy step, the killer approached a large Chorten, built at the center of the monastery and lodged carelessly at the edifice's steps with a thump, heavy breathing accompanying the actions. *"Time must've stood still for everyone here now,"* the killer thought as the hooded figure tried to open the deep recesses of the memories, trying hard to pick an event so paramount that shaped the killer's future and the current events that it was now profoundly part of.

A light sweat broke from the temple, and the initial bead of involuntary salinity slowly disintegrated into hairline tributaries reaching into the cheek before gravity did the rest, and the sweat hit the ground with a minuscule and negligible splash, sending the puddle below into a tiny tremor. The laws of the universe were set in motion, and the outward ripples of the puddle soon came back with a mighty centripetal bang. Somewhere in the universe, the force was symbolic and connected with a recall so powerful that the killer's floodgates of memories swung open with a tidal wave of enormous emotions.

****

In another time and space, in the remotest part of the Denzong hills, Ozer and Ma's friendship bloomed. Engaging in their pastoral lives, their bond grew stronger with each new day. Their age of innocence and brotherhood developed, just like the nearby brook with its sudden burst of perennial fresh water, which started and never stopped.

"Ma, we are good friends, and we would never try to hurt each other, right?" Ozer said as he held Ma's hands and tried to look for an honest answer. Both of them were 15-year-olds and without families, with some village homes providing the only menial labor and food sometimes. Being orphans, they grew up together in a ramshackled orphan house and would act as shields for each other. Together, they roughed out their early years against foes and obstacles with grit and bonhomie. Although their very genes were ingrained with copious amounts of questionable behaviors owing to their environment, Ozer seemed unfazed and uneclipsed by the ill effects of it. Instead, he was always inquisitive and willing to learn. The wealth of knowledge that he derived by virtue of his inquisitiveness and uncanny talent added to his rationality and maturity.

And growing up, Ozer had been different and had found a brother and friend at the extreme end of the spectrum. Ma was the exact opposite, a rampant and quick bloke in his words and actions, and he barely made time to think. Street life had bent him into a shape so rough and tough that he hardly required an iota of courage or second-guessing to commit a crime. His moral fibers had disintegrated at a young age, and Ma, as he drifted into adolescence, had found solace and comfort in drugs and more crime. Through numerous felony sprees and drug use, Ma had turned into a perfect example of a felon. His sure-shot approach to doing things without regret hardly gave him time to have a momentary glimpse into his conscience.

It was after Ma confessed his indulgence to his friend that Ozer learned about his friend's terrible affliction and attempted to guide and free his brother from his bondage of habits.

Ozer looked into Ma's eyes for an honest answer. "In what vicious grip has my brother landed?" Ozer thought ruefully as he noticed that Ma's eyes had a vacant stare confronting him.

"My actions, my consequences," Ma retorted unapologetically every time Ozer tried to advise his brother.

Ozer looked into Ma's teary eyes and tried hard not to feel sorry. But being more brothers than friends since their infancy, Ozer had to eventually succumb to the harsh realities of bonded relationships. And as he looked hard for an answer from Ma, Ozer's emotions and entrails churned inside him with such great force that even his ducts gave way to runny tears. Ozer involuntarily took Ma in his arms and gripped him tightly. As if the words of fear, loathing, and forgiveness had been spoken silently all at once, the conjoined bodies of the brothers showed harmony and love.

****

A loud gong shattered the calm and tranquility of the Chorten Monastery area. The killer woke up with a start, the ears ringing terribly from the sonic metallic signal calling for prayers. The sands of memories still trickled fresh in the mind but were cut off abruptly. The killer adjusted the robe, and although still in a sleepy daze, the killer knew that there were matters so crucial and important that it could afford to lose the afternoon slumber. There was a hint of a vibration inside the robe. Shaking off the last remnant of lethargy and inertia, the killer reached inside the robe and produced a small, black, portable metallic cell phone from underneath it. Eyeing the caller on the screen, the killer did a double-take, excited and thrilled. It had one number, but that was all that was required. With some trepidation and excitement, the killer pressed the button and pressed the cellphone to the ear, longing quickly for a voice that was soothing and familiar.

After some moments of longing in the air, the killer spoke. "Yes, my teacher," the killer answered, involuntarily bowing in response to the call, with the mannerisms suggesting an acute obsequious demeanor. The killer prepared to give the news to the teacher and mentally arranged the thought premises quickly. "Yes, my child," a bass voice with a hint of treble answered from the other line.

"Gyan-la, as ordered, the final task has been completed," the killer said with a hint of pride stationed in the assertion. A loud and deep inhalation of satisfaction emanated from the other end of the receiver.

"Very good, my child," the voice echoed from the other end. "You have indeed set off an event so important that ignorance and downplay from their side are now impossible." A long silence hung in the air, and the teacher resumed, "Now, the rest of the plan must also be handled with utmost care and precision, and I have complete faith in you. "

"Thuchi Gyan la," the killer replied, the hands holding the device trembling with excitement. Right from the time they had made acquaintance, it had been such an honor just to be in his presence and listen to the sermons and teachings of the philosophy. The killer, at the behest of the teacher, had mentally accompanied him to numerous faith and Dharma gatherings around the world. *'Such is his power. You don't have to be physically present with him, but you can mentally experience the magic of meditative retreats in full.'* The killer was astounded at the methods and innovative ways the teacher adopted for the teachings of the Dharma. One would not always have agreed with his somewhat radical ways of translation and preaching, but it was enough for the killer from the numerous sessions to supplicate to him. "Such a brilliant and brave mind," the killer had thought then and still believed in him now. "And to think that I would have a chance to work for a cause so powerful and significant that, at one point in time, I even doubted my participation in it." But now, with him at the center of events and execution, the killer knew better than to question the Supreme Teacher's role.

"It is time that the people know of our deeds and actions. Actions that had to be committed in order to stave off the loss of faith and belief in our religion,our philosophy. It had to be done to eradicate even a minute amount of pretense and sham our religion now suffers from." The voice paused for a brief moment, a heady cocktail of emotions and tensions being borne by the wireless electronic waves between the receiver and the killer. "The men of God will see reason in our actions, and they will acknowledge the fact that their practices and learnings up until now were hollow and futile." The voice paused again before resuming, "The heavens opened up and rained millions of letters from the one true God and Messiah. We must fulfill Vajra's prophecy; the onus is on us." The killer listened intently to every word the voice was saying, each second thanking the stars for becoming the chosen one to do the master's and God's bidding.

"Now the time is right," the voice resumed again, "to carry forward all your remaining duties and tasks carefully and quickly, so that we are in a position to relay not only to this region but to the entire world the message that underlines our doings. I sure hope you know where to go and what to do next." The voice cleared his throat on the other end and signed off on a chilling note, "You have been bestowed with this great divine challenge, and I guarantee that you will find a path towards enlightenment. The goals of Buddhahood and Nirvana must be attained by actions alone, not mere words in the texts...The teacher concluded. "Thuchi Gyan la," the killer thanked the cell phone, and the call ended abruptly. After drawing a long breath, the hooded figure started walking downward from the monastery. "The work of Vajra needed to be done, and my work and duties shall never go unnoticed. Instead, it shall echo until eternity sees mankind off," thought the killer and the figure began trudging and descending toward the temple exit swiftly.

ENTER THE BARDO.

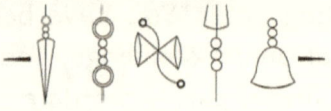

Brahma paced agitatedly along the length of the corridor outside the main temple...'Sol and Alex, come in...' he impatiently barked an order...The events of that day and the days preceding it had been too brutal and shocking for Officer Yangtso Brahma...The barbaric acts perpetrated had not only shocked the State but the news had seamlessly crossed borders and into the shaken hearts and minds of people worldwide . . . The aftermath was also a relentless assault on his patience, challenged equivalently if not more only by the media breathing down his neck questioning the tardiness in investigation and his dedication towards his work...The onus to crack the cases thus was on him, as a lot had been riding on his career lately...The physical and mental toll the training days effected on the officer had been somewhat allayed by the news on the cadre only to be at the vanguard of a brutal and senseless criminal investigation immediately afterwards...The idiom on the frying pan was not lost on him...But the officer Yangtso Brahma took it upon himself, driven by an overwhelming moral desire to see the cases through.... It was also after all a matter of the descendant of the soil standing up in the face of such challenges and hoping to succeed in the endeavor...

An array of jostling reporters from various media houses always had their cameras and microphones trained on him the minute he was outside his office...The incessant open-ended questions on the updates on the investigation had driven the investigating team irate. . . A forlorn expression crossed his face as he impatiently waited for his sub-ordinates to report to him. . . *'they better be here quickly.'*

The officers as expected were nearing Brahma as soon as he had relayed the order...Watching the two of them arriving with urgency Brahma noticed a semblance of calmness returning in him...The officers were accompanied by 3-4 armed guards...The furrows on Brahma's forehead finally increased a bit at the sight...

"Yes, Sir," an ever-obedient Sol and Alex saluted as they neared and stopped a few feet away from Yangtso Brahma...Their hands clasped firmly at the Motorola Walkie Talkie...His constables following suit...

Without batting an eyelid, the officer spoke hurriedly albeit clearly..."You know, the Department was already faced with the task of solving crimes that were committed before this, right?" Yangtso Brahma said with a stern tone..."Similar crimes, along with the modus operandi." He turned towards the temple and lit a half-burned Cohiba that he had doused a few minutes earlier...The combustion of the cigarillo let out an aerosol fume distinct to the brand...The inhalation of the toxicants filled his lungs with the needed nicotine and tar...The fumes dissipated into his lungs, making him somewhat relaxed and focused...

"Sol you and I know that the crime scene was tampered with...That it had been washed and cleaned before we arrived here," Brahma resumed, after taking another drag and then facing Alex and the guards...

"What, Sir? Are you sure?" Alex replied perplexed...The tone a mix of query and shock...

Brahma nodded. "It is clear that someone had found out about the murder before our knowledge...A great deal of effort was put in to wipe out evidence of the same, this person cleared the room of the incident and cleansed the surroundings'... *'tampering and clearing the evidence'*...Sol spoke out softly to Alex who nodded...

"Now who would do such a thing, Sir?" Alex queried, looking at the officer directly and then turning his gaze away...

"An interesting question, Alex," Brahma replied..."Who would do such a thing, and why?"

Brahma took a last drag of the cigarillo and extinguished it firmly beneath his boot...He then turned to both of his officers...

"Time is critical right now, boys...We have to move ahead with great certainty and urgency if we are to nab this murderer and any complicit suspect(s)..." Yangtso Brahma looked at Alex intently and paused for a brief moment to relay his orders.

"You...take these men with you and conduct a procedural yet thorough interrogational routine with everyone from this monastery... "

"Right, Sir," Alex obeyed...

"Spare no one in the questioning," Brahma continued and, with a final directness, added, "Not even the head Abbot or Khenpo of this monastery..." Alex bowed in front of his officer and proceeded to follow the orders...

"Especially the Khenpo of this Gompa," Brahma iterated...

ENTER THE BARDO.

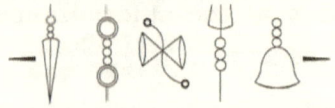

A classic 500h Lexus LC automobile tore its chassis through the streets of the last suburban town, serpentining its way uphill towards the capital. The chauffeur, dressed in Buddhist regalia and high Tibetan mountain boots, slung a long, single-edged dpa'dam across his shoulder, which was ensconced inside the garment of his gown, suggesting that the driver moonlighted as a soldier or a guard for the occupant inside. The gilded scabbard housing the traditional sword was both a work of careless art, with a slapdash of rubies and sapphires straddling the outer cover, and elegant as well, with a shiny amethyst on its crown. He received the cell phone with his left hand from a small portal behind him. A pudgy individual with a sharp widow's peak, more of a result of closely cropped hair than anything, jutting through his head, adjusted himself in his seat after handing the driver the phone. The lone occupant had shaved his head a couple of months ago, ready for an event so significant in his life that he had thought and believed in the very purpose of his life therein after. . . *'Thank you to my chamberlain'* He rubbed his left eye softly and looked out the window of the speeding Lexus. With a great deal of difficulty, he came to a level with the window and could now see outside.

Outside, the scenic nature just whizzed by instantly every second in a kaleidoscope of lights and waves. The vast arrangement of vegetation by the highway disappeared behind the moving vehicle as it sped past with great speed. The scattered yellow rays of the sun broke through the canopy, forming a dapple of marks and spots on the highway. The newsy, noisy commercial capital started to welcome him after a hiatus of many months. The streets were lined with shops, with people ready to embrace the challenges the new day had to offer. Vendors with their street urchins wheeling the carts were getting better at evading the oncoming vehicles as they prepared to hawk their wares and partake in the challenging albeit bountiful commerce of the state.

From among the many moving images outside the car, the one that captured the occupant's attention was that of young and tiny children reluctantly walking to their respective schools. . . *'Ah! children'*, the occupant perked up suddenly, a sardonic smile lighting up his face. . . *'The innocence and nubility of them need not be bent to suit the needs and selfish interests of the masters. . . for they are immature souls; their age and wisdom are just too small to comprehend and bear the responsibility of the philosophy. . . '* The individual shuffled in his seat as the driver swerved sharply on a curve, the tires skidding, before resuming again along a straight road. *'This age of theirs,* he resumed, *' is to dwell in the magic of positivity and optimism that life has to offer. . . Believe till they mature that everything is possible. . . Have fun laughing, singing, and playing with their families, and learn the basic edicts of values and education, which are necessary instillations. At this juncture and time, things should never be forced upon them. They shouldn't be allowed to handle things that they have no idea or comprehension of. They are young and impressionable minds, and bestowing upon them the duty of fronting a philosophical ideology as complex as religion is nonsense and a great insult to the Dharma. '* The Lexus made another turn as it neared the main town area and made a quick dash upwards towards Tibet Road. *'The negligence and highhandedness of supposed Dharma protectors should've been stopped a long time ago. Their very thinking and solution to certain religious problems should've been stripped off the bud. Owing to that, the idea of Buddhism has witnessed the proliferation of sacrilegious and impractical practices. The very sacrosanct texts have been tampered with and given totally different, useless, and wrongful dimensions, and because of that, it has resulted in the production of pretentious and artificial religious heads and devotees all over the world. '*

'From the beginning of my life to this day, I felt I was destined for more, and because of our Supreme Teacher, we are now at the threshold of time to create history. We change the world today and our philosophy forever. For the Buddha, the Dharma, and the Sangha. . . '

The car decelerated, and the engine, which had produced a large amount of torque and speed just a while ago, hissed before coming to a halt in front of a 7 star Hotel. . . *'Better late than never,'* the occupant thought. ' *Time to beat the shamans and the impostors out of our faith. . . '* The sturdy-built chauffeur alighted first and held the door as the occupant struggled out of the tall vehicle. The chaueffeur guardingly covered the occupant as he walked into the hotel. . . *'If not now, then when; if not us, then who. . . '*

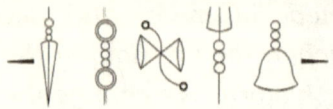

"But how is it possible for someone to do that?" Karma wondered aloud. "And Gyan-la, the very texts of the holy Bardo Thodol are stepped in esotericism...they have wider and layered meanings..." Karma now faced the senior Abbott and tread cautiously... "If I am not mistaken Gyan la...shouldn't it be read only once..." Karma paused... 'in a person's life. '

The tranquility of nature outside could be matched albeit inversely only by the pandemonium inside the confines of the monastery...Karma Wangden was gradually beginning to fathom the gravity of the situation inside...So far a semblance of clarity as to the event had begun to make sense to him but he was still far removed from the whole picture...It had yet to be unraveled wholly to him ...He jogged his memory...*'a murder, young Tulku, messages, Bardo Thodol...what next...'*

"Yes, my son," replied the Khenpo, looking directly into Karma's eyes to emphasize his point. But Karma's gaze did not reveal any further query so Lama Tashi continued. "Yes, Karma, the very essence of the texts have wider meanings and connotations...the writings are not restricted to a literal meaning but have varying layers to them. . . However, contrary to common beliefs, it doesn't just apply to a singular event in a man's life..."

Karma Wangden stood mute and held his dumbfounded stare...Whatever he had learned after arriving at the monastery today had been baffling to him... *'and here is another one from the master himself...the texts of the Bardo Thodol don't apply to death alone...'*

Lama Tashi strolled towards the walled murals, peering intently at one of the paintings on the wall. It depicted Guru Padmasambhava, adorned menacingly with a trident in one hand and garlanded with hundreds of slayed demonic skulls. "The main underlying theme," Lama Tashi resumed after some time, "of the texts of Bardo Thodol serves as a guide or a path towards a better life, or more importantly, towards enlightenment...The obscure scripts of the holy Paycha or book should be used as a guide by people to teach them how to live their lives as long as they are here on this planet. Most of the texts are esoteric and can be interpreted on varying layers, and it takes even highly ordained monks a lot of time and practice to understand the real meaning behind the writings..."

"But a general understanding tells you that the texts are guidelines for those who are nearing death or have already died," Lama Tashi continued. "No subject is feared or looked upon as near taboo as the subject of death. . . Thanatophobia is real..."The Abbot continued, "and the script serves as a mighty comforter to the one who is nearing an end...most importantly, it provides solace and satisfaction to the living and the grieving, knowing that their loved one is on a journey into a new life."

Karma Wangden wasn't in a position to think clearly. His otherwise peaceful and mundane day had started with a jolt. A call for help from the Zurphu Monastery's Khenpo, the sudden swarm of police in the area, the congregation of people, and the eventual news of a murder inside the temple had completely shocked and bewildered him. At that immediate juncture, he doubted his ability to help his Gyan-La.

The connection between the murders and the texts of Bardo Thodol was unclear to him still. . . Although the Abbot Lama Tashi was beginning to demystify the events and he was on a path of learning... it was too slow as his master was constantly conflating and fusing issues for his protégé's simple comprehension...But it wasn't making things easier...Needless to say, it kept confounding Karma Wangden... Lama Tashi's actions of tampering with the crime scene and erasing the evidence were even more confusing... *'Why would the Gyan la do that?'* The student kept asking himself...Karma Wangden felt that he had been unknowingly drawn into a labyrinthine like situation and he needed answers fast. . . His master wanted his help but the needle of suspicion would point towards him when the police found out the truth...For all he knew Karma Wangden was heading towards a black hole of confusion...But he also knew that he had to trust his master and lead him through all the questions no matter how perplexing they might be...His services had been called for...and he was here for him...

Karma placed his hand on the Khenpo's shoulder and said, "Gyan-La, I don't know exactly what you ask of me, and I haven't the faintest idea of the whole situation. . ." He took a deep breath and hugged his old teacher before whispering, "But I'm here now, and I will help you. I will do everything you ask of me. But before that, I have to request something from you. "

Karma let go of the Khenpo and took a step back, looking directly into his eyes. "You know, Gyan-La, that your actions could lead to your arrest...There's a chance your involvement in the murder might be established...the integrity of the crime scene has been tampered with...by you... I hope that you have some kind of a solution after we evade the police outside and leave this area... "

Lama Tashi looked at Karma and smiled. Despite not being well-versed in the procedures of the law, the Khenpo understood the urgency of the situation. He knew they had to escape the police personnel before the authorities interrogated him. Lama Tashi spoke, "We will have to leave quickly. But first. . ." He turned and walked down a corridor to the end of the room. Bending down a few metres away from the wall, the Khenpo turned and he gestured for Karma to do the same.

Karma followed his teacher's instructions, not entirely sure what was happening. Lama Tashi began feeling the wooden floor beneath them with his old sturdy fingers, searching for something specific. After a moment, he found what he was looking for and inserted his fingers into what appeared a rudimentary keyhole engraved on it. With a strong pull, he lifted a small square door from beneath them. Karma was astonished by this hidden compartment.

After opening the door, Lama Tashi descended a set of stairs, with Karma following him. Karma was left in awe when he saw the room below, well-lit and filled with advanced electronic surveillance equipment. Hundreds of computers were displaying images and videos from various areas of the monastery. Lama Tashi guided Karma to a small closed cubicle with its monitor.

These monitors were live, providing real-time coverage of different areas. Lama Tashi explained, "It's essential to have security surveillance, even in holy places, due to recent incidents of vandalism and theft. These devices help protect our sacred spaces. " Almost immediately Karma Wangden blurted out the obvious... "The tapes could show us..." before he could finish,the Abbot cut him out... "Yes records,the tape...I checked..."

Lama Tashi went to an electronic box attached to a wall, pressed a few buttons, and a plate emerged with a circular disk. He quickly handed it to Karma and said, "I'll explain it to you more...later... " But it's impossible to break through the police blockade and escape without getting noticed. Even if I drive at top speed, the noise alone would give us away easily."

Lama Tashi stood and thought for a moment, his mind racing, praying for a solution. He knew they had to evade from the temple premises , but avoiding the police was the immediate priority.

Finally, he asked Karma, "You have a bike, right?"

Karma nodded, and Lama Tashi took away the keys from him. Without delay, Lama Tashi exited the room with Karma following closely behind. They descended the spiral staircase and entered the monastery's dormitory.No sooner had they done that,the duo stopped dead in their tracks...Karma Wangden and the Abbot caught a pair of shocked eyes staring at them directly...They didn't flinch...Careful not to antagonize him any further ,the Abbot tried to initiate something with the figure directly in-front of him...

Karma Wangden and the Lama had just spotted a young monk standing away from the chaos outside,directly in front of them and signalled for him to come inside.

"Inchung Dorje, I have a task for you," Lama Tashi said authoritatively as the teen monk joined them near the window. "We'll explain later, but first, you must help us. "

The Inchung bowed before the Khenpo. "Lus Gyan la, I am at your command. "

The Khenpo, Karma, and Inchung huddled together, and after a quick discussion, a plan was set in motion...

ENTER THE BARDO.

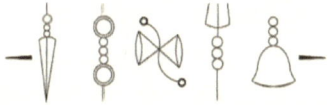

Sol and Alex paced around the table with the monastery faculty seated nervously in front of them. The room was quiet. The silence was interrupted by a faint static on the cordless as it caught different frequencies. However, Alex switched it off and held it ready for an urgent message in case something materialized during the questioning. Seated in a horizontal row across the pew in one of the prayer chapels, the venerated senior nun Ani Trezang prayed with her thenga, her eyes welling up at the events that transpired. She was one of the very few senior nuns that had stayed at the monastery since a young novitiate and had been a witness to its various transitions and changes. '*But none like the present carnage.*' Senior Ani Tresong wiped her tears with a soft whimper. Apart from her, she was accompanied by the late Tuolku Tenzing Wangchuk's Chamberlain Riithang Rimpoche, Stanzin, and one other senior priest, Lama Ghongsor, second in command to the Abbot Lama Tashi. The two officers initiated the interrogation and quickly stepped it up, trying to cover all the loopholes the answers brought with them. But after a tiring session, both found out that all their alibis and answers held water as far as they were concerned. But both knew better than to close the interrogation in a hurry. 'So, Ani Tresong, apart from you all present out here, is there anyone else who else is present at the top of the order in this monastery. . . ?' Ani Tresong just played her beads nonchalantly, rarely looking up.

Riithang Rimpoche cut in, sensing a great deal of difficulty from Ani in answering it. 'Officer, apart from the ones present here, there is Lama Tashi, the Abbot, who is the senior most in the order whom you'll be meeting shortly, and then. . . ' Riithang Rimpoche paused, and suddenly a big pat, more like a punch, met both officers' backs with a resounding thud. Sol and Alex heaved forward from the blow. The force cut their air supply for a brief period of time. But before they could recover themselves, two huge hands held them on their elbows and made them stand. The figure from behind greeted the officers with a huge smile. Before they could answer in retaliation, Riithang Rimpoche quickly interrupted and held the officers back. The figure towering before them was a huge senior monk draped in a civara who walked with an imposing limp, his right hand holding a stick that balanced his gait. He towered above everyone else in the room and recklessly sat atop a stool, eyeing everyone, especially the officers. He nonchalantly grinned at the site of them before proceeding towards an incoherent volley of verbal religious texts.

'Sirs, please excuse him. . . He is a senior old Lama whose mental acumen has seen better days. . . Quezong Khenpo, as we all call him. . . He claims he knows everything, but we doubt that... Over the years, we have just found him loitering around the gompa, talking to himself, and exploding with such incoherent babbles the rest of the time. Please excuse him, sirs. . . ' The officers settled eventually, but their backs were still hurting from the thunderous blow. 'He surely means no harm, and we are sure he was also present in his meditative retreats, just like the rest of us during the time of the incident. . . '

Quezong Khenpo, having finished reciting the mantras, which were surely out of context for the situation, got up instantly and walked up to the two officers. Sol and Alex readied themselves this time to evade whatever came their way. . . ' Quezong eyed the two officers and exhaled a hot breath down their faces: 'Duality, the dual nature of things, day and night, hot and cold, good and bad, man and woman, ugly and beautiful. . . ' Before he finished his rattling, he completed with another nonsensical phrase, 'winner, loser, competition, and religion, the last one, how come? . . . haha. . . ' He snarled and exited the room.

The two officers looked at each other, confused and hurt.

****

Yangtso Brahma walked up swiftly towards the titanium diavel. His gait was a movement of authority and urgency. Upon nearing it, he reached into his pocket and extracted a small, oval metallic device from inside. He kneeled down and stole a few glances sideways. Noticing no prying eyes on him, and with a move as smooth and fast as a wily fox, he stuck the device on the bike's cowling. *'Let's see you try and outrun us,* he hopefully thought. 'Everyone, rally around, ' Brahma ordered the police to gather around in front of the main temple for a final briefing before they stormed the temple and the attached premises.

ENTER THE BARDO.

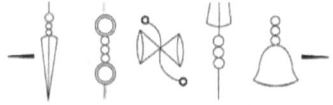

The killer drove with a frenetic pace as the vehicle descended from the capital towards the lower-lying areas of the capital. . . Driven by a relentless determination to complete the mission, the car careened dangerously on the winding roads, often skidding perilously close to the edge. . . The hands-on wheels and the foot on the throttle coordinated perfectly with the brakes playing second fiddle on the journey. After a sharp turn on the curve beside Ortem Plaza, the foot hit the pedal and drove swiftly downwards towards the destination. . . The figure slowly stole a glance from the cowls of the robe to a pair of media vans making its uphill journey, jostling in traffic. . . *'For the news,* ' the figure snarled. . . '. . . *and I've been a delightful witness to the macabre turn of events. . . firsthand. . .* '

'I have to reach my destination soon,' thought the killer as the old fiat ambassador went full throttle. . .

****

Dense monsoon pouring dampened the hilly tracts as Ma and Ozer's friendship bloomed. . . Their homes were one of the many huts that perilously mushroomed in other stony escarpments along the Denzong hills. . . After all the nomadic Buddhist practices were adopted by their elders in the group. . . Fodder gathering and hunting became a staple part of their pastoral lives. . . The two friends would spend hours exploring the areas under the valley, angling with their rudimentary fishing equipment and chasing elusive riverside birds and mynahs and an assortment of other biodiversities that they preyed on and that their area had to offer. . . Ozer was the collector of the two and Ma's curiosities would often peak as Ozer would showcase the loot safely deposited in a copper box that he had collected over the years. . . For there lay among the treasure trove, two rusted albeit sharp fishing hooks which had according to Ozer been instrumental in catching a large carp that he claimed that he had ever seen. . . The box also contained a half-burned candle, a somewhat hard carapace of a mud crab endemic to the region and a couple of marbles that they would shoot at now and then. . . Under the setting sun and atop the stony escarpment the two brothers embraced each other and vowed never to let go of each other. . .

'Until eternity sees us off,' Ozer said as he held closely the emaciated body of Ma. . .

The alpine vegetation in their areas started to etiolate like the summer warmth as the cold winter crept in with an icy vice. . . The trees and even the mosses and nearby lichens paled as the challenge to sustenance grew amidst the oncoming winter. . . The two friends after many moons made their foray into the city life, hoping for such a migratory success but here was where Ma succumbed to a life of agony and pain after just a couple of months. . . A tragic accident had torn them apart, and Ozer had been taken away, leaving Ma in a world of darkness and despair. Ma's life had spiralled into addiction and crime as he struggled to cope with the loss of his brother. . . Fleeting moments of yesteryears flashed in his head as he convulsed under the influence. . . The fast life in the city didn't relent and Ma knew that he had the devil running in his veins now. . .

Ma had been the one between the two to tinker with danger and test fate. . . 'Ozer you never know if you're living fully until. . . '. . . 'Until what?' a scared Ozer asked Ma one day as he held the steering wheel of the motorcycle as the two sped the highway in full race. . . 'Until you taste death up-close,' Ma whipped out a knife and quickly cut the brake wires. . . Before

Ozer could say anything, they were already doing 120 plus along the heavy traffic. . . Ozer had no option but to hold on as the bike careened and swerved viciously. . . Luckily it hit a nearby swampy lake, the duo escaped with minor injuries. . .

And often as Ma relapsed into a world full of voices and visions, Ozer was there for him. . . It had all but taken an instance of a near-fatal overdose that Ma realised that he had been throwing caution to the winds too damn often. . . Ozer instilled a regime and faith in him to cure Ma. . . The dying friendship instantly rejuvenated into a much stronger bond. . . The core of their newfound relation strengthened with each new day, much like a digital helix of a strong DNA formed by two strong forces. . . Thus, this fortified bond was witnessed between the brothers. . . And Ma kept his end of the bargain with him slowly but surely and with conviction laying off the decadence and debauchery. . . The memory painted a picture of their friendship and how it had grown from the depths of despair into a profound connection. . .

Gradually, he began to take interest in what was being offered to him by Ozer in the form of books and knowledge that was in abundance. . . Ozer was now a collector of something more profound and sacred. . . The two brothers often discussed with each other about life, the world and religion in particular. . . Their philosophies and arguments often proved to be enlightening to each other at times. . . Fate had sealed their friendship with an everlasting benediction that even the difficult of times wouldn't tear asunder their bond. . . Such had been the revenant tale of their resurrection and friendship.

. . . Nothing is permanent and everything is nothing. . .

But being subject to impermanence, as all things around, the universe played a vicious trick on them and the very jealous heavens stole into their friendship without mercy. . .

Loitering around the Chorten Monastery during the annual Pang Toed Chaam and enjoying the ritual in all its full regalia Karma Wangden had been hit with a sudden unfortunate news. . . 'Karma, the news is about Ozer. . . there has been an accident. . . it was a big fall. ' Karma couldn't believe the news, he stood there, a mute listener. . . 'It was a quick death, ' the messenger had relayed, ' Please stay strong. '

In between failing senses and flailing arms, Karma had forced himself to visit the site of the crash. . . As he looked down into the gorge below, he could only think of the cruel joke that life had played on him. Stealing from him, his only companion, heaven's cruel joke as pitiless as the deep dark chasm below. A vehicle now a twisted, crushed heap of metal, Karma looked into himself and his life and succumbed to the reality. . . His inner fortitude now resembled the vehicle, inanimate mangled remains of a chassis...No engine, directionless, useless. . .

Karma struggled with the news of Ozer's unfortunate and untimely death, it was as if the very juice and life inside him turned visceral and venomous. . . The torturous emotions and memories truculently nibbled at him and decimated him from the inside day after day, night after night. The times again turned hard for him and with no one by his side after that, he succumbed mercilessly to the dark pull of strings, he was a puppet now once again, the weakness birthed by subdued chemicals now playing the role of a counterfeit master. . . The chronic fixation and the cravings had reared its ugly head and so also had begun the parasitic nature, with some nights spent under the shower in a state of acute paroxysm. . . Then followed a life of crime for Karma, until it culminated in a dank sunless Government Detox Centre, where help had come from the most unexpected of places. . .

ENTER THE BARDO.

****

'The time to act is now. . . I cannot believe this opportunity that has been bestowed upon me by my master, the Supreme Teacher. Only a few chosen get to do the Sangay's bidding, and I've been called for this purpose. ' The killer hit the gas on the ambassador and throttled past the traffic downwards towards the destination. . . *'Today we vow to uproot the sham and the pretence going on for centuries, '* thought the killer as the vehicle swerved dangerously speeding on curves, *'Today we do the Guru's tasks as prophesied'.* . .

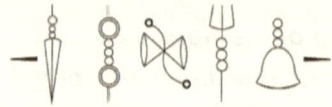

Although the Zurphu monastery is a fortified area of worship, with sentries in the form of ITBP personnel manning the premises with great precision, there was a glaring lapse for all to see that day. The incident had rocked the state and the entire world. Akash Nag, the officer in charge of the security personnel outside the monastery, let out an angry snarl every time he barked an order to the sentries. The burlesque officer in his fifties was obviously directly responsible for the failure of the monastery's security. But he kept calming his nerves down and tried to allay himself on a technicality. . . "But it happened inside the monastery, which is not entirely under my jurisdiction." The officer tried to take stock of the melee outside. The peaceful philosophy of Buddhism had succumbed to the heinous and ruthless murders committed in the last few weeks, in quick succession. The Gompa, being a place of worship and religious piety, had never warranted such a security presence. The number of monasteries that straddled the state had negligible armed personnel guarding the gompa. It was as if the heads and the trustees of the Zurphu monastery had taken a leaf out of the Vatican in Rome.

The Vatican, the seat of the Holy See and a place steeped in Catholic Christianity, provided a veritable fecundity in terms of art and architecture for aficionados, tourists, and pilgrims alike. The Vatican held sway in matters pertaining to not only religious aspects but financial ones as well, for billions of faithful worshippers around the world. Also, the expansive and aesthetic architecture of Yore and its innards housing works of famous artists like Da Vinci, Botticelli, Raphael Santi, etc. meant that the holy place had to be guarded. *'An opulent prison for the Gods of Men. . . '* The Vatican did it with the Pontifical Swiss Guards, people who were recruited by the Panel of the Vatican themselves and trained to execute the orders of the Papacy. Swiss male citizens who are devoutly Catholic, sworn to celibacy, and rigorously trained under the Swiss military to protect the Vatican.

Although the monastery had humble beginnings and the artists never rose to the level of the Renaissance, there was a need for security, and the paramilitary in the form of ITBP personnel who provided it. The reason was a big confusion regarding the ascent of a reincarnated lama, and the issue had turned the holy place into a place of contention between two warring factions within the Kagyu lineage. The incident, in fact, had been a mocking circus of sorts, thwarting the very ideals of compassion and order. It had all started when the Kagyu lineage homed in on the next Karmapa, Orgyen Trinley Dorjee, as the head of the sect. The reincarnation was well endorsed by one of the most famous examples of the reincarnated lamas, His Holiness the 14th Dalai Lama of Tibet. The new Karmapa, thus instated as the successor of the lineage, had courted much controversy and gave birth to a new faction, denouncing and decrying His Holiness's endorsement. The statement of protest reverberated throughout the religion's power corridors and beyond. The world bore witness to the blatant defiance of the Dalai Lama's word. It was unprecedented.

For the first time in the history of philosophy, a schism was detected—a division so significant that it threatened to put the Dharma at stake. The new division had opened up a Pandora's box of religious doubts,questions and troubles, which any layman probably considered to be the Achilles heel of the Dharma. That particular incident had hurt the Dharma. It had sparked arguments and significant discussions when it came to controlling the Monastery. The once peaceful monks had now become warring tribes hell-bent on following the orders of their masters and establishing their dogma as the ultimate philosophy. A ritual and philosophy guarded so secretly for ages were now under threat. The event itself raised critical questions in all walks of life.

"We thought this was the only true philosophy that would free us," said a dejected believer then. "A faith without any shamans or self-styled godmen. But this division in the sect is because of the issue." He sighed. Where does it leave us?" The question thus echoing the sounds and thoughts of billions of believers scattered throughout the globe.

A static walkie-talkie went off as Yangtso Brahma walked around the other restricted areas of the Zurphu Monastery. His steps forward were adorned menacingly with brute intent and the desire to nab the suspect as fast as possible. "Alex, take three personnel along with you and recon the entire premise," Brahma barked an order as he flicked the switch on his wireless. "Yes, sir, we are sending in more personnel and armed guards as well, like you requested, sir," an obedient, albeit barely audible voice said. Brahma roughly stowed the wireless on top of the parked police vehicle. "Let's see what you have in store for us," the officer thought as he peered into the vast, expansive sky above.

"I want all the exits blocked. Round up all the people in the monastery as fast as possible. I want to interrogate them one at a time. The IPS officer walked straight up to the main temple and eyed the stationed Titanium Diavel bike carefully as he did so. Upon entering the scene of the murder, Brahma looked around for something amiss. He found none. The butter lamps and the smell of exotic Buddhist incense filled the prayer room; its scent was all-pervading and continuous. He looked at the statues of gods, brilliantly embellished with priceless gems and valuable jewelry. Everything he observed was right in front of him. It hadn't been touched, let alone taken by someone. "It definitely isn't a case of heist. Every valuable seems to be in order, just like the other ones." Although it wasn't a case of a religious heist, a spate of looting and desecration of the Chortens, currently filled with gold and wealth, had shocked the local denizens recently. Yangtso Brahma thought as he looked around for some answers, prima facie. As he neared one of the statues inside the pedestal, which he knew to be of Guru Padmasambhava, he feigned a slight bow, a muscle memory rather, and was about to exit the room when something caught his eye. He adjusted his position and tried to get closer to the statue cased inside a big glass. What he saw gave him a big relief. "I was expecting this." Right behind him, and on the left-hand side, on account of the reflection on the glass box, a small, round, black, and shiny device lay perched on one side of the temple door. Quickly walking towards it, his hope was confirmed. His sight greeted an object—a round metallic device attached to the temple door. "A surveillance camera." Two significant answers in just a matter of minutes, Brahma thought as he carefully touched and looked at the tiny light flashing inside. "Let's see what you have in store for us. "

Just then, the ominous silence of the place was torn apart by a loud sound. Yangtso Brahma stood up, alarmed, and exited the room quickly. The engine of the Ducati Diavel roared loudly and made a sporting leap towards the temple's main gate. The officer looked at the spot where the bike was previously parked. The place was now filled with roughly strewn pebbles, with the smell of burning smoke and rubber burnout filling the air around them. The bike made a quick dash towards the exit, and before Brahma could think of a solution, the Ducati had done what it does best. It left everyone wondering behind about its speed and pace. The bike's ergonomics for speed and torque helped the rider as it tore into the open highway with great speed and vanished into the meandering curves and tree lines quickly. Yangtso Brahma roared loudly an assembly of orders to all the personnel near him, after which the monastery converted into a scene from a movie and threw up a din of swirling vehicles and tornadoes of dust, everyone chasing the bike and its occupants.

"It's time," Lama Tashi said, drawing a long breath. Karma Wangden nodded and heaved a sigh with the duo finally shaking off the police and he knew that things had to be comprehended better and solved fast and at a great pace. There was no time for delay...

The Diavel stormed forward gaining traction and speed every millisecond...

ENTER THE BARDO.

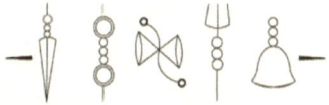

'I knew it to be true, 'the IPS officer snarled. 'It's all too evident now, my hunch was correct, 'Brahma surmised as he time and again shifted his position in tune with the speeding bolero vehicle. He rummaged hastily inside the dashboard and a couple of seconds later, lifted up the wireless and got set to send an order to the personnel in the other vehicle already some distance away and in-front of them. With the other hand in simultaneous action, he flipped open a small rectangular grey electronic device and switched it on. As soon as the device turned on, the shiny screen on it came alive with an array of lines and sketches drawn cartographically. Brahma looked at the GPS device intently and searched for a moving marker inside the screen. Almost instantly, the sketch of lines and diagrams of highways, roadways and landmarks of the area got interjected by a tiny albeit visible red dot blipping its way forward, snaking and arching at every twist and turn. 'There you are, 'he thought and immediately relayed an order to his men. 'Make sure you cut that bike at the next police

outpost, before the cantonment areas.....'. . . "Copy that Sir, we will try to,"the police attendant replied as he pressed his jeep's metal to a maximum and followed fiercely the tail of the Ducati, a good 100 meters away from them, speeding and whizzing past into oblivion. The police cavalcade with all its authoritative din and urgency definitely ruffled a few minds in the valley as onlookers lined the highway at each and every turn to find out.

Yangtso Brahma eyed the fast moving police vehicles in front of them and tried to keep up with them. With his often accompanying driver at the wheels, whom the officer judged had seldom been involved in a high police chase, given his frantic expression, he nevertheless urged the constable attendant to a full throttle. Upon continuous descent from the whirlpool of arterial highways above, Brahma from afar noticed the bike careening violently for some time before coming to a halt at one of the crossroads near a big hotel, a high and swanky joint for the high rollers in the State.

Even from far and amidst the mists stealing into the day, Yangtso Brahma could significantly mark out a silhouette of an apparition hurriedly dismounting the bike and making a quick getaway into the nearby woods surrounding the hotel. The weak foliage surrounding the hotel doing nothing to weaken the officer's view.

'You know we have little time to do this,' Karma told the Khenpo.

'Yes, I know that, and we must ensure the completion of task as soon as possible,' the Khenpo replied breathlessly as he tried to keep up with the speed of things he was embroiled in.

Within minutes of arriving at the location of the abandoned motorbike, Brahma ordered his men to fan out and nab the rider, with him following them in quick pursuit. As soon as they began a bloodhound trail of the suspect into the nearby thicket abounding in shrubs and bushes, the combing police personnel in a random horizontal chase homed in once again on the elusive figure in front of them making a quick dash away from them and into the thicket of the woods. Sensing that the fugitive might make a getaway, Brahma upped his tempo and the once athletic officer felt his legs and body muscles and his sinewy limbs open up, after which he saw himself getting segregated from the crowd, the only person now who had an advantage over him, being the fugitive.

Before long, Brahma was already trailing him by only a few yards and the fugitive with no endurance inside him gave in to the chase and stopped. He turned around and looked at the officer.

Yangtso Brahma was flummoxed. As soon as he encountered the face before him, the eagerness and the uniformed motive of nabbing a criminal went south as he began to decelerate slowly. His will now wilting by a millisecond, rapidly. Because that was when he knew that he had made a big mistake.

The sound of the roaring motorcycle, the supposed suspects fleeing from the scene according to him and the mighty police chase to nab them had all been futile. For standing infront of him wasn't the suspects he had hoped for. It wasn't the original rider who had made an entrance into the monastery, and it sure as hell wasn't the Khenpo of the monastery.

'What happened Sir, did we get them?' the Inspector pantingly enquired as he reached up to him.

'Them. . . yes them, ' retorted Brahma and cursed himself vehemently.

'How could I not figure just a lone rider, when it should've been two. . . ' Brahma lit a cigarette and muttered silent imprecations.

'They're still inside the temple, ' said the Officer, his words mixed with emotions betraying feelings of exasperation and getting into a heady and tired cocktail of panting breaths and physical exhaustion.

The officer took a short rest at the nearby boulder perched precariously and thought, 'This one is yours. . . I give it to you, but you don't know what's coming for you'. . . The officer got up and immediately proceeded to drive towards the temple. . . *'Fast Inspector. . . '*

****

Five dead bodies lay unattended in the morgue, the blood spattered sheets trying their best to withstand the effects of the Autumn wind. The very stench inside did little as in his grief a tall built individual identified all the 5 bodies, his very gait and visage consigned to helplessness.

'You are lucky, the last occupant in the vehicle is still alive', a medical attendant hurriedly relayed the message to the man, trying to assuage some grief in him. With such a gruesome sight before him, the word lucky didn't sink in.

He eyed the attendant and followed him.

'Your wife has been in and out of coma, it has been a really traumatic experience for her, you better see her and talk to her fast. . . 'Talk to her fast, 'thought the man, 'why fast?'. 'At this point, considering the magnitude of the injury, anything untoward might happen'. The man followed the attendant into a cubicle in the hospital and looked at his wife in the bed.

'My love, 'beamed a voice reassuringly. 'Please come closer my dear'.

The man was crushed at the site of the person in front of him. 'Why, ?the only word that was unspoken. He tried his best to conceal his ever building sorrow, second by painful second.

The assortments of medical instruments filling the room pinged at intervals, the only solace for the man, pointing at his wife's life hanging, albeit precariously. . .

He sat beside her and looked at her. A kind of surprise hit him. Although the accident was brutal for her and the other families in the car, he could see that she maintained a visage so calm and serene.

'Guess this is it...' the wife let out a sigh.

He just sat there looking at the bedside machine that indicated her lifeline. . . a series of ridges and flats drew every time on the screen. . .

'*Ridges are good*, 'he silently thought.

'I would give anything to be with you again. . . to hold you in my arms and to go to the end of the world with you, 'mustered the man. . .

'Please, 'he iterated, '... 'please don't leave me. . .' 'Please come back to me, I swear I'll ...'

The man broke down. Between the incessant sobs and tears a sweet voice beckoned.

'Don't you worry my love, I'm right here. . . don't you ever think that I'm leaving you. Just promise me that you'll love our kids and raise them to be right. Instill values in them, proper ones, alright. . . '

'Yes, I'll do that but I want you here with me. . . 'the man hugged her tightly and kissed her. . . It was a connection the man had never felt in years.

All of a sudden, an array of disorderly beeping of the machines started. . .

The man looked at her and tried talking to a woman losing consciousness. . .

'Please stay, don't do this, '. . . the room filled with attendants trying to revive the woman. The defibrillator working overtime. . . Nurses and doctors rushed around the room trying to revive the dying woman. . . 'Please leave her hand, and stay away, 'they shouted but the man wouldn't allow it. With bloodshot eyes desiring for her return, her one word, one smile, one everything, he held on tightly even as the medical personnel tried their best to dissuade him. . .

'Please, just talk to me, just say something. . . 'pleaded the man. . .

A white portal, so shiny and ebullient opened up in the space above, and she knew she had to follow that path. Her instincts told her that it was time. She knew now that all would be answered and she would know the truth in death...

An incoherent babble hit the man's ears as he hugged his wife tightly. . . He had hoped for a word or a sentence, but all he could hear were some words and phrases which were nonsensical.

The lifeline machine indicated a flat figure and after much effort, she had passed away peacefully. . .

The linen covering her was filled with copious tears the man had shed that day...

ENTER THE BARDO.

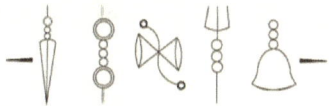

On seeing the police cavalcade exiting the monastery, Lama Tashi sighed and hurriedly summoned Karma Wangden to follow him. The gathered crowd had disintegrated and dispersed as soon as the police had made a hastening chase after the bike. Their desire and the penchant for unfolding events and answers following an incident inside the gompa had taken a backseat with the departure of the police. A handful of them stayed behind hoping for a return of the chaos at the monastery. Lama Tashi along with Karma quietly stole into one of the main temple shrine and locked the door behind him.

All alone and quiet inside the room, the khenpo walked up to one of the metallic cupboards and opened it.

Karma still dazed and shocked, couldn't fathom the entirety of the predicament he was in. Now with his Khenpo inside one of the rooms, resembling a storehouse of the monastery, adjoining the place where the body of a tuolku had been found, Karma looked at the Khenpo impatiently as he fished out a notebook and handed it to him.

'Switch it on, 'the khenpo directed to Karma.

Karma Wangden nervously received it and switched the device on. After the screen had played host to a desktop, the khenpo retrieved a cd from underneath his robe and handed it to Karma. The screen toggled for some time and the contents of it digitally played in front of them. Karma slowly leaned in closer to the screen and watched it. The timer on the extreme right hand bottom corner elapsed slowly with each passing second and the video just exposed the still playing images of the temple room. The camera and the images being projected on screen lay idle as a dead mouse. It had a wide view of the statues of Gods, with the butter lamps and their lights casting a brilliant golden aura over the pantheon of Gods. After some time, the camera slowly panned, indicating movement inside the room.

The main content of the disk startled Karma Wangden. 'What'?. . .

What he saw in the video after that left him mind-boggled and scared at the same time. The video showed a dark hooded figure with the body of a small child slung over his shoulder. It entered the temple and carelessly threw the body on the floor. Karma focused on the video even more as he watched the figure drop some things on the ground near the body. '*Paper pamphlets*?' Karma guessed, hundreds of them. Slowly the figure arranged a pattern of solid shapes near the corpse and directly after , looked at the murals behind it and stalled for some time before resuming again. After completing the arrangements on the floor, the figure lifted up the body and placed it dead center, with the arranged objects acting as a periphery for the body all around the concrete.

Then the killer rummaged through a bag slung over the shoulder and produced a giant flex indicating a picture. '*A painting, a fresco*'? Karma was at his wit's end. With precision, he placed it in front of the body.

'Gyan-la, what are those objects on the floor, encircling the body?' Karma asked after remaining silent for a long time. With a pointed finger on the screen, the khenpo quietly directed Karma to look into the screen and watch the clip. The screen slowly played the movements of the killer on the floor, as the figure kept himself busy performing some ritualistic act beside the body. After sometime, the figure arose and moved a good 6-7 feet away from the body, the general behaviour indicating pride at what it had done inside the temple room. As it did did so, the screen came alive clearly with the images being projected on it. Karma looked at the Khenpo who in-turn shook his head as if signaling the obvious to Karma.

The body had been wrapped in a traditional Buddhist attire with a Shyamo or a cap crowning the corpse's head. With rigor-mortis setting in, the body of the child tuolku had stiffened, but the killer had forcefully and with great amount of strength, contorted it manually and it now lay in a position of meditation. The objects strewn around the body, Karma now found it to be the termas or dough effigies neatly aligned in a circular position around the body. With Karma Wangden and the Khenpo, in mute witness to the events unfolding before their very own eyes, they had no other option but to subject themselves to the continued video's screening. The figure exited the temple in a hurry after a while and the screen playing the video again resumed to idleness, with a dead body and some effigies getting added to the scenario, properly aligned around the body.

'Karma, 'the khenpo spoke in a hushed tone, 'The video which you just saw now should be able to ring in a few images from your memories. 'Karma looked at the khenpo surprised. He didn't understand anything, let alone conjure up anything from his mind. 'I don't know what exactly are you talking about, Gyan-la. I haven't the faintest idea. '

Lama Tashi slowly placed a hand over Karma's shoulder and said, 'You were a part of such rituals many years ago, my son. When you had just recovered from your afflictions and you had accompanied and helped me so many times. 'Karma looked at the khenpo and still couldn't understand or recall anything. The Khenpo continued, 'Remember Karma, the times when you, under my aegis, helped me at various religious rituals. You went with me on various occasions and learned a lot from me regarding such rituals. And from amongst those, I hope that you remember the times when we had to work for a berieved family, close our ears to their mournful wails, shut our eyes to the countless tears that flowed, because we only wanted to bid adieu to the departed and grant comfort and solace to the aggrieved families. '

Karma Wangden as soon as he heard those words, jumped up and gripped the khenpo's hand tightly. How could he have forgotten those things. It all made sense to him now,completely.It was as if the incremental knowledge the Khenpo was blessing him with this morning,standing against direct information, was all but wise and made sense...

ENTER THE BARDO.

All the talk about the intermediate stage, the esotericism and the body inside the temple and the Khenpo removing it slowly started to make sense... The memories of him helping the Khenpo right after he cleansed himself of all demons definitely had given him a chance to appreciate this life and embrace it fully. The ritualistic events in the past too had a profound bearing on him, especially the ones involving death and funerals. It had taught him to live a life filled with hope and strength and above all fearlessness. 'Of-course, 'Karma thought, 'The arrangements that were done, that they'd seen in the video was about how a dead body should be kept so as to communicate to the soul and show him a path in the afterlife. 'The khenpo nodded quietly, half pleased on the thought that Karma had understood.' But there was more to it and Lama Tashi pointed his finger towards hundreds of scrawled pamphlets strewn on the floor near the body.

As soon as he read those words, calligraphically written in a Buddhist text, his hair shot back and the words literally sent chills down his spine.

It was a direct threat and not only that, whatever the Khenpo had uttered about a prophecy that rained from the skies now stood out to be true. For years, the authenticity of such prophecies had been debated and questioned. But now in hundreds strewn all across the floor, Karma had no option but to believe in the ominous threat inscribed on them.

Now the question remained and it played in the minds of both the men. 'Who would be quick in their endeavors?' The killer who had committed those murders and used the ancient texts as a threat or the Khenpo and Karma on the other side of the fence with the police in hot pursuit of them as suspects.

'And one more thing Karma, 'the Khenpo produced a rolled parchment of paper and handed it to him. 'See it for yourself'.

Karma Wangden took the parchment away from the old frail hands of his master and started to open it. The parchment a modest 9*9 by dimension easily fitted into his hands.

When he finished unrolling it, what greeted Karma's eyes shocked him into oblivion.

'What'? the only syllable escaping his mind. What he was holding was one of the most famous of Buddhist Paintings which adorned every monastery in the state and outside the country.

The famous Dharmakaya, also known as the painting of the Bardo Thodol.

ENTER THE BARDO.

Now it dawned upon him, the fresco, the parchment laid down on the floor in-front of the tuolku's body.

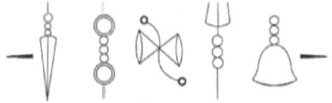

When it came to the oldest monastery in the state , the Dubdi has always been a direct answer. However with much arguments over the years as to its year of establishment, there always has been some kind of controversy as to the oldest monastery in the state. . . Records and dates point out to a monastery built in the 1600s much before the Dubdi monastery. The quaint religious lodging nestled in the hills of West Sikkim of the Kartok Gompa provides one such contention when it comes to the State's premier monastery.

The crisp morning air of the Dubdi monastery pervaded the temple complexes in its entirety. A slow movement of an individual traversed the path leading up to the monastery.

'Here I'm. . . finally, 'thought the killer stepping onto the fresh morning grass path of the Dubdi monastery. The tiredness and famished state of the killer was instantly rejuvenated as it neared the temple premises spinning the Dharma Wheel one at a time.

'The work has to be done, 'thought the killer silently. The loud roar of the Gyalings filled the environment of the temple in their religious cacophony as the slow collective steps of the thousands of devotees with muted and inaudible prayers thundered into the area. The repertoire and the huge collection of flags and festoons neatly and colorfully decked in vast arrays signified the initiation of an important event in the monastery.

It was a special prayer event held annually signifying the start of a great religious event at Tashiding, a silent town some few kilometers away.

Eyeing the surroundings and the usual gatherings around the Dubdi, the Killer slowly merged into the crowd, his fingers and his mouth in tandem, joining the chorus of prayer chants pervading the atmosphere.

'Glad, it has started. I just have to be more careful now and complete the task beforehand prudently, 'thought the killer, 'People especially the authorities have already noticed I reckon.'The killer suspected given the incidents that he had perpetrated within such a short span of time.

As he neared the oval greenery fronting the main temple monastery, the killer along with the myriad devotees now stood witness to a start of the event that was of profound significance and importance annually in the State. The event heralded the start of a religious retreat so big and auspicious that it witnessed thousands of participants from the state and waves of pilgrims and devotees internationally. . .

The religious festival and a retreat that occurred annually at Tashiding monastery was big in terms of its history and the patron saint associated with the event. Tashiding Monastery, a remote Gompa in West Sikkim suddenly transformed from a calm uneventful countryside to a place bustling with religious pilgrimage all around, all in an instant. The village also bore the same name as the monastery on it . Communalized by a number as less as a town, the place was purely bucolic and serene in its settings, proving to be a suitable 'Dharma' place. The monastery was situated at the hilltop of the Tashiding hills and the roads leading to it from adjacent distances from opposite side of the hill provided a majestic view of the Gompa. . . *truly a jewel in the crown*. A place steeped deep in Buddhism and it's philosophies.

The temple was fully dedicated to the Nyingpa sect of Buddhism with Guru Rimpoche or Guru Padmasambhava at the helm.

'To achieve, we must sacrifice'. . . The wise words of the teacher again echoed in the ears of the killer.

'Such priceless words of wisdom and knowledge. . . such rationality.'

For a while he was transported back into time inside the chamber of the Supreme Teacher in one of the monasteries.

'What we do now, will echo till eternity and there will be a crusade against us and our radical ideals.'Silence crept into the room. 'But to achieve something, we must be willing to let go of our fears and prejudices. Believe that whatever will be done, shall only be aimed at saving the Dharma and nothing else. History has been replete with instances of actions undertaken to save various religions. The holy wars fought in the name of their beliefs and Gods were moral actions taken to safeguard their traditions and practices. It still is evident today. These were and are brave souls, the soldiers of God, courageous groups who've donned the mantle of warriors for their Gods and for the protection of their religious ideals.'

A sudden surge of inspiration was felt by the two individuals seated beneath the supreme teacher.

His every word registering with great force into their minds. His conviction planted at every syllable, every idea, signalled strength and character. The killer and the other individual sat transfixed, waiting for further pearls of wisdom from him.

The Supreme teacher drew a short breath and stared at the murals covering the room. With a whisper that was audible he muttered, 'If not now, then when, if not us then who' remembering the wise motivational words of Rabbi Hillel, a 1st Century Jewish leader, giving a clarion call for action in a time of crisis... 'We are at the precipice of destruction, hanging precariously for existence. The ignorance and the utter lack of trust from the higher echelons of power will surely grind our philosophies and ideals to dust. The work of hundreds of masters over generations will all be wiped away instantly. It will be a big mockery of the Dharma.'

'Through great exercise and preparedness I have chosen you two individuals to carry out tasks that will reshape our philosophy for the better. Though the steps taken may appear to be harsh and even brutal, please believe in the greater good of God and the Dharma.' The two minds seated looked up to the teacher with great respect.

Although, it had been a seminar in secrecy, but it was enough for the dual minds to gravitate towards their teacher's words. The Supreme Teacher than walked up to one of the seated disciples and hugged him tightly. With piercing eyes locked onto him he said,

'You have to execute the most important of actions. Never give yourself to doubt, never surrender to inaction. Never shy away from your duties. For it is for the greater good of the Dharma.' Saying that he planted a kiss on the forehead and raising his beads, muttered silent prayers.

'Whatever he says, I'll do it, 'convergence of the two minds present at the chamber of the supreme teacher was all but evident.

Standing and mingling in with the crowd, the words spoken by the Supreme teacher in that chamber reverberated through the ears and replayed again and again. 'I'm a warrior of the faith and I'll do what it takes to achieve what's good for the faith, 'thought the killer jostling for space, with the hands holding the robe to veil the face.

It was indeed true that history bore testimony to the fact that all the bloody wars and battles fought in the name of religion were aplenty. The textbooks of school going children were scrawled with such episodes in history.

'Yes, the teacher did tell us about battles fought for religion and I fully believe in their endeavors to protect the beliefs,' the killer eyed people around carefully.

It was true that right from the medieval ages, the events of 'religious tyranny' in history to uphold one's beliefs was pretty evident. The blood soaked crusades during the Middle Ages aimed at suppressing factions opposed to their beliefs was one such instance...

'...The Gods of Men, with supreme powers, had made sure of establishing their faith as the ultimate religion. Any act of theirs was a testament of their unwavering faith and firm devotion. Therefore any instance of heresy was met with brute force. The Inquisition was one such instance in history...It was in this respect, mass tortures of scientists, rationalists and thinkers of the time were executed . The bloody crusades against Islam and its followers that raged on for many years paint a gory and horrific portrait in the annals of history...' The killer contemplated on the wisdom of the teacher...

History had been replete with instances of religious wars and persecution throughout. From the bloody Crusades, to crucifying the enlightened minds including the great Galileo when he had hit a scientific benchmark with his heliocentric theory, later forcing bright minds to band together and giving birth to Renaissance in Europe ...Such brilliant minds and their ilk always faced the heated religious anvil of suspicion and the powers that be had always held sway.

'That was how they established the faith over centuries. Any dissent or heresy was met with great force, thus solidifying the faith even more'.

'And why talk about a single faith only, 'thought the killer,*'talk about Islam and the followers . . .the religion that embodies peace and compassion has been divided'.*

The killer thought vehemently as the justifications for the cause erupted with each passing second.

'The Sunnis and Shias, 'thought the Killer, *'What are they?'. . . 'Aren't they brothers from the same sect fighting each other. And if such ideological differences caused animosity on a ruthless scale between people from the same faith to uphold and protect one's values, then our war against such hegemonistic powers is warranted and justified. For in-order to bring order, there must be chaos first.* The killer's lips escaped a smile of satisfaction upon the contemplation.

It was true that the Islamic world was vehemently divided between two sects of Islam. The brutal war footages filling the television screens bore testimony to that. The only division, a vital division that threatened the very lives of millions of them on each side of the fence was infamous.

The war was being fought everywhere in the world. It was not only for the protection of one's religious ideals and practices, but it was especially for the belief in those ideals. Most important of all it was also against tyranny and oppression as well. The contours of struggles were marked with interconnectedness, with the ultimate similar connection and aim being to establish one's dogma or credo.

It was happening in Yemen with the Houthi rebels stacked up against the Saudi led coalition...Whether the media portrayed the cause as political or not,the religious ideological difference stood out... The rivalries between the Israelis and the Palestinians were old and never seemed to let up. After non-agreement on a 2 State solution by Israel, the small handful of Palestinians refused to budge from their demands. And as settlements started by the Israelis at West Bank, vocabularies like Gaza Strip and Golan Heights had become common place. Again the cause of the Palestinians were supported by Hezbollah, another fiery group believing in the cause. The mass killings in the name of religion and ideals were heavily evident in places like Chad, Sierra Leone and Uganda where rebels fighting the Government had even employed little children to do their bidding. . .

'All of these incidents have purpose and objectives, and the underlying theme or moral compass always points towards protection of beliefs and faiths.'

'I'm sure whatever they are fighting for has reason and justice. Warriors of God,' thought the killer contemplating on the actions.

'And I'm trying to achieve the same with my philosophy.' A steely determination and steadfast resolve emboldened.

'Even if I'm considered an outcast. . . the pariah. . . the outsider. . . So be it. . . but I'll never betray my beliefs and my faith.' A small trickle of a sweat broke in the killer's brow, 'I'm in this for the Dharma, and in no way shall I abandon it in any way. I shall see through all my objectives.'

The crowds dispersed as the prayer ceremony at Dubdi Monastery came to an end. Hundreds of devotees lingered around the monastery taking in the sights of the Gompa with their smartphones in tow.

But the killer had no such desires. 'Materialism and show boating is for the pretentious, I'm here for a cause greater than that. I'm above them.' The Killer exited the monastery and jogged swiftly towards the ambassador parked near the monastery. The mind slowly disengaging from the mundane allures of life which had the multitudes in its vice grasp, the killer took comfort and solace to be the one chosen to do the Lord's work. The very visage and countenance expressing ruthless passion and nothing else.

'Each and every action of mine beckons and directs me towards the greater goal, 'the killer revved the car and hurtled towards Tashiding...

****

The swanky Ritz Carlton hotel room, filled with all the amenities one desired was one of the best of its kind in New Zealand. With the base laid with 30 foundational columns, it boasted of an edifice bigger than the country's PM lodgings situated at Premier House. The hotel was sprawled along 10th Kensington Street and usually hosted celebrities, sport stars and business tycoons alike. The familiar sight of a gang of Paparazzies trying to hide their equipments and themselves behind ornamental shrubs lining the hotel always greeted the guests. Their attempt at chancing upon and ambushing Celebrities at the hotel, a normal routine.

A man on room # 621 sat cross legged on his Tempa Pedic bed and breathed calmly, inhaling and exhaling with great control and restraint. A silent prayer chant escaped his lips and he played with his beads for an instant. Slowly he opened his eyes.

Kelsang Rimpoche, the venerated and highly respected re-incarnated Gelug lama, was a highly recognised monk known worldwide and a great follower of the Dharma. His teachings and his seminars on Buddhism went to packed houses filled with devotees and often he was beckoned to address gatherings in the west and in various Ivy league colleges and institutions around the globe.

'Faith: The need in today's youth', was one of the many programs he attended. A Gelug or the yellow hat sect meant that the roots of Kelsang's faith originated and had its genesis in a place known as the roof of the world, Tibet, with a renowned sole religious head, known globally, and with his government and Kingdom in exile.

Identified and ordained at a young age as the incarnation of a late great Rimpoche, Kelsang had been a prodigy when it came to studying and understanding the Dharma. A precocious student right from the time of his grooming and learning, he was considered to be a great Boddhisattva, or the enlightened one reincarnated to serve the Dharma . His religious debates often were a one sided affair against the counterparts of his monastery. His sharp and witty mind leaving his opponents perplexed and in a moral conundrum.

Kalsang Rimpoche got up from his chair and slowly drew open the curtains of the nearby window with his hand. Below, hundreds of devotees waited in great anticipation to seek his blessings or *Kawang.* He was happy to witness the throng of devotees outside of his room. *'The Dharma really has succeeded in bringing mass people together. Their very ideals have been now etched with the teachings of the Buddha and his philosophies.'*

The propagation of the Dharma and its export to foreign nations was definitely received well. In that the western population was now turning towards Buddhism and trying to understand it's Philosophies and receiving them well. The very rational of edicts applied and connected with their minds, so to speak. At present it had become a worldwide phenomenon. . . the embracing of Buddhism and it's teachings.

Kelsang Rimpoche after a weekend's stay at the hotel was already yearning for the place he called home. Although a calm soul, but a series of rapid and unfortunate news from his country and more particularly his hometown had left him drained, disillusioned and highly disturbed. *'What is happening'?*. . . thought the Rimpoche as he contemplated on the images of the lifeless bodies of recently identified Tuolkus that was emblazoned on the screens of every media houses.

Already dressed in his embellished civara with the saffron vest accentuating his Buddhist attire, the Rimpoche now took upon a final patch of grey, so to speak, to complete his religious sartorial choice. A giant yellow hat which conically tapered towards the front, a hat worn only by the highly ordained monks. It was definitely a full regalia. As He started to make his way outside of his room, 4-5 monks or attendants bowed obsequiously and with their robe loosely held to cover their mouths, lest it would be too direct a communication with the Holiness, ushered him towards the hotel's exit. After a couple of days in the country, he was hurriedly trying to make his departure from it and into his home. . . the land blessed by the Gods,a blessed land of plenty...With no prior engagements in India, he had but one special event to attend and it was the annual special event at West Sikkim, particularly at Tashiding. The annual religious event was worshipped and attended by devotees from various stretches of the planet. From the austere Hinayanists Sinhalese pilgrims, to Thai monks and from Nyingma Bhutanese devotees to worshippers from far flung South East Asian Nations like Phnom Phen and Laos and most of Indo-China, the event was embraced by all and sundry.

'I hope the message, this time is good, 'thought the aging Rimpoche, thinking about the chalice and the level of content in it. *'Not a single trickle should be out of balance. For the level prophesizes the yearlong events that'll follow this blessed land. That's how it must be and that's how it shall always be, with the Guru's blessings'.*

As he neared the exit of the hotel, a number of other known Khenpos, old but learned lamas bowed down before the Rimpoche in total respect and utmost devotion. He touched their heads one at a time, slowly advancing towards the gate as he did so. One last curve before the exit, Kelsang came across three tiny tots, happily enjoying their new found friendship in a manner that was innocent and puerile. These were the newly identified re-incarnated ones, asked to make their presence felt at the seminar, thus inspiring the hundreds of devotees present. The presence of recently ordained tuolkus were a thing of fascination and intrigue for the non-

Buddhists. The theme of re-incarnation and rebirth was viewed as rituals steeped in magic, esotericism and downright otherworldly. The Rimpoche often met with skepticisms in the form of rebuttals towards such concepts at various seminars and programs.

"But the concept of rebirth and re-incarnation hasn't been proved, and this is just blind following of a leader." One such critic or interviewer interjected once, when the Rimpoche had been delivering sermons about Karma and its effects on the afterlife. It was a packed seminar in the United States, where the devotees ranged from usual Buddhist hags, their old partners. But the Rimpoche was happy to know that it was also peppered with a handful of youths, both Buddhists and some white teenagers who had come to the seminar.

'And this theory of being reborn, why is it Buddhist exclusivism?', 'Are we to believe that such things happen only in your religion and philosophy. Why not in other religions and faiths? Are we talking about exclusivism and elitism here?'

The whole hall had been deafened with the silence after the questions. The sea of gimlet eyes and probing minds for the answers from the Dharma leader were as inquisitive as ever. The interviewer took in some pride as he had been successful in putting forth some 'real' questions. He laid back on his chair and readied himself for an answer, a tiny hint of a smile escaping his lips.

Kelsang Rimpoche, sat cross legged, facing a sea of eyes and bodies before him. He had come here to deliver some sermons, basic guidelines on happiness and compassion and how everyone was entitled to it. But the QnA session had turned a bit hostile with all the questions aimed at trying to floor the leader.

But Kelsang Rimpoche knew better than to crumble under such pressures. Years of practicing the Dharma, the incessant debates during his youth and countless meditation sessions had trained his mind to become calm at the face of such aggressional probity. Not new to such interrogations trying to undermine the faith, the Rimpoche knew better how to deal with such inane queries.

He scoured the sea of eyes before him and asked a simple question.

'Anyone here believes in Science?'. . . After a moment of mass hesitation, some hands randomly threw up, the first hand being that of the person with his condescending tone of questions. The devotees were perplexed and confused as to whether to surrender their beliefs or not. *This is a religious seminar, after all,* thought a young blonde sitting at the front row.

'Good, and may I know where we stand today when it comes to conflict between these two themes?' Kalsang Rimpoche sat playing with his beads, a beatific smile across his face, waiting for an answer. The question was thrown open to all present and seated in the room. After a prolonged moment of silence, an uber enthusiastic voice replied, 'We are at a crossroads, Rimpoche la, I believe the truth that separates these two subjects can never be found. The violence that has been witnessed in the past trying to stifle Scientific thinking and inquiry has gone down and what we are witnessing is sort of a change in tolerance level. I believe that they aren't at loggerheads instead they complement each other and try to learn from one another .' The reply that came was from an attendant who wasn't a monk, but a teenage student, a young bespectacled Asian probably studying in the country.

A big sigh escaped him, a bit audible to prying ears.

'Correct, it isn't that both of these subjects have absolute answers, but a camaraderie has been forged over the years, so to speak, complementing and helping each other.'

'How, please care to elaborate, ?'The individual with the original question dug in further.

'I'm guessing you are a student of one of these subjects...Science to be particular?'

'Majoring in <u>physics</u>, from the NZU of Sciences, 'came a direct reply, tactless and conceit writ large on the admission.

'Good, and to be basic about your subject, can you please tell me about Newton and some of his laws?'

'It's easy, come on man, 'thought the man. Isaac Newton was a famous figure in Science. His work symbolized an entire era of scientific reasoning and development. Almost all the developments in Science could be viewed through a Newtonian prism. The study of a famous incident, wherein an apple fell on Newton's head while he was contemplating upon the motions and behaviours of celestial bodies and which later inspired him to theorize on Gravity as a universal force, one of the landmark achievements of science, was something anyone in his or her common capacity was aware of.

But there was more to his achievements than just Gravity.

'Wait, where shall I begin. Newton's gravitational theory, his work on optics, which was at the forefront of the light studies, thus proving it's complex heterogeneity through the famous prism experiment. . . , 'he rattled off some of the scientist's achievements in his head quickly' *'...and his seminal treatise entitled Principia Mathematica which was the motherload of scientific achievements. . . Laws of motion, theories and laws which actually laid down the foundations of Classical Mechanics and which was well received by the scientific community and the world, laws of Gravity, his work on Calculus, although there was a contention as to its discoverer, where the honor is also shared by another brilliant German Mathematician Leibniz. . .* 'the man paused for a second... *'again the telescope. . . and yes the binomial theorem etc.'* . . . List exhausted. . . the man looked up and prepared to voice his thoughts.

'Well, his achievements are aplenty and it has really helped modern science and industries in furthering their objectives. 'The man took in a deep breath and continued, 'As you can see, his theories and postulates have helped build machines making work easier and they've inspired and influenced generations of great minds like Einstein and Sagan. . .'

'Ok, let me just stop you there, ' the Rimpoche interjected, his interruption more a request than an order. The man looked surprised as he hadn't finished.

Let me ask you a question first, correct me if I'm wrong, please. 'The Rimpoche looked at everyone and asked a simple question to the man.

'What is Physics'?

'Simple', thought the man. 'It is the study of science where the subject matter deals with mechanism, magnetism, force, radiation, atomic structure, 'a short pause, 'you know I can go on and on about my subject. '

Kelsang Rimpoche gave a faint smile. 'Yes you are right but may I also offer a response to this question. 'The crowd waited with baited breath. '*A Buddhist teacher about to lecture on Physics*', a collective thought.

The man feigned an honest wait and brace.

'It is something which deals with the study of nature, the interactions, interconnectedness and also tries to explain how something comes out to be...'

The crowd nodded in unison except for the man.

'Basically it is something which is rational, a body of science which keeps asking questions about nature and life and tries to ascertain answers, organically.'

'My son,' Kalsang Rimpoche motioned to the man whose very disposition still betrayed dissatisfaction. 'While we are on the subject, let me state one of Newton's 3 laws of motion'.

'He knows this?', a collective sigh again. . .

'Correct me if I'm wrong, but the 3rd law states that to every action, there is an equal and opposite reaction, right?' Some of the youngsters in the crowd familiar with the law nodded in agreement.

'Now I'm aware of the fact that Newtonian axioms and postulates weren't until the late 17th Century. . . but what if I told you that ancient texts, religious texts already bear those theoretical maxims.'

The crowd was stunned.

Kalsang Rimpoche paused and began, 'The religious texts, the ancient words of wisdom, from the Bible, to the Koran, and from the Kabbala to the Sutras of Buddhism, all speak of following the basic guidelines as spoken by the Buddha, Christ or Allah.'

'In simple words, the common theme running in all these says, that if you do something bad and evil, like steal, kill, lie or hurt someone with all these sins, you'll face damnation.'

'But how could it relate to the 3rd law, ?asked a young Chinese girl seated 3-4 rows in-front of the man.

'I knew this question was coming, 'the Rimpoche took in some time in collating and organizing his answers before speaking out, the traits of a learned and erudite individual. The entire room felt an air of palpable tension as the seminar had just turned into a big science expo.

'Do you think, there is a heaven or a hell? I mean the way they describe things in the Bible, like an underground chasm filled with all the sinners and ghosts and apparitions and ghouls trying their best to get their claws on you.'

A muted silence filled the room.

'Whatever, these ideas of hell are basically human constructs. Manmade ideas to make man fall in line with the church, temple or the mosque. But the general instruction and its meaning running across these scriptures of 'evil shall befall evil men' and 'thou shalt not commit a sin without consequences' are all related to Newtonian law.'

The man with the questions, ruffled his hair a bit and waited for some more explanation. Kelsang Rimpoche tried to slip an example for easy comprehension...

'If you commit a simple crime. . . let's say steal someone's phone', what do you think will happen to you. . . immediately?'

'Feel guilt at first, but fine later, 'a middle aged potbellied man joked.

Laughter roared through the room.

'Yes, that's true' the Rimpoche said, you might feel good later on and extra good if you sell it for a few hundred dollars. The regret and guilt might not catch up on you and chances are you'll stick to that bad habit of lifting people's things up with impunity. . . But what if you get caught, and sooner or later you will, trust me. It'll bring shame and embarrassment not only to you but to the ones near you. Your family, friends, the people who matter...The effect... And because of your actions and the consequent effect,you'll face isolation,humility,abandonment and bouts of regret...

'That's one idea of hell', replied the man.

'Exactly young man, as you sow, so shall you reap. Not only history, but ask the experienced lots around you. They have more experiences about certain things coming back with a bang, because they initiated something. It could be good, could be bad. If a simple act of stealing a phone, will bring you ignominy, what about killings and other heinous crimes. A lifer in a maximum security prison anywhere in the world will vouch for that fact.'

'Because, 'the Rimpoche's voice boomed loud in the mike, surprising everyone with the sudden change in decibel, 'there is one word, one energy that is capable of bringing fruits and poisons to you depending on your actions. '

The crowd didn't budge an inch.

'That word is Karma. And it doesn't mean fate, mind you. Karma means deeds. And Karma is basically the principal law governing Cause and Effect...your Newtonian Law... The good deeds will make you feel good and bring good things to you, but the bad ones. . . well, might as well take a guess. Whether physical, mental or spiritual, thoughts and actions initiated on various such levels will come back with a result, no doubt.

'Don't believe me, look around you?' The whole system around you is built to pin your dreams on an exercise...The theme of the seminar now roared fully... 'The exercise of belief and faith. Faith in your work and dreams. It could be anything, trying to be an athlete, or an actress etc. . . . the underlying theme is believing in yourself and putting in the work. . . The result as they say will follow. . . This is the truth. . . If you channel your mind and your body towards something you want to achieve, it'll come to you, no doubt. This holds true for all your thoughts and action.'

There was a mild roar of approval. All the talks about achieving your highest self, the chicken soup for the soul and the tomes and works about trying to achieve the highest all hinged on two things. Belief and work. And these two done properly would set in motion your actions which would be your deeds and bring you success or the 'fruits' in time to come.'

'And coming back to your question, 'the Rimpoche pointed at the man.

'Buddhism's philosophy is just basic, just rational and logical. The belief is solely depended on a man's karma or his deeds and the more merit he earns in this life, the more easier the afterlife and the next becomes for him.'

He went for another hour on the afterlife, the intermediate stage and re-birth and the crowd including the man with the questions gave into the lucid explanations presented by the teacher, a toned down demeanor, now evident.

'Before I finish, let me ask you your name Sir.
'

'Case Arden', the man replied.

Somewhere in the deep recesses of his memories, he stumbled upon names, these were baby names given by him to families who'd recently given birth, as was customary in Buddhist families.

'Ah yes, if I don't go by spelling alone, the Buddhist names, mainly having its origin in Sanskrit, an ancient language in India, your name can be interpreted as 'The man who always Rejoices and the second name means treasure, 'said the Rimpoche bowing down before all of them.

Case, bowed his head down and became a believer, along with all present.

'And since your second name means treasure, it would do you good, to not only stick to your pedantic reading of science texts, but broaden your horizon as well, be a voracious collector of treasures in the form of knowledge, in-order to be a true follower of your subject.'

Case scratched his head looking down.

'You know Quantum Mechanics?' asked the Rimpoche suddenly.

'Wait, so he knows the study of physics at the sub-atomic level too'? Case was spellbound by his Holiness' question.

'Please don't expect me to lecture you about it, I myself am trying to study and comprehend it, 'said the Rimpoche trying to allay the shock prevalent in the room, more so in Case's case.

"You know ancient Indian texts and scriptures have provided a huge playground for Western Scientists to test their theories and axioms from. Not only Hindu scriptures, but texts and ancient heliographs from excavated sites have provided so much of intrigues for the curious mind. If I'm not mistaken, some of the cutting edge theories of science have been directly found to be taken from the pages of such scriptures."

'What do you mean Rimpoche la?' asked the same Asian student who had answered a few hours earlier.

"I believe that the greatest and sincerest of minds often don't have time for petty differences as to who did it first or who should be credited with the achievement... They come together to fill the void left by the other."

'Do you know a certain Raja Ramanna?'asked the Rimpoche.

A blank response drew from the crowd.

'I was expecting it', thought the Rimpoche. 'It's an Indian name'.

'Almost 20 years before all this, the leader of a big Buddhist sect in India received a letter from him, whereupon he expressed his surprise and shock to find some Buddhist scriptures, esoteric as it may have seemed to others but were similar to the ones he was studying or trying to study on the subject. Except those scriptures were a thousand years old, much before he was born.'

'And you know who Raja Ramanna was. . . , 'still a blank from the crowd. . . 'He was India's foremost Nuclear Physicist. . . '

Some sections of the crowd familiar with the tropes of science and scientific terms drew a collective gasp. *'How is it possible, Science is Science and religion is all faith and spiritual, how can the two meet, '?* again a collective thought.

The Rimpoche began with his speech, 'Raja Rammana was so fascinated by the script that he personally wrote a letter to. . . you know whom?'

Again no response from the crowd.

'It was addressed to His Holiness the 14th Dalai Lama of Tibet. '

A stunned silence entered the room. Many queries mixed and incoherent, *'How come him, a*

Buddhist monk. . . and a scientist asking for his help. It's all farfetched', the room erupted with such mumbles.

Except it was not far fetched.

"The communication between the two thus laid the foundation for the annual seminar at Jawaharlal Nehru University or the Dharamshala, Himachal Pradesh where hundreds of Professors and Scientists, domestic as well as International converged to discuss upon the Quantum theory or the Madhyamaka Philosophy. Of course, His Holiness approaching a problem had a different religious side to tackling the problems like the Uncertainly Principle, Wave Particle duality, the slit experience or the Schrodinger's Cat."

That last line from the Rimpoche floored Case. These experiences about uncertainty and whether there really was a cat in the box were all experiments at the forefront of modern science. . . Quantum Mechanics.

'Ok now it's brass tacks, 'thought the teenager.

After some discussions filled the room, especially from teenagers alike, Kelsang Rimpoche resumed his speech.

'See I in no way want to extol the virtues of the Buddha or make believers out of agnostics or even atheists. And I in no way want to plunder the believers of other faiths and religion. I just want to lay the facts as they come. Because these are rational and logical things which any individual in his/her right mind would assent to it.'

'I just want to say and particularly to people like Case that even hardened science people, your inventors and discoverers always espoused looking at ancient scriptures and recognize the beauty and intelligence in them. They were certainly at a convergence. They knew, the ancients had answers to possibly the most difficult of questions. '

Kelsang Rimpoche paused for a second. 'I'm not saying you have to believe in God to read them, I'm just asking you to read them.'

'And in concluding I would like to add that a certain Robert. J. Oppenheimer, famously quoted, 'I'm become death, the destroyer of worlds.'

Nothing registered with the crowd of people seated there.

Kelsang Rimpoche knew that and added, 'The famous figure known as the father of the Atomic Bomb, who worked on the Manhattan Project that tested the bomb, Oppenheimer uttered these words out after the testing of the deadly bomb at New Mexico in the year 1939. . . 'The gathered crowd had little idea about the statement of Oppenheimer, until the Rimpoche concluded, 'He was quoting those words directly from an ancient Hindu script. . . the Bhagwad Gita, a chapter from the Mahabharata.'

Stunned Silence again.

ENTER THE BARDO.

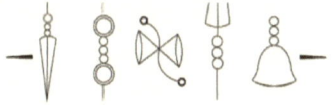

Although it was pretty evident that the paper pamphlets as rightly guessed by him were strewn randomly in the vicinity of the body but the strange texts drawn on the floor being projected on-screen unsettled him and sent chills down Karma's spine and for a moment he was speechless. The obscure lines scrawled on the floor at first didn't make any sense to him. But on close scrutiny, it had all become nauseously evident to Karma. He was now speechless and shocked. *'The murder and the circumstances surrounding it, surely puts Gyan-la and myself at the helm of the suspects' list,'* thought Karma. 'And even if we were to evade the police now, for how long would that be possible.'. . . Karma Wangden slowly stood up from his crouched position and sat in a stool next to the Khenpo's.

The winter sun did little to steal away the coldness of the place.

'Gyan-la, 'Karma said quietly, how can we do this alone? As far as I know, we are already suspects absconding and on top of that, we are expecting to solve this brutal case and heinous murder ourselves with no leads.

'I know I have my fair share of experiences with some practices, which I've conducted in the past, but this is. . . I don't have the words. I think and I'm sure that the past murders over the week were all related and this one is the final nail in the coffin. I'm sorry Gyan-La, but aren't we being too foolish or stupid to do that. I mean I already told you that we could take the help of the police.'

Lama Tashi understood Karma's predicament and impatience but could do little about the present state of his mind. It was natural for a human being to abandon calmness and serenity of the mind and involuntarily drift towards the chaos of nervousness in times of crisis. But Lama Tashi knew that what had unfolded before them this morning, was something vile and truly ugly. Not to mention so evil that it would have negative reverberations for the faith which would echo till eternity resulting in loss of faith from the billions of devotees throughout the world. 'Karma, 'the Khenpo spoke after a moment's silence, 'Since my youth I have pledged to uphold the dharma and protect it from the hands of zealot vandals, vested groups and people who act as vigilantes and patrol the area and act unilaterally to impose their sense of righteousness on others. I took a stand then, and I take a stand right now, that I will not stop till I find out who the killer is and bring him to book. The promise of riches, and unspoken billions and trillions of dollars as charities and which is controlled by the leader of any Buddhist sect draws out wolves in droves for a share of their pie, and for that they'll go to any length. '

Karma knew this to be true. All religious organizations in the world scattered throughout the world including the church with the Vatican sitting at the helm, renowned synagogues of the Jews, the mosques of Muslims and different other big Buddhist sects and their huge monasteries in multitudes in domestic as well as foreign shores had reserves and donations in huge numbers pouring in from everywhere and this resulted in these organizations sitting on top of huge mountains of mobile cash. The skeptics pointed the thing that was ironical was the fact that in trying to run a God's house and propagate teachings of the Lord, mountains of wealth were supposedly necessary, contrary to commandments of frugality and non-materialistic teachings of such religious orders.

Karma Wangden flashed upon an old documentary where the narrator had mocked the teachings of the various religious organizations, supported visually by comical animations and with quotes in dramatic high decibel in the background viz., *'He is God, the all mighty, the powerful, the Alpha and the Omega, and he is going to burn you in the depths of hell, fry out your innards and make the experience so visceral for all your sins and crimes,* 'Karma had tried to control his laugh then but to no avail, because the narrator had concluded with such mordant wit and humor ripping off lines from the famous texts from the book verbatim, following sardonically, *'But he loves you. . . And he loves money, Oh yes, lots of money. . .'*

Such was the hyper-tense commentary on the 'zeitgeist' of the times...But what the documentary failed to understand that these huge corpus of funds were used for noble purposes, like building a hospital, retreat centers and conducting mass transportation of such funds to different parts of the world to build schools, nurse impoverished children in war torn areas where famine and strife tore families and countries. These institutions with alliances with the Government had played a great role in helping areas and people not only during emergent times of crisis but in the overall process of development as well. Of-course these institutions were audited like any business organization and the money used for noble purposes throughout the world. But Karma was also aware ofthe dark pull and influence of such financial muscle.

'It can pull any man, men, groups or even organizations for a chance at 'wetting their beaks', or even try to be at the helm of affairs. And for some of them any length is short and insufficient.'

'More than that, I vow to stop any group associated with it.'The Khenpo panted after uttering the last sentence, his respiratory innards flexing and tensioning after every exhale, made evident by the heavy bobbing of his aged sternum.

Karma quickly held him before it got too aggravating for the Khenpo, with the latter finding some comfort in Karma's flailing albeit consoling strong arms. With the Khenpo's respiratory rhythm now normal, he proceeded to sit up straight. After a moment's gasp, Karma tried to make sense of the Khenpo's last words.

"Gyan La, why are you talking about a group, ?"Karma said. 'I mean this could be just an individual wavering between fanaticism and lunaticism with no big agenda.'

'No my son, I'm afraid you are wrong.'A strong hand rested on his protegee's shoulder and resumed with a shaking voice, "When I entered the crime scene, it was directly evident to me, scanning the room, about the forces in play here. I decided your eyes be the first after mine to see and second my judgement."

Whatever the Khenpo had been saying, was starting to make little sense but one thought kept eating away at his cranium. 'I still do not know how the Khenpo expects me to solve this and most important of all, why is he hell bent on solving this himself?'

'It is unto us, 'Lama Tashi breathed slowly, 'and we should stand by our duties and give into action Karma. '

'Stay steadfast Karma, for we have to find answers from a veiled enemy.'

The confusion and chaos of the situation definitely irked the young man but whether he was fogged by doubts and confusions earlier, one thing was now certain in him , 'I'm not going to abandon him.'

'Forgive me for my nonchalance and nervousness earlier Gyan-la, I was at my wit's end, 'Karma clasped the Khenpo's hands in his and said in a reassuring tone, 'Let's do this together and I have full faith and trust in your knowledge. 'The duo looked at each other with a gaze filled with fondness and dependence and touched their foreheads.

A large and beautiful door sculpted with all the Buddhist themes and deities swung open inside one of the rooms inside Zurphu Monastery. Karma Wangden and the Khenpo took hurried steps as they tried to reach upon an object as quick as they could with Karma in tow. 'I've never been in this room, 'thought Karma excitedly. Nor had anyone to be precise, except for the head priest or any top Rimpoche guarding the monastery, no one was allowed for the treasures inside were too valuable for the common prying eyes. The place was supposed to be the storehouse of everything sacred and ancient. According to legends, since no layman was allowed to tread upon the highly restricted room, it was the custodian to everything valuably religious and holy. The room was supposed to contain relics of great masters of the faith, last remnants of highly enlightened individuals. It was room to great treasures of the Dharma, in that it contained teachings and codices and letters of late Rimpoches or masters right before their death, thus predicting their next locational birth. The letters also contained hints as to the time and year of birth, along with the signs that would accompany the letter allowing and helping the current help of the master before death to find the re-incarnated being again. It was a whole cycle.

The moment Karma entered the room, he knew he was at a place highly guarded and secretive. The walled murals outside stood in no comparison to what was here in the room. Every deities' form, and line came to existence as one laid eyes on them. The famous Tibetan Lharigpas or the artists, the exact same one who had designed and worked on the original monastery in Tibet had accompanied the then Karmapa and had commissioned the build and the painting of the interiors. He had definitely turned heaven and earth, so to say, to embellish the rooms. From Guru Rimpoche's wrathful presence, to the Dakinis posing as if ready for an Armageddon of sorts, the visuals were both visceral as well as alluring.

Karma tried keeping pace with his Khenpo, all the time gaping at the murals and the holy objects lined along the pavements. As he walked past each one of them, he came across things that were good only in his theory, for he had never personally been in contact with them. 'A conch shell supposed to be used by the late Karmapa, some remnants of his teeth after his holiness' cremation, the late great Karmapa's work on Dharma, his writings and his seal and pen, accompanying them made Karma stall in his thoughts and think, *'all the greatest relics, the achievements by the late master, the evidence as to his living and dying were all before his eyes, neatly arranged in the comfort of a room, inside a museum like room in one of the most famous monasteries in the state...'*

As they neared the middle of the room, Karma could see an entire enormous arrangement of ancient scriptures and books. What faced them was a high 20-30 shelves arrayed precisely, with all the rows filled with bundled religious texts sacredly ensconced in the warmth of the cupboard. Such shelves filled the room, lined back to back in a giant arc, with the middle being occupied by another giant embellished vault, it's quadrilateral edges aesthetically lined and stylized with gold. The door of the vault crisply decorated with the 8 lucky signs of the faith.

'Come here and help me, 'Lama Tashi produced a bunch of old rusted keys as they neared the large walled cupboard in the middle.

After a quick turn of the key, they opened it, a big rusty grate accompanying the action.

The enormity and the numerous texts bundled together in heaps before them startled Karma.

The Pitakas, mainly the Vinayaka, the Sutta and the Abhidhammas, the main suttas or books on Lord Buddha were shelfed uniformly. These related to the Theraveda or the original sect of

Buddhism much before the division of the philosophy into Mahayana and Hinayana. There were other texts that contained writings from other great Buddhist masters and Rimpoches. Their scripts attained over a lifetime spent in meditating, revising and updating the works of the Dharma selflessly. His eyes scoured the sea of scriptures, trying to ascertain the one the Khenpo had been trying to look for. *'Well, I hope we are here for the scriptures*, 'thought Karma, *'but which one'*. He tried to follow the Khenpo's eyes but couldn't place his vision homing in on anything in particular. But one item stood out for Karma as it was neither a text nor it resembled any relic according to him as displayed in the other parts of the room. *'It looks like a part of a costume but he couldn't figure out which part.* ' As soon as he figured out that much, and upon nearing it, he was half sure as to the contents of the glass case. And as soon as he was standing a few inches below it, he was now dead sure as to what he was staring at.

'Legend...only in TV have I witnessed it. 'Watching his reaction, the Khenpo agreed with the master relic safely placed in a bulletproof case...

'*The legendary Black Hat of the Karmapa,* ' Karma Wangden stared mutely...

****

'How can I be such a fool?' Yangtso Brahma thought as he kept hammering the dashboard of his vehicle with the driver striving hard to evade those angry blows during the momentary gear shifts. The vehicle charged fast through the arterial curves and narrow turns with the car almost running off the course many a times, it's skidding tires nearly giving into the deathly chasms below the road. As the jeep again quickly meandered its way up the slithering highway, Brahma was itching to get his hands on the Khenpo of Zurphu Monastery, who he thought definitely might have some answers for a lot of questions regarding the incident of not only that morning, but the past ones as well. *'Oh you better be ready, for what's coming'*, Brahma snarled at the thought.

ENTER THE BARDO.

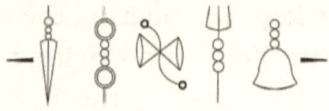

A static crack from a company issued radio went off startling Aditi Mukerjee, the field correspondent of English bulletin IBC News, who was trying to catch a quick wink in the confines of the monastery. Her media mobile resembled the hundreds stationed curiously outside the gates of the monastery, the media carnival at least a mile away from the main shrine. Although, upon seeing the police cavalcade in hot pursuit of a speeding motorcycle downhill had pushed the uber story mongers to follow the cavalcade instantly, their dishes attached at the top roof of the vehicle, trying their best to stay engaged in the pursuit.

The cameraman had thought about following the noise, but Aditi, the senior correspondent had prevailed in the situation. '*Just a routine drill...must be. After all, all evidences will eventually lead here*', thought the experienced correspondent.

The Doklam issue of Chinese infiltration bid as her premier virginal assignment had kept the news correspondent on her toes. Graduated with distinction out of a famous Communications and Media House some years back, she was ready to take on the media world by storm. Where some would've opted for a cushy job at the office, relaying bulletins and stories from the comforts of the space, far from Ground Zero, Aditi wanted to be an on field reporter. Being in-situ of the events and report. . . fearlessly bringing news to the multitudes sprawled across the geographical locations in the confines of their safe homes.

Her tours included extempore trips to violent war and strife torn places like West Africa, places like Chad and DRC, where tribal killings had terribly escalated into ethnic cleansings. Being directly at the place of action, her nubile mind had witnessed the horrors and brutal images of war and civil strife which would forever remain etched in her mind. But remaining true to her calling, she had reported with affirmation at every order from her bosses. Pack and leave, unpack and then pack and leave again. Her idea of *'living out of a suitcase box.'* After the issue of incursions that put the National Security at stake, Aditi had been the first correspondent headed towards the Indo-Bhutan border. She had provided much needed reporting, talking to Indian soldiers and wilfully venturing close to the LAC, where various unjust OPs had been marked in Chinese paint. Once the issue had simmered and thawed down a bit, some incursions in Sikkim had immediately made news and it was again reporting time for her.

She in a way thanked the Gods for a change of venue, as the images of war and strife had been a constant assault on her senses. *'A nice little break into the land of Gods. . . again. . . for the 2nd time'*, Aditi had thought. This was the second time her work had brought her to Sikkim, the first time being for an equally important one. *'Hope there is a breakthrough here this time. And I hope a really genuine one, no sensationalism or trivialization,* 'her mind a bit disconcerted about the entire episode that had taken place then.

As she had bundled herself in the flight towards the Himalayan state with her cameraman plonked next to her, enjoying his neat quota of in-flight spirits. *'This is good for altitude,* 'Mahesh had downed the two tiny foreign liquors...even hers. It was duty as soon as they had landed in the capital and they'd immediately started for the border areas, high atop North Sikkim. Then after some days patrolling the Lachen and Yumisangdong valley with the border troops, a spate of incidents had occurred in the capital. *'Well someone's really putting the name to test'*. Aditi thought looking at the giant mountains swathed with white, which arose on all four sides with such majesty, that the noon glare and resultant refractions, gave them the appearances of large deities protecting the land.

It had been about a few weeks since the back to back murders and the recent one had surely culminated in bringing the world media to its feet and here. Their cameras trained at places of incidents with a hawk like stolidity.

'Probably must be some muddled frequencies. . . jammed in the ether, 'Aditi reclined back in her makeshift hammock made with the suspended blanket, the ends latched securely between the two points at the back. Her cameraman, also a designated driver, started to take stock of the inventory of films with them.

A static again, 'He...ll. . o'the break in the syllable infuriated Aditi. 'Not again...just switch off the transmitter Mahesh.' He followed her order.

But the effort by Mahesh to follow her was now interrupted by a definite message.

'Aditi, is that you?' A soft voice spoke out. 'How would you feel to have a front view of the spectacle about to unfold later tomorrow?'

Aditi sat bolt upright. *'Did it just say my name?'*

Mahesh looked at her, answering the obvious.

A lot of noise passed through the airwaves and the frequencies often collided and cross connected. But a name was being called out clearly. It whispered the correspondent's name. . . clearly.

She took the receiver nervously in her hands and spoke, 'Yes, who is this?' She paused for a moment and asked the pertinent question, 'How do you know my name?'

'Never mind the person here and the knowledge, 'the speaker let the line hang in for an instant and resumed, 'You have to hurry and make your presence at the address felt in case you want some real news. '

The voice relayed an address and Aditi jotted it down quickly.

'Remember, we are just defenders of our faith and beliefs, and we are doing this for the greater good of God. '

The line went dead. . . Aditi froze,'She said a 'spectacle tomorrow'. . . 'What Kind'?, was all Aditi thinking.

Without batting an eyelid, she ordered Mahesh to gun it, with her driving shotgun.

'What kind of a message was that, 'the constant thought overpowering her, *'and what spectacle was she talking about?'*

'What did she mean by defenders of the faith? And how did the caller know my name?' A swirling mix of questions hovered around her head with no answers.

'Oh by the way. . . ' the journalist did a doubletake.

'It was a lady, the voice was that of a lady's, ' Aditi recollected suddenly as her media van throttled past the winding roads, in a downward spiral leaving a cyclonic trail of dust and hurtling stones behind.

ENTER THE BARDO.

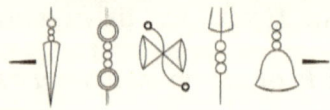

The individual in room 36 at Hotel Sonam Delek stripped himself of the clothes he had been wearing. A modest pair of shirts and a trouser. The room was filled with the left-over aroma of food. Some stray bones from a fried culinary cuisine lay strewn carelessly on the table. The overpowering aroma of ice cream and desserts diffused inside the room, overwhelming it with their pungent odor.

Lying stark naked in front of the mirror, the individual viewed himself, a lithe body facing him.

'The secret to enlightenment', the individual thought, *'the secret to Buddhahood does not lie in this body, for it is merely a mortal shell. '*

'It is one's deeds and one's karma that decide your fate now and in the afterlife. What will you be? Where will you go? How will you live? Where will you be born? These are questions that can be answered absolutely:' A smile tore up in his face.

'We must abandon it, for death is inevitable. But karma ensures our name and destiny. This life gives us purpose, and we should stand true to it. It is what makes us immortal and assures us a place in the realm of the gods.'

'Remember, the body will wither and die, but the deeds will live on; they're never interred. It lives on.'

The sound of the Supreme Teacher echoed.

For a moment, the kiss on the forehead inside the Supreme Teacher's chamber from memories past sealed the truth and belief in their mission. *'It is for the greater good of God, and remember that it will free you forever from Samsara,'* the teacher had assured...

'No matter who or what you are, what backgrounds tell your story, no matter what age or disposition you swear by, very few obey when they are called to action'. A pride swelled inside him for a second: *'And the supreme teacher has chosen us two to do the bidding. Until the bright light sees us off'*.

Disengaging from the thoughts, he opened his Louis Vuitton trolley, a limited edition picked up from a posh boutique of Paris some years ago. The only choice in terms of clothes he had were his most promised and important pairs, according to him. And it was just enough.

'This is just what matters—no more, no less, no excess, or in the extremes, just what you require.'

Slowly lifting his monk's robes and other assortments of his monastic dress, he placed them on the bed and started to dress, each twist and bun of the drill done with utmost precision and respect.

'I'm now on the threshold of a phenomenon that will make me immortal and a Buddha.'

'Our forces are just too strong for them to stop it now. The wheels are already in motion.'

'The actions that will be taken tomorrow by us will ensure a promise, an act that will go a long way in establishing our way of worshiping the gods. The tyrannical rule of a few zealots, supported by a few devotees here and a few extras in the West, will be drowned out by our actions. They will bend down to our ever-increasing band and groups of disciples, which are organized and scattered everywhere in the world. Western society is no longer the forte of the Dalai clique alone. We are here, we are ready, and we will never allow adulteration of our practices any more. The time of tyrannical rule in faith is gone, and the time of rational thinking and logic, as espoused in Buddhist philosophy, is the only way.' The individual hurriedly finished

dressing, stood up again in front of the mirror, and looked at himself with pride, a sense of immense purpose welling inside of him.

After a few minutes of contemplation, he was descending the stairs of the hotel with his driver in tow, bowing and leading the way. 'Whatever the payments and expenses, they shall be repaid instantly, ' said the driver, placing a telephone number with the receptionist. Amanpreet at the reception table knew little about such protocols, and being new to such incidents, she gave in easily.

As the individual made his way through the corridor of the hotel with small steps, the driver's obsequious behavior in trying to forward him towards the vehicle surprised the onlookers.

'Oh, he must be a great manifestation, an image of the Buddha, ' mumbly queries hit the chamber as the individual made his entry towards his vehicle.

'Such great beings, ' a Swedish tourist clad in traditional Buddhist attire said.

With him comfortably lodged in the Lexus, he knew where to go, and the driver, in tow, fired the engine towards the destination.

'It has to be done tomorrow, ' thought the individual as he ordered his driver to gun it.

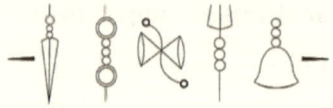

'I know it must have come across as a pleasant shock to you, 'the Khenpo said following Karma's gaze to the Legendary Black hat of the Karmapa of the Kagyu Lineage.

'You must remember that it is no co-incidence that your eyes are privy to such objects. '

'Co-incidence?' thought Karma, *'everything is Gyan-la'*. . . 'I never knew I would be here today trying to solve a crime by helping you. And my presence in this room was never premeditated.'

'Yes it was, this day, this hour, your presence here was always pre planned and existed much before today. '

Karma feigned an understanding, but the Khenpo's words didn't make any sense.

"Remember a simple act as kindness, a random thought, a cursory conversation and even the most rudiments of human behaviour shape a person's future path. Any random event occurs and we call it a co-incidence. It could be anything, any event, chancing upon a friend at a strange location, meeting someone whom you wanted to much earlier and the person materializing before you. A chance, probability or the frequency with which these events occur could be seen as random but they aren't."

Karma scratched his head a bit. "Remember in our philosophy, the forces of Karma, the cause and effect relationship between thoughts, actions and energies being projected by the mind and body are dynamic and interdependent. This is well supported by science as well. These thoughts and actions of ours already rotate the wheel of cycles dependent on those variables and create an event in our lives at moments, which we consider random."

The Khenpo was beginning to make sense. The science behind such effects although hadn't been quantified, but the results were aplenty everywhere.

A student getting academically successful because of his discipline and rigorous work ethic, a professional getting fat paychecks working for an MNC owing to his belief and actions. Although, these examples were also filled with stories of failure and desperation, one thing stood out in common along such exercises, the thought and the energy directed towards such mundane activities irrevocably and unconditionally came back with a result to the person with universal precision. It was the energy and thoughts combining and sending a signal back to its original sender. Call it the Laws of Attraction or Positive thinking or Power of Manifesting...it was prevalent throughout the world,with unerring frequency...

"That is the power of the universe, my son, and remember the power of Good shall always outweigh the evil."

Karma Wangden, with his eyes still glued to the black hat, cased inside a robust bulletproof plexiglass, nodded in agreement.

"Which brings me to my next question?"

'In keeping with all these philosophies of cause and effect and Karma, 'the Khenpo stopped for a moment and completed the question, 'What if there are no co-incidences?'

'What if you were destined to be here with me, here at the monastery, here in-front of the greatest treasures of our faith and below the legendary Black Hat. '?

'What if this episode was already written?'

A blank drew across Karma's face, but something was eating him up from inside. It wasn't the forces responsible for events, as the Khenpo had just explained to him. It was something else.

Finally he mustered the courage and asked, "Does that thing really fly, ?" Karma pointed at the Black Hat...

A diffused laugh escaped the Khenpo.

The Legendary Black Hat of Karmapa according to Karma had a long history as to its origin and present state. The history filled with magic and realism, sometimes often a line blurring the two had been passed down from generations...It was steeped in Buddhist traditional history filled with magical beings also known as the Yogis and Yoginis of ancient Tibet who performed feats and miracles that was outside of ordinary human being's cognitive sense.

Not merely a cheap conjurer of things, but Karma knew that there were actual reports of such ancient Lamas of Tibet who could defy gravity and perform a sprint across great distances with ease. Such feats were well recorded and reported by famous names in World History. The one name that stood out was a Russian Philosopher and an occultist named Helena Blavatsky. She spent most of her time travelling Europe and embarked on several tours, simultaneously developing the likeness for esotericism until a claim by her that an encounter with high Gurus transferred her to Shigatse in Tibet, where she learned to synergize religion, science and philosophy. Although many term her a fraudster and a charlatan, but she went on to become an important part of India's history as well where an alliance with the reformist body Arya Samaj played a role in the independence movement. Basically she was at the vanguard of the theosophical movement at the time, a movement well founded in India by Annie Besant, one of the proponents of Indian Independence. Theosophists simply had brotherhood, living in harmony, a coming together of Science and faith and most importantly the effort to tap the underlying and latent immeasurable powers of man. The latter being a result of Blavatsky's experiences with the gurus of Tibet.

A whole bunch of Buddhist leaders and spiritual heads had studied enough about Blavatsky and her times. Silence was always a standard practice in the faith when asked about such episodes. Also the theosophical society had a belief in coming of the World Teacher or Maitreya who would come and guide mankind through the evolutionary process and preach a ton about humanity, compassion and love. The Maitreya term connected Hinduism and Buddhism completely.

After many years of spending precious times with the Khenpo, Karma had learned one thing and that was every faith had in its scripts the prophecy that a new enlightened being would come and free mankind from all sufferings. It was written in the Bible about Armageddon and the return of the Son, the rise of Hierophant in Ancient Egypt, and about the return of the Lotus born, a manifestation of the Guru himself in Buddhism to eliminate sufferings of all mankind.

In a way Karma Wangden personally had less reservations about such things. History was replete with wise souls, born way ahead of their times talking and preaching about humanity and love. They were all beings talking about the idea of love and compassion. Lord Buddha, the Christ and even Krishna, these were people who recited words of wisdom into the ears of normal beings and tried to bring a measure of order and love in those turbulent times.

Of course their discourses were often met with skepticism and insult, but they stood their ground and went about doing the good work.

"Which brings me back to the question, does that thing fly,?" Karma kept looking at the hat.

The lesson on the famed Black Crown of the Karma Kagyu school of Tibetan Buddhism had been lapped up by Karma Wangden during his stay with the Gyan-la. The Khenpo had diligently detailed every aspect of the history associated with the legendary Crown, often peppering the anecdotes with magical instances and events which had kept Karma glued to the stories.

The biggest shock had come when he had found out that the Karmapas were actually teachers and guides to an influential and powerful empire during those times.

'What? the empire of the Ming Dynasty. . . . ?'Karma had reacted. . . 'China'?

The shock from his student then didn't surprise the old monk. After all, much of history of the philosophy had been lost over the years and only ardent devotees had tried to peer into the past of their Gods.

Karma knew the legends of Yogis and Mahatmas, great spiritual adepts like the back of his hand. People who possessed immense powerful wisdom, a mystic or the Mahatma from the mythical Kingdom of Shambhala, possibly straddling the Tibetan plateau according to various conjectures and accounts but no real geographical or physical state. The land had inhabitants in the form of wise men, adepts or seers who populated the place. The Hindu scripts of Vishnu Purana talk about the coming of Kalki, as the last incarnation of Lord Vishnu from this magical place. Although no actual physical or geographical locations of Shambala were discovered by various Western Expeditions, accounts from explorers like Alexandra David

Neel, a French Buddhist, Nicholas Roerich the famous Russian painter and archaeologist who was so much involved with spiritualism in the country pointed towards a place with great magic and spirituality. From theophysicists, explorers to even the Bolsheviks in the early 1990s allegedly trying to combine Buddhist Kalachakra tantra with communism, with a view to creating that perfect specimen of a human being. Albeit the rumors abounded that such expeditions could've been used for harnessing such great powers and be eventually used as weapons of destruction, the place stoked a lot of interest then and it still does now.

Hearing about all these the Khenpo had asked a question to Karma some time back, 'Do you know, the name of the place has attained great status and currency in modern Popular Culture?'

Karma obviously had no clue.

"Modern culture now terms it Shangri-La."

Lama Tashi explained to Karma how one such yogi or adept after attaining Bhumi or the highest form of Boddhisattvas had been blessed by gifts from the elated Dakinis or Female Buddha Deities and offered him as a gift, a hat or a crown made from the strands of hair of the Dakinis.

"Of course the coming of the lineage of Karmapa was well predicted by Lord Buddha in one of the sutras and it was Dusum Khyenpa who was the 1st." Karma listened intently...

"Then the 5th Karmapa, upon vision from the Ming Emperor had asked the Holiness to prepare a Crown filled with valuable stones with a giant Ruby at the centre. Thus started the Black Crown ceremony of the Kagyu lineage, a device thought to be powerful enough to grant the witnesses at the ceremony a feeling of great positive energy and emancipation from negative ones." The Khenpo drew a steady breath and continued, "The practice of the Black Hat Ceremony stopped after the passing away of the 16th Karmapa, Ragjung Rigpe."

Karma Wangden was aware of this fact. In the early 1990s, the 16th Karmapa had bought valuable relics of the lineage and lodged them safely at the Monastery in the Sikkimese capital. The abode of the Kagyu Lineage had been blessed by valuables all stored in the central monastery for occasional display to devotees at particular sacred events. Rumors had it that all of those relics from the past had magical powers, especially the Black Crown.

"Then the passing away of a Religious Titan," Not only him, but the entire Buddhist community, domestic as well as foreign had

collectively mourned the passing away of a great Rimpoche. However, the mourning evolved into murmurs of dissent soon after and the lineage was in danger of being torn asunder. The aftermath had witnessed unfortunate schisms and split between leaders of the same lineage.

"The entire incident was a scar in the face of the Dharma, Gyan-la,.."

The Khenpo nodded.

"The Black Crown that held in it the powers and energies of positivity and spiritual contentment were hidden and it's real location, made unknown to the general public."

Before Karma could react, the Khenpo added a final nail.

"That the Holy Black hat is here is known just by a few of us in the monastery…"

Karma just stood there, a mute witness to Lama Tashi's final statement. The events that had unfolded in the temple premises after the 16th Karmapa's death were acerbic to say the least. It was damaging the credibility of the faith, the twin foundations of faith and belief of every religion or philosophy were being violently shaken by powerful voices of dissent. And as there were two different re-incarnates, an army of followers spawned and followed their respective leaders.

Karma still remembered the time when boots were ordered in the ground.

"A familiar sight now, the monks, the tourists, the devotees, and soldiers with high powered rifles patrolling the premises of the monastery. . . a holy place about to erupt in violence..."

Karma often regretted the oxymoronic scenario.

It was trying times for the Dharma and the patience and anxiety of the times were pushed to the hilt with many just praying for a peaceful solace of a solution...

'It was tumultuous times for the faith, and the need for true preaching and practicing the Dharma was replaced by constant power struggles' Karma had been an adolescent then and the debauchery of his time did less to bring his focus and energies into the issue.

"But I have a chance now, to serve," Karma thought, *'to dispel such dark forces trying to sabotage the faith.'* A deep breath and a sense of purpose was felt that invigorated his system.

The Khenpo pulled across a large table, Karma helping him all the time. His frail body which had seen better days seemed to still eke out some strength hidden in the old sinews of his riper self.

Opening up a notebook earlier held by the Khenpo, the duo tried to again look at the surveillance videos and make sense of it. *'At least 'I' have to make sense of it,'* Karma thought.

The video played again with the inner confines playing host to a figure with a body slung over his shoulder.

After the exit of the dark hooded figure from the main temple shrine, Karma sat transfixed in his chair looking for any hint the video might be able to offer. But the damning digitals had done little to throw answers at him. He looked at his master and tried to elicit an answer from him.

He quickly went back to his memories and processed them, each event following up in his mind, one after the other. *'So there is the body and the dough effigies neatly aligned around the body, as the killer had and tons of paper pamphlets strewn all around the body, '* With great focus, he peered into the video trying and prying for an answer.

He was at a cul de sac. . . *'Where will this this lead now, '*? a lone thought escaped his mind. The Khenpo meanwhile was looking at Karma expecting a miracle from him. . . to solve this. Between the digital reels and revision footages, a thought suddenly hit Karma.

An idea as spontaneous as it could be was yelling at him.

'Gyan-la, can I have a look at those pamphlets that can be see thrown all over the floor?'

The Khenpo on listening to his request was more than happy to cater to his demands. With a wry and an appreciative smile, he quickly went over to one of his duffel bags and produced what was a page from the hundreds stuffed inside it. All of them bearing the same scripts and texts as the one handed over to Karma.

Karma Wangden held one of the Pamphlets in his hand and looked at the texts scrawled across it.

'The script is Tibetan, Gyan-La, 'Karma reacted to his teacher.

The Khenpo nodded and asked him to try to read it.

Although well versed in the language, Karma had been many touches away from the reading of the Tibetan script and his current predicament slightly embarrassed him.

'I must do this correctly, or else the Gyan-La might correct me with full punity, ' Karma thought as the teacher student relationship during recitation practices often turned sour for the student making the mistakes. He slowly laid

down one of the paper pamphlets in front of him and tried to decipher or rather translate the contents of it.

The Tibetan script lay before him, the scrawls and the calligraphy trying their best to convey the meaning embedded in those texts. *'If only it had been in English, '* Karma Thought, silence filling the room and also the space between the two.

The parchment lay idly as he started to read from the text. Wherever he faltered with his lines, the Khenpo would reassuringly help his student.

After some minutes of intense reading, Karma Wangden was pretty sure about the exact nature and origin of the texts that the paper was trying to convey.

'If I'm not mistaken. . . ', a pause, 'these papers are the ones that was said to have rained in thousands from the skies, according to its history, 'Karma said aloud.

The old monk laid a hand on his shoulder and pressed firmly as if in affirmation to his student's words.

'The famous messages that was thought to have rained from the skies in ancient times. The one believed to haverained them from above was none other than the Lotus Born, ' Karma

Wangden's memory about these letters or prophesies were crystal clear in the mind like the collective consciousness of any Buddhist devotee.

The Lotus Born or more famously revered and known as Guru Rimpoche or Guru Padmasambhava was a great learned saint who lived in the 8th Century and who was responsible for introducing Buddhism in Tibet. Born in Oddiyana, the region straddling the borders of Tibet and Afghanistan, the Guru's stature asa Tantric Buddhist practitioner, teacher and his subsequent teachings over the years have been accepted and found relevant during the current turbulent times. Worshipped alike by all the four sects of Buddhism, his seminal works on different aspects of the Dharma are still considered treasure troves of tomes filled with his immense clarity and purposeful mind for the benefit of all sentient beings. Every single monastery and places of worship depicts him in a seated position, looking menacingly, holding a Dorje with a trident slung over his body. The reason being that apart from being a learned and saintly practitioner of the Dharma, his innate nature was often said to erupt with such ferocity and anger when faced with 'demonic' adversaries in the region. Due to close resemblance between various edicts of Hinduism and Buddhism, many consider him to be the incarnation of Lord Shiva and Lord Buddha respectively. His story of him depicted as a slayer of evil has often been found on walled murals in monasteries throughout the world, with his angry visage trained at the onlookers with much artistry and skill.

Now holding the parchment in his hands, Karma found out that they were mass copies of the original texts. *'Being used immorally by immoral souls'*, Karma regretted the thought.

Although the original first copy of the text was safely preserved in the museum of Namgyal Institute of Tibetology, Gangtok, such copied texts from the source were often circulated aplenty during religious events.

Karma Wangden had been a follower of ancient texts of world's religions and after devouring tomes in myriads of various religions and practices, he had always noticed the similar announcement of an impending Armageddon or End of the World. He knew what would usually follow in such 'crystal ball' texts so to speak.

It would always point out to a time in the future about an apocalypse, impending doom where mass death and destruction would follow. An era or time where everything would be in total anarchy. Lawlessness, mindless wars, killings and diseases in pandemic proportions would fester and there would be chaos and marauding carnage everywhere. Everywhere the organized system of governance would fail and it would take in people in its vicious cycle and grip of ruin and pain.

'Countless such post-apocalyptic sensibilities had been explored by filmmakers in modern popular culture,' Karma recalled. Some termed it the present reel about the real 'future-history'.

Of course such prophesies had another side to it. A more comforting side or more of an assurance. The prophecies also talked about a help that was imminent, a divine hand that would save thousands and billions more,with it's benediction... A saviour that would land upon Earth and destroy such evils in whatever form they were. These premonitions that were written usually portended about future catastrophes and they were filled with unimaginable horror which ultimately and allegedly tugged vehemently at an emotion that fed on such incidents of death and destruction. Karma knew what that emotion was.

That emotion was fear. And fear usually made believers out of men.

The human construct and the idea of hell was no where more famous than in Dante's cantoes of the Divine Comedy...A famous Florence poet and philosopher.Many experts termed it was actually a response to dwindling footfalls and attendences in the faith that the powers during the time, in a bid to re-group and gather the strays,employed the skills of a famous Florence citizen and poet,Dante Aleghieri...And it was Boticelli who drew the famous L'Mappa'Hell,drawing the 9 rings of hell by depicting it as a sub-terranean funnel for the wrongdoers and sinners as described in the eponymous Divine Comedy.It's therefore a lesser known fact that the modern idea of hell was laid down by Dante...

To say that it struck the spines of people would be an understatement...Similarly there are instances in other holy books like the Torah,the Quoran guaranteeing 'fiery hell' for the sinners...Such graphic preaching naturally made believers out of men instantly.

People always fear the unknown.

But to say that these tactics were used as weapons of faith would be wrong...as it went a long way in bringing a measure of order and discipline in any given society.

"So the question really was,whether they were all scare tactics or the sacrocanct truth of various holy books and scriptures."

Being a man of faith,the question kind of alerted the Khenpo...

After a moment's pause,he spoke , "Karma, to say that these were mere tactics to instill and work the fear psychosis of people and the masses would be wrong."

Karma Wangden gave in to the explanation of the Abbot with rapt attention...

"It's safe to say that not only these ancient texts and scripts have provided some semblance of normalcy and control, but these very writings were talking to us at a level, we were trying to understand."

Karma did a rejig.

The only words that people understand are ones that hit them at the core of their primal senses. These words in its esoteric aspect aims at either fear or happiness.

"Since these words were written a long time ago, there was few logic and rational consciousness, so to speak. So the only way to reach the minds of the people was by uttering words and sentences that could appeal at the time."

The Khenpo was slowly making sense. The various teachings of great masters, including Lord Buddha, knew that people of his times wouldn't've comprehended and ascertained the real natureabout his preaching and therefore their oral transmissions had quotes which connected to a human being's primal emotion. The teachings and scripts often talk about turning into a possible cretin or an unfortunate animal in the next life, if people committed a crime or a sin in the current life. Any intellectual during that time period wouldn't've even understood if teachings in its original format would've been done. Some would've termed those statements hazy and unclear calling them outlandish and without any base. But on closer scrutiny, one would know the real meanings hidden behind such sayings. Human knowledge kept evolving with consistency and a simple physics theory by Einstein, something as simple as a Brownian motion which didn't break into the 'craniums' of the scientists of the day, today forms a simple chapter on an 8th grader's Physics book.

"So since the primitive minds didn't know about the cause and effect, and the consequences of one's Karma, the esoteric and heavy language wouldn't have made sense." Such was the power and high intellect of his mind.

The Khenpo drew a gasp as he made sure of his student's comprehension. "But remember, there always has been and always will be greater minds in this world, people born way ahead of their times."

But to understand it's immense potential as a tool of faith, one has to read and understand the underlying layers hidden in the message.

"It all depends on how you see it and it will test you and your faith in the Dharma."

Karma scratched his head trying to take in the words of his teacher, *'Why does Gyan La always talk at a subliminal level, instead of just calling a spade a spade.'*

ENTER THE BARDO.

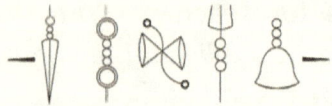

An important religious head with a huge conical yellow hat, flanked by the armed police, New Zealand's finest, the Delta Z, trudged slowly across the tarmac of the airport. The Delta-Z's involvement in this simple mission of providing security was not a tough choice for the Government of New Zealand. They were the country's finest military outfits who carried out their missions with death like precision. The individual had three 6 Ft, muscled and armed personnel with semi-automatics in front of him and at the back. Each relay of their message was done through an earpiece, silently relaying positions and objects in the vicinity. Far atop the control tower, a sniper with an AWP loaded with a 9. 0 caliber lead, lay in position, an overwatch, scouring the expansive asphalt, trying to protect the important Buddhist head headed towards the lone chartered plane lodged for an imminent flight off the country. A group of stragglers, some stray disciples trying to break the security cordon, just to get Kawang or blessing from His Holiness, having missed the chance at the seminar, waved profusely, a sea of hands at random intervals waving, at the person trying to mount the plane.

The figure turned towards them and waved back. He could've retraced and met them but the protocol had to be maintained.

'An ever increasing sea of Western followers, that's good, 'thought the figure walking up towards the plane.

After the secured group reached the plane's stairs, the religious head turned towards his security and thanked them, folding his hands into a Namaste.

A sea of sirens from various stationed security vehicles dispersed in randomness, the plane now a visible lone object at the Tarmac.

As it soared through the stratospheric spheres of the atmosphere, gaining elevation consistently, Kalsang Rimpoche wasn't his usual self. Although the seminar on the Interconnectedness on Happiness and Compassion had gone well throughout the many cities in the country, but the constant bombardment of ill news from his country kept him on the edge. *'Who and why?'* the thoughts kept materializing. All the random acts of murders of innocent tuolkus recently ordained had disillusioned him to a great extent. The story of the scribe from another country about how this could be related to killings in the name of religion went over his head. Nothing made sense because his Philosophy, the Buddhist Philosophy had at its central core, the word Compassion. *'Compassion and staying happy and the ultimate aim being the end of suffering of the people*, 'thought Kalsang as he tried to peer outside into the distant horizon, past through the hazy and smoky Cumulo Nimbus for an answer that he wanted so badly himself.

As soon as he ventured past those images outside the plane the skeletons of the past and the evils of the present suddenly filled him with immense regret, the incidents as if freshly embedded in his memories, clawed their way through the dark recesses of his mind, a violent reminder of the truth. And it was not only Buddhism that was suffering from mankind's cruel actions done in the name of faith. The evils of men and their illogically evil ways had occupied regions and myriad other faiths with full impunity and wrath.

'What has this world come to?' the Rimpoche thought.

News of barbarism, and mindless wars were part of everyday vocabulary.

His inner conscience had been wrecked by news of immense warfare between tribes and different groups for ultimate supremacy throughout the world. Every day, he woke up to news about organizations trying to put a stronghold against their rivals, groups committing deadly and horrific acts against their targeted adversaries.

'Whether it is a good thing or bad, about trying to uphold one's ideals, the way of violence is truly wrong, 'thought the monk as he contemplated on the tiny ring of beads on his hands.

The turbulence at 30, 000 feet and it's accompanied violent shaking of the vehicle at such high elevation did nothing to scare him and as he adjusted his robes within the confines of the aerial plane, he was hit by thoughts and memories, memories that culminated in a meeting in the distant past.

Kalsang Rimpoche had been one of the leaders, the spiritual guru seated in a circle at a large table inside a monastery, in some unknown location in India. Having trekked the uphill beaten path, the Rimpoche was relieved when his eyes met the lone light high atop a hill. The climb had been dangerous, with deep chasms of violent depth on one side that extended to an abyss that was a combination of pit less greenery and boulders. '*Guaranteed death,* 'the Rimpoche had thought thinking about the terrifying terrain. The Rimpoche had asked his driver to wait at the base of the hill and he had slowly walked up groping and holding the wall on the opposite side of the path. His every attempt at the ascent tried every last vestige of his depleted and old muscles. The strain more on his diaphragm with his lungs working overtime to control the breathing.

A monastery lay at the top of the hill, far from the confusion of everyday life. Although it was mostly deserted, its sole custodian visited often on a monthly basis to make sure that the presence of the idols inside were safe, the growth of the bushes outside and overall maintenance work were carried out every month. The custodian who was an aged monk and highly revered in the region, made it his responsibility to attend the monastery every month without fail. A temporary detachment from his usual quotidian practices and preaching of the Dharma inhis monastery provided a wonderful sojourn for him. *'Solitude and nature in plentiful around me,* 'thought the monk, *' also is a form of meditation and retreat for me,* ' the old custodian completed his thought.

A rustle of the dried autumn leaves broke the usual silence that enveloped the area. The slightly overcast sky picking unto the last remaining light of day. Today was different from all the other times. After a few hours of patient waiting, the solitude and the serene atmosphere had changed. Today he was not present at the monastery as a custodian but as a member of a group. Today he was not going to be alone. He knew an urgent meeting of the Dharma's top leaders had been called extempore. *'Is it that time for us now,* 'the monk thought.

As the custodian played with his beads chanting mantras, a familiar robed figure ascended the last cobbled steps and reached the monastery.

Upon confirmation, he shouted, 'Kalsang, you're here.'

Kalsang Rimpoche was more than happy to see the old monk who'd been his guide and more so his friend all these years. Gasping and panting he lunged for his friend and hugged him tightly. It had been some years between them and the distance away had really increased the bond between the two. 'Many years away from you, and you still haven't lost the charm in your eyes and face my friend.'Kalsang held the old monk's face in his hands lovingly.

'I can say the same thing about you, 'the custodian monk replied.

The years between them definitely produced moments and emotional yearnings to reminisce upon old times and talk about them, but today was different and both of them knew the gravity and urgency of the times. A sudden frown erupted in Kalsang Rimpoche's face. 'Have they already arrived?'

The monk lifted his finger, indicating that they were upstairs. Both of the monks had to cancel all their pending and scheduled works and had to rush to answer the call. Important meetings were called before, but there were advance notices sent to the leaders. But this was different and sudden. It was a direct call from the highest offices under His Holiness Dalai Lama.

Each member, each leader had been contacted through a telephone and been relayed the message. The urgency in the message had kept all of the contacted leaders on their toes.

Kalsang Rimpoche and the old custodian knew that they wouldn't be the only ones today at that monastery. All the four heads of the sects would be present at the meeting.

Both of them made their way upwards towards the room. The ancient flight of stairs fashioned out of an adamant oak creaked as it tried to manage the weight of the bodies stepping on it.

As they entered the room, both of the monks were greeted by the other two present and seated. The usual venerated exchanges followed amongst the leaders of the sects.

At 85, Kelsang commanded some form of respect from the other leaders. The room went quiet for a second as all of them silently played their beads and chanted prayers. A slow collective murmur crescendoed, sounding enchanting with the resonances filling the acoustic vacuum in the room. Each one then placed the beads on their heads, prayed inaudibly, and sat back straight as they braced themselves for the serious issue at hand.

Three heads costumed in their lamaic robes and regal attires already started withthe discussion.

"It is unprecented that a call for a meeting was asked," said one monk as he drank a strong black brew from roughly boiled local tea. He continued, "Every time a meeting of this nature is called, an official letter is dispatched to us with the Holy Seal directly from His Holiness."

Everyone present there agreed. A meeting of this kind was done on a momentary basis, with their agendas simple and true, albeit important. The cause includes, inter alia, targeted donations and the amount to be decided for various monasteries in the country, developing the cultural performing arts, or TIPA, and establishing schools focused on efficient monastic pedagogy for the new entrants or junior monks. The meeting included discussions about donations and mass reserves of cash, mostly foreign, which ran into billions and billions of dollars under different sects. The meeting, in a way, tried to hash out or find solutions to important administrative and financial issues pertaining to the faith, the monasteries, and other charitable works conducted in the Dharma's name.

But the phone call that had hit each one of those leaders present in the room about a few days ago sounded outrageous and, at the same time, ominous.

"If this threat is real, then we must act. I know we shouldn't take it upon ourselves, but we can always seek help from the authorities."

'Don't you think that we've done enough in seeking help from them in the past, 'said the custodian, looking at the leaders sternly.

'And what did we get from them?' The old monk recollected his thoughts and spoke, 'The highest court of the land ruled against us in the most important of cases involving the Kagyu lineage, which brought a lot of despair to us and millions of devotees worldwide. '

All the gathered agreed with the words spoken by the custodian.

'But it was an isolated incident, and better minds might prevail; we can never forego our faith in the justice system of the land. Like our faith and credo, it is without fear or favor and rational, ' said a pudgy leader, pointing to everyone as he made his remarks.

'Isolated incident, you say?' asked the custodian, a firm overtone visibly audible.

'And what about the government's order and the subsequent raid on the holy monastery in Himachal? '

All of them stayed silent. The news about such a raid at the 17th Karmapa Orgyen Trinley Dorjee's monastic residence came as a big shock to Buddhists all around at the time. Local as well as international news channels worked overtime trying to get that media bite from the policemen involved. It all started when a senior IPS officer of the state, based on alleged confirmed tips, raided the temple premises and uncovered millions and millions of dollars in donations, some of them in Chinese currency. Given the geopolitical state of India and China and the relationship between the two, the matter of Chinese currencies stashed in the vault of the monastery was enough to raise the doubts of the officer and his investigating team.

'A probable Chinese spy in the garb of a Buddhist spiritual leader?!" read aloud headlines from prominent English dailies, and the uber-enthusiastic news presenters, with their larynx on steroids, fanned and supported such issues and claims made by the police.

Of course, the news came as a huge shock. It hurt the sentiments of the local and international devotees when certain comments against the petulant nature of the incident and the highhandedness and inaccuracies of the authorities were even made by top religious leaders of the faith.

And they were right. It was a familiar sight as far as the fundings of religious institutions were concerned to find a hefty amount of donations by discipiles, and it bore testimony to the fact that places of worship usually received donations aplenty from various walks of life. Add to that a philosophy and a religion that has grown exponentially over the past few years, a faith resting on the twin pillars of rationality and logic, and there was never going to be a dearth of such devotions and, most importantly, donations. After the issue had cooled down, so to speak, another leading English daily with a veteran correspondent wielding the pen termed it a futile and funny exercise on the part of the authorities. The article detailed the source of such donations, the Holiness' credibility and infallibility, as well as the stupidity of the officer who laid the raid. Where most of his writings compared the escape of His Holiness the Karmapa from Tibet as nothing short of magical, from the glaring military eyes of the Chinese, the writer also likened the disturbances as a big achievement of the Chinese government at the cost of the inane stupidities of the Indian authorities. *"The Chinese must be laughing at the Indian Media Circus on the issue,"* one of the lines from the article read.

The heads of sects swallowed up their pride and accepted the truth. After all, the exercises of the authorities had been baseless and without any iota of truth in them. The matter erupted and ceased as fast as it had materialized.

'But this threat is something we've never experienced before, and it threatens all the stakeholders in the faith—you, me, and the ones present in the room. And most important of all, the millions of devotees worldwide.'

'So what should be done to deal with it?' Rimpoche thought as he mentally went about the possible catastrophic aftermaths of such a threat.

'Threat, ' the Rimpoche pondered over the word with full focus. The assembly talked about threats. Not from any individual but from an organization.

It wasn't new for the faith to receive such threats. And though the frequency of such incidents had shown a spike in recent times, the faith as well as the top echelons were hardly intimidated by them.

'We've received such threats in the past, ' the Rimpoche reminded himself, *'and nothing untowardly has ever transpired. '* In fact, threats had been a natural order of things for the Dharma. And high on top of all of them were the foreign threats, particularly from the Chinese. With the Communist nation frequently exasperated by His Holiness the Dalai Lama's meetings with the world's top leaders for the just issue of Tibet, those well-known high-level diplomatic or strategic ties with the West had inevitably caused the Red Army to issue warnings to each and every country, categorically stating that Tibet would always be a part of China. Of course, there were talks about fringe elements, such as the clandestine death squad of the Chinese rumored to concoct plans for the assassination of the spiritual leader. India had silently answered back to the Chinese

by providing Zplus security for His Holiness, thus guaranteeing his protection and long life.

The Rimpoche stayed strong in his thoughts and kept on with the discussions with the other monks. *'As far as threats were concerned, they were directed in heaps, but we've always tided over them.* ' The leaders present in the room kept up the discussions, also trying to hatch a proper solution if ever a need arose, for another hour. Kelsang Rimpoche could sense a hint of downplaying nonchalance from the other senior monks. It could be nothing but a hoax or a threat. But something told him that it might be serious after all.

A strong turbulence hit the flying vehicle at some unknown elevation, and Kalsang Rimpoche was immediately transported to the present. A swirling intensity of rabid thoughts kept engulfing him, and before long, a strong pain radiated at the back of his head and proceeded with total potency forward, like a band around his head, each instantaneous second and the accompanied pain wreaking more trouble as he failed to control his thoughts. *A vicious cycle.* The lama held onto his beads and clutched the rubber handle next to his seat with full strength. After struggling a bit, he was able to control the outcome of such a stressful situation. He started breathing steadily, and after a moment's time, a uniform respiratory process replaced his anxiety and the palpable pain gradually. He looked out the window of his chartered plane. The clouds did little to offer him a horizontal view, but the Tasman Sea, or more informally, the Ditch, as used by the Australians or the Kiwis traveling to each other's country, threw up a huge expanse of blue water in his eyes. He instantly thought of the infinite marine life that existed in that oceanic ecosystem, where a smorgasboard of millions of species were surviving and dependent on each other. *You can have a variety of narratives about living beings being independent of one another, but the central concept of our philosophy will always* stand *the test of time.* "Pratityasamutpada,"Kelsang Rimpoche said aloud after completing his thoughts. "Or interconnectedness."His level of religious erudition and reflection on this core concept of dependent co-origination or relational theory was well appreciated in religious circles. From the theme of Shunyata, or Emptiness in Mahayana Buddhism, the man was well aware of the fact that everything present on this planet was mere composites or cogs in a bigger machine. The components merely exist in relation to one another and are reducible to impermanence when viewed at a subatomic level.

The Rimpoche kept his head down for a long time on the whizzing undulating sheet of water below where countless exercises in everyday marine biology were currently being conducted unhindered. The circle of food chains and acts of pro creation kept recurring every moment inside that enormous pool. Every single act played like notes in a symphony, where every act or note was dependent and would result in an outcome.

'A simple change in tide would result in the migration of hundreds of marine lives present there, but it would eventually ensure a system, an organized symphony which would crescendo in a natural order of things. Everything is connected,' thought the Rimpoche as he looked down at the depth of blue below. This symbiotic relationship between various or all aspects of life and the interconnectedness of things between species and the environment where one was living was at the core of the philosophy of Buddhism. Where one's actions and thoughts would create an effect for the universe at large.

Kalsang Rimpoche had studied and preached about such relationships numerous times at many venues during his long career as a practitioner of the faith. He had always insisted on correct and mindful action. Actions which would be beneficial for all as everything was connected. He talked about everything and everyone being different parts, playing important parts in a big idea. Everyone moving towards a goal, an objective towards realising our fullest potential. And in the end it was all about attaining happiness, ending suffering and fostering compassion. Even a single organism was a collection of protons and neutrons further indicating that even and at a cellular or atomic level, we were all the same, tiny entities in a giant galaxy with billions and billions of stars, with a purpose to forego our egotistical minds and self-deluded persona and love ourselves with a purpose.

'If there is born a sense of purpose to help others and the environment, one must go forward, but if not, then one should at least try his best not to harm the natural order, 'Kelsang thought for any being in this planet should be benefitted through our actions so that there is synergy and harmony in the entire ecosystem or in an entire organism called Earth.

"The fear and the possibility of catastrophic consequences of such a threat, if executed, was visible in the faces of the monks present inside the room that day, including mine. And with reason." The thought of what was discussed that evening in a room high atop a monastery, and the impending gloom struck across the visage of those wise men had deeply troubled Kelsang Rimpoche. *'Never had such a group made a stand in that manner in the past,* 'the room could sense

the collective thought. 'What if those things, those threats come up with a tangible result? What if the group does carry out their 'rightful' vendetta against us?' The old custodian had spoken then and questioned everyone.

'What needs to be done now?, 'asked an elderly monk, 'going by recent incidents happening around us, a new age of mockery of sorts is taking place. All our present predicament will cause a mass lampooning of our beliefs. '

'Agreed, 'said the other elderly monk, bowing down before others, acknowledging their presence.

'Whatever that needs to be done to stem such violence and sins perpetrated in the name of religion must be stopped and those responsible shall be held with consequences and punity. '

Kalsang Rimpoche knew that the situation had indeed turned careless. Buddhism had moved a long way from the philosophy of immaterialism and twin strengths of wisdom and compassion.

"But these unfortunate events of excess and debauchery were nothing in comparison to what had transpired with the infamous incidents occurring in one Rakhine State in South East Asia with the inhuman 969 Buddhist movement," the monk said, vehemence in his tone and speech.

'We know the gravity of such events and His Holiness the Dalai Lama has himself intervened, a move political as it may seem, in trying to stop such violent acts in the name of religion, 'said the same elderly monk.

Kelsang Rimpoche knew that the events mentioned had soared to such negative heights that it drew the ire and reactions of International Human Rights such as Amnesty. Not to mention the article on the Times which termed the leader at the helm in the country as the Face of Buddhist Terror.

'Such things should never be condoned, 'Kalsang Rimpocche said aloud.

A loud murmur of assent reverberating from the leaders present at the table.

As another strong turbulence hit the flying object at an unknown elevation the occupant inside shuddered with it thinking of the result or the consequences that the old monk friend of his had warned them about. Because the aftermath of inaction following confusion on their parts following their meeting had resulted in a spate of murders that took the Buddhist world by storm. The group had indeed carried out their gruesome tactics without remorse or care for the law, much less for the Dharma. Everything that they had relayed to the heads of different sects were being brought to fruition. And that morning the final act had been performed. As the media men trained their cameras on a lifeless body of a young tuolku in one of the oldest Himalayan Monasteries, the television visuals and reporting had been gut wrenching for the Rimpoche. If he had thought that he had known enough, he certainly was wrong. The floodgates of repressed images and emotions of earlier slain tuolku's had vehemently introduced Kelsang to a dark side of humanity. His very faith and beliefs began to wobble before those horrific images. *'Lifeless tiny rigor mortis bodies with distended bellies carelessly lodged inside a Government gurney. The sight now a matter of sensationalism, a subject of the media's attention and news, '* Every tear from Kelsang's eye fell and hit the turf below. Fear and doubt now crept into his mind, rationality already leaving him as he thought about the group's power and resources to infiltrate and commit such sins in the name of faith and that too in the house of God.

His bitter world interspersed with violent memories and carnage were suddenly interrupted by a voice from the cockpit. It was the lone pilot briefing the lone occupant in the plane.

"This is Captain Alfred Rudiger here. We'll be landing for refueling at the Sydney airport in another 5 minutes and immediately fly towards India from there. The weather looks pleasant and dry, after some sporadic turbulences, so sit back and enjoy the flight. Another 5 hours and we'll be flying over the Indian Ocean. Over."

Kelsang Rimpoche steadied himself from all the fatigue and strain the recent actions had brought to his mind. *"I just hope the culprits get caught soon. But most important of all, the festival yes, it should throw up a good omen at times like these. Yes, we desperately need this."* The Rimpoche for the last time held his beads and kissed them as he readied himself for the landing. He quickly rummaged through his handbag for some meal that was already prepared for him by his aides at the hotel learning about no in-flight meal for the Rimpoche. Rolling out a tin foil, his nostrils instantly filled with the smell of the sweet Tibetan Phalay bread, a small dot of a drool visible along the sides of his mouth. He poured himself a nice hot cup of tea and enjoyed the light lunch, the bread dissolving quickly with a sip of the finest brew.

He rolled up the leftovers, closed the flask, disposed the cup and proceeded towards packing the leftovers in his bag. A flicker or a shine of a material hit his eyes from the dark cavernous confines of the bag.

He put his hand in and lifted the object up. *'denzaphaphram'*, it read.

'Well someone definitely forgot the all-important medication,' with a smile he packed everything inside after he was done and prepared himself for a short siesta inside the plane.

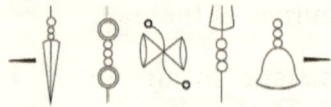

It had been a full hour of hurried and mindless chasing. The chaos and confusion and the ultimate futility of the exercise had transformed the already bad mood of theofficer into the worst. Like a volcano about to erupt. *'First, they contaminate the crime scene, remove crucial evidence from it and then mislead the police on a trail for the probable suspects.* 'Lodged in the speeding vehicle IPS Yangtso Brahma, sat impatiently on his seat as he neared the final curve leading up to the monastery. The incessant winding curves now gave way to a narrow bamboo lined rough road stretching a good mile and a half till the monastery's main premises. 'Stop the car, now, 'Brahma ordered his driver and prepared himself for the walk upwards towards the monastery. 'Lus Huncha Sir, 'the driver obeyed and came to a screeching halt alongside the rough stretch. Brahma dismounted the vehicle swiftly and briskly walked upwards towards the Gompa, ordering the driver to follow suit. The officer with gait as sure as that of an athlete's, trudged past the cobbled path easily, expertly maneuvering each next step, dodging and preventing the roughly strewn rocks and puddles with ease. The driver behind him tried his best to match his senior. The dense bundle of trees and arched bamboos along with the ancient unkempt shrubbery on both sides ofthe road acted as a dark tunnel made out of vegetative foliage. The bent of the growth providing clandestine anonymity to the exercise in question. *The chase for the killers.*

After covering a good 30-40 yards, the officer felt the first trickle of sweat down his back and paused in his tracks to open his coat. The winter sun had done enough to the body in action inside the thermals of his coat, as the officer tried to fight the nagging prick in his body that was redolent of the wintry heat. Brahma stashed his coat in the seat and barked an order to the driver. "Alex I want you to cover me at all times." The driver nodded nervously. "If the suspects are still inside the temple premises, then it'll be a challenge for us. Any prying eye could relate the news of our arrival to them, making the escape easy."The driver nodded in agreement. Their frantic police chase of the probable suspects on the bike, which resulted in great embarrassment had alerted the authorities and especially Brahma and hinted at probable accomplices in the monastery itself. *'It could be anyone, a senior or even a junior monk, or the temple's help in great numbers assigned to carry odd chores for the monastery,* 'thought the officer as he contemplated on possible actions once they were inside. *'But what if they all were in this together, an organized group of sorts, right from the senior monks to everyone connected with the monastery, hand in glove. . . how can that be, it's absurd, '* Brahma quickly quashed the illogical thought as soon as it had birthed in his mind.

"Whatever happens Alex, you report to me instantly at the first sign of those suspects, you understand, ?Yangtso Brahma impressed upon his junior. Alex nodded again...nervously. "We have to keep this raid on the temple as silent as possible. Any hint of noise will alert the people and might as well alert the suspects. We have to operate on negligible decibel."

Brahma rolled up his sleeves and got ready for the final ascent or rather the break in.

As he resumed towards the monastery which was now a few meters ahead of them, the dense greenery slowly gave into the light. 'Now listen, 'Brahma said with a stern tone, 'remember, the old head monk is frail and old, but I'm definitely not ruling out his involvement. And from whatever that was witnessed this morning, the old one has some sort of affinity for the biker. So I'm not ruling him out either.'Alex took in the words of his officer and agreed. 'Both of them must be treated as high probable suspects in this case and any attempt on their part to escape again must be foiled with force. Do what's necessary and try to nab them as quick as you can. There's just us now, but the help of those Border Police force will make the break in easy, 'Yangtso Brahma said as they neared upon two sentries at the monastery gate.

'Yes Sir, 'Alex said instantly, a sign of confidence entering him after sometime, at the presence of other armed personnel.

As they neared the premises of the monastery, Yangtso Brahma took out the walkie-talkie and relayed a message to one of his officers who was trailing them.

There was a burst of static and an officer some few kilometers away from the temple seated in his vehicle answered, 'Yes Sir, Samar...copy...over. 'The line went silent for some time and Brahma spoke, 'Samar, we've reached the monastery. . . as soon as you reach the spot where our vehicle is parked, do not stop. . . just speed up to the Gompa as fast as you can. . . '

Samar the young officer hung up the receiver and relayed the message to his driver and asked him to gun the engine. The driver followed and throttled the vehicle with great speed and intent.

The two sentries with their INSASs slung for action were surprised to see the officer and the driver walking up to them. Both of them straightened themselves and looked straight beyond. Yangtso Brahma acknowledged their salutes and called them out to him. As they huddled, the officer got to know about a lot of information as to the number of personnel stationed there.

'Sir, the protocol says, just 4 armed personnel, 2 at the back and 2 at the front. Going by how less incidents have been happening these days, the boots have been reduced, 'said one of the armed police force member.

Brahma thought for an instant, *'Just 4 here and the temple premise is massive, we need more forces. If only Samar and his five team members reached here sooner.'*

The officer with a fast pace of steps entered into one of the cylindrical bunker meant for the armed personnel. The slightly elevated security's den gave him a good view of the temple and the surroundings. The media vans could not be missed with their dishes arrayed for signal reception on rooftops. *'Close to 10-15, along with some local reporters,* 'Brahma did a guess.

But his assessment came off as a bit of a relief compared to what thronged the place a few hours earlier. A lot of the idlers and the curious crowd had faded away into their own little worlds, the place which again promised incidents like in the past, had turned down their expectations. Only a few remained now, with one or two seated atop a huge boulder perched precariously beside the monastery.

'*This shouldn't be a problem,* 'the officer thought as he made sure of the situation, still scoping the place like a hawk from a squatted position.

He called out to one of the armed personnel and whispered a command in his ear. 'Right Sir, 'the personnel answered and with a quick turn, he casually walked off towards the temple, no sign of nervousness or hurried demeanor visible in his gait.

'Sir what did you tell him, 'the sub-ordinate inquired.

'We have to make sure that the rear doors and the exits have to be sealed. No one and I mean no one should be allowed to enter or exit the monastery. Yangtso Brahma turned towards the solitary armed personnel and issued an order, 'Listen I want you to maintain strict order as we move into the monastery, my team might be arriving here any moment and I want you to man the gate firmly and open it only for the police vehicle that'll be coming at great speed. '

'Right Sir, 'the personnel agreed.

'Remember, it'll be hard to keep them at bay as they'll sniff things easily from a distance, 'Brahma pointed to the media vans parked on one of the adjacent sides of the temple gate.

'But we must enter with a strong and sure intent, and make sure no one gets a hint of what we are trying to do. Understand, 'Brahma concluded.

'Sure Sir, 'the personnel was ready for action.

'Just two points of egress and entry, 'the officer did an assumption, 'the back has been sealed and we are storming from the front…I hope the suspected duo better have strong reasons to justify the crimes.'

With that thought, he slowly trudged past the last few 100-150 meters into the main gate of the monastery, the personnel and the driver behind following the officer, trying to match his ease and regular temperament.

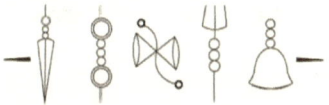

Over and over again the Old Monk's protégé went over the text and tried to ascertain the clue that was supposed to be in there. Karma's teacher had told him about such clues hidden. *'So where is it?'* Karma's thoughts ran frantic and wild.

After reaching a wall, he finally gathered some courage and asked his master.

'Gyan La, whatever I've tried here with sincere intent doesn't say anything about the motive or the impending destruction that you talked about earlier.' Karma regretted the tone in his voice.

'And these texts are replete with warnings that portends a calamitous or catastrophic event. Some kind of an 'extinction level' kind of thing. 'He gazed at the texts once again and resumed, 'nothing of that sort has happened, so why warn people unnecessarily.'

The Khenpo knew that to understand the statements of the pamphlet in its entirety one need only stop for a moment and reflect, reflect on the current state the world was in.

'Every form and scripted hint of an apocalypse in the future, present in every holy book, of any religion or belief is happening right now. The scenes that've been pointed at such books with premonitions of death and destruction were there for everyone to see. The news and the channels are filled with all the gory details. Tribal Wars infamously known as the Rwandan genocide have seen ethnic cleansings between Hutu and Tutsis, the mindless killings engulfing all of the African continent.' Lama Tashi rushed with his words to make a point.

'And why only warfare, abject poverty and famine have crippled nations like Somalia and the entire cluster of nations known as the Horn of Africa.' Karma suddenly hit at images of emaciated bodies of men and children before UNICEF Ambassadors, their state a stark reminder of the hunger and immense poverty the region was in. 'Such incidents have killed, displaced millions of people from their homes and their livelihoods. And the rampant diseases like the dreaded new strain of Ebola that had hit Sierra Leone sometime back all make the prophecies true. Add to that the ever violent and unpredictable effects of Global Warming. . . , 'the Lama stopped to catch a breath, 'It's like as if we are purposely pushing ourselves to our own extinction. . . to our graves that is.'

The Khenpo was finally making sense of the real meaning behind those scripts. Whether those ancient texts were really clairvoyant in nature, some mystic powers attached to them, it sure did study mankind and made some accurate prophecies. And the effects were being felt by the ones at the vanguard of such incidents. The rest of them, the unaffected ones so to speak in a state of complete and total denial. Their denial pronounced, more so out of nonchalance and ignorance.

After some thoughts on the Khenpo's words, Karma spoke out, his words more of a question than a mere statement.

'So Gyan La, if all the manifestations of the premonition hold true judging by their occurrences, then where is the saviour when the world needs one. I mean if the prophecies talk about death and destruction, it also talks about the coming of a saviour. What about him and his imminent arrival? As far as we know, the destruction has been wrought largely all around the globe. ?'Karma fumed at the last sentence.

'These are manmade problems. So praying to God and asking them for the help is useless. Humans should fix them.'

Karma Wangden did a doubletake.

'I'm just quoting His Holiness and his thoughts on the troubles the world is in, 'he smiled as he proceeded to make sense of the words to his confused disciple.

'Now remember Karma, the idea of a saviour in the future with lots of magical powers at his arsenal shouldn't be misinterpreted as the coming of an all-powerful individual. 'Karma scratched his head.

'Remember we were talking about subtle messages, of the texts having layers and in that your answer lies. If you ask a devout Christian to quote from the Bible who the saviour is, then he going to say and I quote 'Look into yourself and believe and I shall come before you'. . . If you ask a devout Hindu who his God is, he'll frantically answer Har Har Mahadev and if you properly translate all those holy lines and texts, it all means the answer all lies within you. You have the power to solve all the problems of humans as they all are human problems. . . '

Karma still looked at him dumbfounded.

'The words of various faiths talk about you as an individual, albeit in veiled layers as the ones who will rise up to the occasion as the saviour. '

Now it turned too tedious and exasperating for the Khenpo's protege, '*Gyan La we have a murder to solve, stop with all this esoteric stuff,* 'he mumbled incoherently.

'The words 'God built you in his image' and Har Har Mahadev are all allusions to the fact that humans are actually the ones who'll rise up to occasions when called upon. That God actually built you in his image and you have all the resources to play his role.

'So when did they rise up to it, I don't see the all-powerful human here, belting out lightening and rods to neutralize opponents, 'Karma's query grew terse as he tried to make sense of his master's words.

The Khenpo looked intently into his pupil's eyes and studied them for some time. It was obvious, all the confusions and the uncertainty writ large on his face. Along with fear. Yet he had his own way of imparting the virtues and he also was just a student of the Philosophy...

The Khenpo detected some anger in his pupil's words and it was well founded. After all, the nature and the perception of such things bore unclear results.

The Khenpo didn't know how to start although he had lots in him to share with his pupil. He looked up to the Black hat that was encased in the glass and meditated on it for some time. The collation of organized answers slowly building up inside him, a clear awareness as radiant as the vast blue sky arose in him and after a few minutes he was now in a position to answer his student.

'Karma, the heroes needn't be people with gigantic physiques and unexplained strength and speed as shown in the screens. It definitely doesn't mean your stereotypical comic book heroes that talk about 'eating fire and crapping thunder.' Karma couldn't hide his smile. 'All that is needed in this world are just normal human beings. You and I and countless billions who populate this planet going about their purpose with right mindfulness and compassion. '

The Khenpo could feel that his pupil was following him intently. "Look around you and tell me the state we are in now. The Neanderthals, the early or the ancients would all marvel at where we are right now. From great knowledge ever pushing towards perfection, the world has been witnessing too many feats unimaginable. We've certainly come a long way from Fleming's discovery of Penicillin, and the annals of history are filled with the human endeavors which have gone a long way in helping mankind. From research in medicines to counter resistant bugs, to building machines that are achieving greater convenience for human beings, the results are there for all to see. They are the heroes, the ones who are working tirelessly towards achieving great feats for the sake of humanity's longevity and mankind's endurance on this tiny spherical blip in the whole of cosmos."

Karma Wangden finally saw truth in his master's words. After all, mundane daily acts of compassion and love, a random Samaritan to distress and the scientific developments doubling and trebling over the years were all pushing mankind towards ease and comfort and lessening their sufferings.

'So my son, the hero you're talking about and wanting needn't be a great incarnated lama or Rimpoche or even a White old man with long hair, hiding high above the clouds. Although their preachings give us hope and belief in our tired and weary lives, but they still are people. It's just ordinary people with courage and valor, who have that sense of purpose in them and willingness to push themselves on a relentless pursuit of perfection, so that they can ultimately help and inspire others.'

'Remember, even acts of courage as epitomized of characters in countless popular culture and even literature for that matter is actually talking about facing their fears and standing up to the occasion when called upon to do so. All of these characters in real, your doctors, engineers, and the sportsmen etc. all are heroes who have shed copious amount of blood, sweat and tears and in their testing isolation, they've come forward and emerged a winner, to set a benchmark for all to follow. If it was easy, everyone would be doing it.'

Karma nodded and eyed his master respectfully.

'Still taking me to school, this old man. '

'And KarmaWangden, these normal people who become heroes exude energy and passion so infectious, that ordinary masses get the chance to draw from their aura and brilliance and get inspired to emulate them. And remember something purposeful and positive usually follows after.

Karma took the Gyan La's words in its entirety.

'So next time you're talking about your saviour, just think of all the people working for a positive purpose throughout the globe.'

Karma Wangden sensed some sort of fire rising in him. Just listening to his words made him forget all about the issue at hand and he was for an instant overwhelmed by his master's wisdom and perception. Indeed the achievements of mankind were nothing short of miracle and their positive results were beneficial to all and sundry.

'Gyan La, 'Karma came back from his state of reverie immediately and asked the most pertinent question that had been at the back of his mind.

'You were talking about a conspiracy, something about a group a couple of minutes before, 'Karma asked casually trying his best to hide his zeal and passion which was bursting through him.

'Pray please tell me everything as it is, without any mincing of words or circles.

He held the text close to him and tried to ascertain the message, trying hard to uncover any hint hidden in the texts. But he was at a cul-de-sac. Every time he held the text, he couldn't uncover it's mystery. *'Some answers should be in there, no doubt. Just read it again and again,* 'Karma Wangden kept going through the scribbled scripts, straining in extra effort to ascertain the answers. After some minutes into the exercise, he just gave up and looked up into the ceiling of themonastery, with its intricate outlay of sculpting and painting staring down on him. For a moment he was mesmerized and lost in deep appreciation of the works of famed

Lharigpas or Buddhist artisans and painters whose dedication and passion of their practice and execution was another testimony to the fact that those paintings would forever remain as a symbol of faith and belief in the hearts and minds of countless Dharma Followers.

But something occurred in his mind that instant that was inexplicable. He just shrugged away the confusion and tried harder again. But he was never freed from it. It was as if the images above were blurred and another stronger sets of images out of nowhere were now superimposed on his mind. Just out of nowhere.

Every time Karma Wangden held the text in his hand and looked up into the ceilings of the Zurphu monastery, his projections on the ceiling murals were stronger. Some image, some figure filled his mind, the effect accentuated by the low light of the room. But just as it had appeared his projections just seemed a chaos of lines and unclear cross sections the very next instant.

'My recollections of Buddhist iconography, of all images and figures of deities, from my memories, must be playing in my head randomly, 'thought Karma Wangden as he couldn't shrug the fuzzy lines and figures occupying his mind. . . *'It just comes and goes in an instant.'*

The Khenpo Lama Tashi broke the silence and spoke, completing what he had begun, 'So Karma, the next time you're looking for a saviour who's going to come for you and salvage all of mankind's troubles, just think of countless individuals, the ordinary beings around the globe going about their lives with right purpose and right mindfulness.'

Karma came back from the confusion encircling his head. The exigent circumstances being used to solve the murders had been controverted into a philosophical longueur. But despite the lecture, Karma exhalted in the truth and simple logic dripping in his Khenpo's words.

'And you were talking about a group a couple of minutes before, 'Karma calmed himself.

'Pray please tell me everything as it is, without any mincing of words or talking in circles. '

The Khenpo knew that his student demanded more and his demands werewell founded. After all whatever he knew, wouldn't've made any sense to his pupil unless he was privy to all the information that he had collected from the crime scene and in the hope of tackling them alone. He knew he was too old to understand everything and had therefore reposed complete faith in him,his protege.

'Ok my son, I get your confusion and doubts, it is natural.' The Khenpo pulled up a chair beside his student and rummaged into his robe and produced another pamphlet and laid it in front of him.

Karma drew a gasp. 'But I thought, from the videos, these were the only one. There's more?' His question more of an urgent query out of rude surprise.

He laid that piece in front of him and real aloud.

The script was again Tibetan and after a moment post completion, Karma couldn't find anything that hinted towards a group's involvement.

'Gyan La it doesn't say anything about a group here. So what is the basis of your guess?'

Karma laid down the pamphlet in front of the table.

The entire text was in Tibetan as Karma Wangden tried to make sense of the words…All the protégé could see was a text neatly stacked akin to a sonnet or a poem…He had come across some metres or Chandas in Sanskrit myriad times when he was poring over famous lines by brilliant writers…He just like a novice at play tried to make some sense of the metre first…

'Could it be in Iambic Pentameter...let's see, some stressed and unstressed syllables...To be or not to be kind of thing'...Karma Wangden blurted out the obvious but as soon as he did it, he thought of himself as a fraud with all his erudite fakery...He chuckled silently not to incur his master's wrath... *'Not even a Dactylic, no...not Spondiac either...'*

Lama Tashiread the first line aloud which clearly pointed at atime believed to be the Genesis of the Dharma as signified by the term Enlightened One.

'But it could be anyone and not an organized group trying to mislead the authorities and everyone in trying to achieve its agenda Khenpola, 'Karma rebutted.

'Read the whole text to understand things fully, 'the Khenpo blurted out the order much to hisand Karma's surprise. So without trying to doubt and test his teacher further he read all the texts aloud verbatim...

'The Enlightened one, his first steps bore flowers,

Leaders of the Lotus Path couched in erected towers,

The Three Great Sights for his eyes and followers,

ENTER THE BARDO.

Compassion reigned centuries in'thrall to Bhante Wallowers,

Privileged but a few breaking the sacrosanct vows,

Atop Nechung's edicts now consigned to ashes,

Testing forbearance and silence the tempest grew,

Enthralled by the lies every generation anew,

Troubled senses discovered a nun there, ravaged

Beneath the Silky Oak's stare,

Old tunic with lustful designs torn, albeit 'guised and

caped in romantic designs' scorn,

Hour of reckoning draws near, like the deity and

Phantoms chased by the Red Army,

The sins await Karma's scales at the Gates of the Bardo,

Space and time blown into oblivion, a liminal space for the mortal soul delirium,

For Mahakala and Yama's realm starts to churn,

As the holy water brim'd displaced from the Urn,

will follow suit into the Bardo, where in impermanence's realm all veer,

Much like vengeance, a steadfast Nun stands austere...'

After completing the text Karma now broke into a sweat. Each translation of the script was now hitting on Karma with more force than ever. He thought the Guru's texts were enough evidence, but he had underestimated the Killer. Every line now started to appear clearer as with every read...

'The Khenpo might've been, all the time, hinting at the mere probability of a truth...there might, just might in-fact be a group involved and it might just stop at nothing to achieve their dangerous motives. They must be stopped at any cost, if the seriousness of the threat is anything to go by.' Karma went over the lines again. Every time he read it, the Khenpo's words made sense to him.

After gathering his thoughts, he finally spoke, 'But it just speaks about the supposed injustices at the end and doesn't speak out any name or group in particular Khenpo.' Karma Wangden tried going through the lines again and again...He silently spoke them in Tibetan and then English...After sometime the metre stuck in his repetitions and he discovered the unthinkable...It was not in any specificmetre or Chanda but an invocation rather as Karma Wangden bore through the texts again...It was a simple chant or a form of recitation ofMantras or prayer but a unique one at that...Ancient Pali or Sanskrit texts barely had any leaning towards the prayers or teachings with any metre(s) known today...They sounded pretty much all the same as the purpose of mouthing of the mantras were purely transmission of the same down the ages...Even the Khenpo at this point could do little to help the taught...But as the teacher and the taught delved deeper into the chants,one thing stood out...That the chant or the invocation was more in a narrative form and it was telling something to the reader... *'...don't see any hint of a group operating here,myTeacher,'*KarmaWangden breathed silently and dejectedlyafter hitting a high just a few moments before,making sure his comments were inaudible...

'The more I read the more obscure the texts get...are there any hidden conspiratorial groups going by any name Gyanla...any group bent against the Philosophy?'

Karma Wangden felt tried and exasperated...

'Again, please pardon me but this could be a lunatic of an individual trying to carry out his own set of dangerous motives...that too alone.' The anger and irritation surely rending the air...

The Khenpo drew a breath and impressed upon his pupil. 'This list of incidents, the spate of murders that were committed involved the high profile child Tuolkus, famously recognised and ordained by His Holiness the Dalai Lama and other top Lineage leaders. The victims as you may know were well supported by security staff all around. Pray tell me, had it been one person, a single killer, where would he have the resources to bypass such tight security and protocol to get to the victims, much less murder them in cold blood.'

The Khenpo's words rang true in Karma's ears. After all the murders had all been committed in various famous monasteries which housed them and security in the form of monks and regents were aplenty. And any visitation personal or in the form of devotees would have to be overseen by the Lineage's top regent or caretaker of the child Tuolku. Someone with resource and backing had to be the one to carry them off with precision and anonymity.

Lama Tashi now threw one final thought that he had observed and said to his pupil, 'Karma, the paper alongwith the texts look funny if observed carefully, for the letters seem obscured for some reason or the other...' 'Is it intentional?' The Khenpo sat down and heaved a sigh... 'Why be unclear when you're issuing a warning, yes Gyanla?' The protégé assented to the observation of his master...*If you truly wanted people to know the truth, why be unclear about it?*

Khenpo Tashi leaned in closer and uttered something in Karma's ear just for a tiny fraction of a second...But that was enough to raise the hair on Karma Wangden's back...The name that was being suggested by his Guru was notorious to say the least...but seemingly possible...

Karma Wangden stood flummoxed and flustered. The name his teacher just uttered was impossible and at the same time given the current state of affairs, not wholly unimaginable... After all the groups infamous rantings and protests against other Buddhist texts were all visible for everyone to read and see.

He now understood the gravity of it.

'This is a direct threat coming from a group that has been infamous lately, 'thought Karma. *'All of their mission statements against the Dharma and especially His Holiness the Dalai Lama have been one of many plagues or unfortunate incidents introducing itself and*

festering like a cancer in Buddhism, eating into the very nature of the philosophy of wisdom and compassion. '

Although the history of enmity, the genesis of the opposition between the group and other four sects of the religion pre dated the early 1930s, it wasn't until the advent of internet and technology that saw a full-fledged penetration of such religious animosity in every household. Every religious internet cookie, every web address created in the group's name was a haven for propaganda and rhetorics in the digital world that was helmed bytop known leaders of the sect, who spewed hatred and venom against the supposed barring of their practices by other Buddhist groups. Every social and networking sites now impressed digital information into the consciousness of the many Buddhist practitioners and followers from all the Buddhist groups around the world. The enmity of-course, Karma knew was steeped in the Tibetan Kingdom's history much before it's forceful annexation by China. A lot of studies into the nature of the conflict had been undertaken by scholarly masters of the faith over the years and almost all of them had unanimously sided with the Dalai Lama with sound facts and logic.

Although the very veracity of their beliefs were being countered with logic and sound arguments by the scholars, yet it wasn't uncommon to find demonstrations and rallies in the country, and more so in the west demanding for full right to worship and freedom to exercise their beliefs and practices.

The said group in question was steeped in infamy as far as their war of words against the other groups continued. *'But the mere war of words could soon escalate into unmindful violence,'* Karma Wangden had once portended when he had first read about the group and their rock like stolidity in going to any lengths to achieve their religious goals. *'It was fanaticism,'* Karma had thought.

And sure enough a date suddenly materialized out of nowhere and the memory of the group's actions some years ago in the nation's capital hit him with full force.

'The group even was charged with the murders of two spokespersons who advocated reconciliation and requiem of the faith some years back, Gyan La. Karma said those words trying hard to swallow the grief, the incident that co-incided with those murders.

'Yes, 'the Khenpo replied with sudden interjection.

How could Karma Wangden forget that? A surge of sorrow filled his bosom. *'For it was the same time my friend, my brother Ozer had succumbed to the accidental injuries,* ' Karma Wangden felt a break in his breath, he looked for asniff for the control of his tears.

He quickly gathered himself and said aloud to the Khenpo, 'Gyan La we have to try to ascertain what the rest of the text is trying to convey. You were right about a certain group or an organization involved here.'Karma stood up and walked up to one of the relics stationed inside a glass case and ran his fingers across the transparent material.

'The words may or may not directly point to a group and support their cause against the Dharma,but they have been been trying their best to foment troubles against the faith. 'Personally I don't have anything against them or their supposedfight for the freedom to follow their dogmatic beliefs or practices, ' Karma Wangden paused for a second and said, 'but going by this message, 'Karma Wangden pointed to the pamphlet on the table with some force indicating urgency, 'just like you mentioned earlier, it directly becomes a suspect on our list...The scrawled texts definitelyis now hinting at some planned events, after the murders, at an unknown place, saying something about akind of disaster, a calamity or a catastrophic event that might engulf everyone in the region in itsfold.' Karma Wangden looked at the pamphlet again and ran his eyes throughout, hoping to elicit an answer. *'Some clue, some hint maybe,* 'he hoped. The Khenpo, the old monk gave an assuring look to his pupil who was confounded as to the contents of the message.

'We do not know what it is, what the group's ultimate plans are but it is definitely sinister.'Karma resumed, his thoughts all the time reflecting on the texts scroll in front of him. His mind trying to ascertain the information that the script was trying to convey. 'Their motives are crystal clear as to why, but what, is still a mystery?'

'paper and the texts look unclear...images playing in

my mind... 'the protégé's mind started catching on the words spoken earlier by his master...

Karma Wangden again looked into the texts trying to find some answers, anything that would help them in nabbing the killer and the source. He peered nonchalantly into one of the empty white walls located to his direct right. Again a spate of images, some contours of lines into figures materialized and it confounded him.

'What, '? a sudden realization now entering him. He eyed the scroll, focusing his vision on the middle of the scrawled texts and immediately forwarding his gaze to the white wall.

In an instant, everything was clear to him and he believed in the words of his Khenpo.

'Angry and vengeful spirit...' he muttered to himself. All the doubts and uncertainties were removed from his mind, body and soul about the group and he remembered the imposing play of images on his mind a couple of minutes earlier and now everything was crystal clear...*A masterful deceit...hidden in plain sight...*

****

A pair of steely eyes scoured the wide premises of the monastery. '*Making sure that no one gets a hint of what we are trying to do, the only immediate motive right now,* 'thought the official, as he inched closer to the monastery's gate.

The officer pussyfooted through the last steps towards the iron gate with the driver in tow behind him. Their each step forward was marked by whispers from behind which reached a collective murmur. Not giving into such disturbances, Yangtso Brahma kept his cool. His steady walk marking a behaviour as casual as any.

As expected, a few of the stationed reporters trained their mobile cameras and hurtled towards the front gate. 'Hey, I think something is happening here, 'shouted one of the scribes, a potbellied Bengali, as he tried to make his entrance from the gate. As soon as the decibels hit the ears of many, some odd 10-15 journos followed the man running a good 5-10 meters ahead of them, their hard attempts at trying to ascertain the story evident from their mindless and chaotic run downwards towards the temple gate. As they hurtled mindlessly forward, they immediately skidded to a stop some few yards away from the gate.

A giant built of a man, stopped everyone in their tracks. A fully armed para commando with strict orders to adhere to was the only obstacle between the media and their much coveted story.

'Stop here, 'the 6 foot 6 inches heavily strapped individual with an assault rifle ordered them.

A big bundle of chaotic noise abruptly came to an end.

'We want to know, what is going in there, 'said the potbellied journalist as he tried to muscle his way towards the armed sentinel. A strong opposing push met his chest and he instantly gave up. So did all the others present there.

'We've been following the incident sincemorning and we've just seen one of the officers entering the monastery. We demand an answer. The press and the people want to know.'The final diktat from one of the journalists emboldened others to speak and before the armed guard knew, a cacophony of questions and protests filled his ears.

'Silence, 'a loud roar erupted from the guard, which took everyone by surprise, probably from fear more and less from surprise. After a moment's time, as the din settled down, he spoke out the orders given to him.

'There has been a strict order to not let any soul, normal or any media persons through this gate. No one enters or exits the temple. It has been classified as off limits. Now I know you all are doing your job, but so am I. Nothing comes before me, but the orders given to me and by God I shall obey them with every mind and muscle in my body.'The armed personnel looked defiant and scoped the sea of eyes in front of him to look for some form of dissent and protest. *The protocol demands for a harsher action, if it veers out of order,* 'the guard thought upon the impending situation that could easily spiral out of control, because some locals, the denizens of the area had also started making their slow curious walk towards the gate.

Luckily the stern tone of the armed personnel worked and before something untoward transpired, some of them backtracked just a few yards away from the gate, a look of utter dejection writ large on their faces. A few of them tried to voice their anger, but their whimpers were way away from the armed guard's earshot. Looking at the retreating numbers away from him, the guard heaved a sigh of relief and manned his position again. *'It worked just fine, the first time,'* thought the guard praying for a non-recurrence of the event.

As the officer neared the entry of the monastery, Brahma stopped a second and swiftly unbuttoned both his holsters, finely jacketed inside a leather strap. The line of leather thinly ran across his back and sternum, with the guns safely slung below his armpits. He quickly hid behind one of the large pillars of the monastery and stealthily drew out one of his service guns. A fully automatic Magnum with a 0.5 caliber lead. With another 20 yards advancement towards the temple, he ordered his subordinate to go out the back. Brahma quietly clipped open the safety of the weapon and flanked the entry door by the side, ready to enter the temple with authority. For a moment, he reflected upon the morality of the exercise at a pious holy place, *'I'm armed. '*

ENTER THE BARDO.

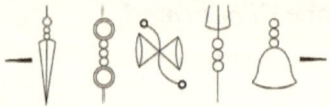

Pelham Psychiatric and Mental Health Care Institute (30 years ago)

"You have to leave her here; the conditions are worsening every day," the psychiatrist at Pelham Mental Health Institute, New York said to an elderly person seated across from her. Outside the huge facade that was known as the country's best psychiatric institute, many families, along with their affected loved ones, lined up to get an appointment with the doctor in the hope of finding a cure for their loved ones.

Having arrived early, Khyentse Dzhogpa had already finished with the formalities of pushing papers and had received an appointment card with the time allotted for his visit that day. Khyentse, like all the other refugees who had made that fortunate foray into the land of their dreams, had embraced the new nation fully. His initiation into the new world, where he had arrived with his wife, who was 5 months pregnant some 5-6 years ago, had been a struggle, to say the least. New land, new beginnings, the possibility of being at the receiving end of the throes of rejection by the new country, all had played in his mind. But where few would've thrown in the towel, he had shown mettle and acumen and started a small fast-food business right around one of the the corners of Avalon Street.The city with it's relentless pace of cut-throat commerce barely let up...Even Khyentse Dzhogpa had it in him the devotion of a hunted to eke out an existence day after day... Of course, he had to grease some palms to get that neat spot for snacking. It had only been about some years into the business that the land of opportunities had lived up to its name.

First, he was blessed with a beautiful girl child, multiplied his mobile and movable feasts to almost all of Long Beach, and as his business rocketed, he opened up some more mobile units and managed to open two restaurants in the heart of Park Avenue. He really had 'worked his fingers to the bone', and with his toil and belief in his Gods, he now boasted of a rich life, that his latent Tibetan blood and genes made him capable of.

But over the course of his time, he yearned for his own people, his Tibetan compatriots, the other refugees who had planted themselves into this great country. He wanted to visit them and be in their company. Thus began a quick search on the web, and after some months, Khyentse Dzhogpa had purchased a nice condo overlooking the best sights at 6068 Lincoln Boulevard. His arrival and the moolah which he had raked in all those years automatically made him a first-class Tibetan in the area.

He was now really a citizen of the great nation of America, and like all expatriates of the Tibetan nation, made full use of his newfound freedom and clout to rouse ample assemblies and decibels for Tibet's Freedom from the tyranny and occupation of their lands by China, the words 'Bod Gyalo' resonating with thousands of Tibetans throughout the country. He began forming associations and attended others, playing a pivotal role in bringing together genuine passions needed for the freedom of their nation. A prominent figure in the circles, Khyentse now commanded respect, and his word was the final say in any matter.

But there was one little thing that bothered him and was a disturbance in his otherwise peaceful and happy life—the health of his daughter.

"We've already given you a warning about her conditions, her convulsions, GAD, and episodes of morbid depression which are recurring with greater frequency might put her in a state of catatonia soon. If you do not institutionalize her, then I'm afraid we'll be unable to control her, and she herself might harm herself. Anything might happen to her, you must remember," the doctor warned.

Khyentse Dzhogpa, now an old man, didn't know how to respond. He looked at his daughter, who was slouched and seated across from him, her twin pair of eyes lifeless and expressionless as she stared into nothingness. He had been there at the beginning of all this when it had started. Violent fits of rage, infinite convulsions, as if the Devil himself had possessed her. The effects ticking like a time bomb about to go off any instant. The parents, however, didn't give up, and in the routine midst of all the faith healers and religious leaders and well-planned albeit violent exorcisms, they finally gave in to the idea of talking to a shrink.

"But will my daughter be as good and cured as she was before?" the old man asked the psychiatrist.

"Because I want to be able to see her as my precious joy once again, as she was when she was fine and good," the old father wept like a child before the doctor and the employees present there.

"Please," the doctor requested aloud, "This facility has very effective state-of-the-art methods when it comes to treating mental patients. I'm sure with a proper and diligent dosage of medicines and a disciplined regimen of exercises and interactions, we'll be able to bring her back from her condition. "

The final words came as a relief to the father. He couldn't wait to go and tell the news to his wife, the mother, at home, who'd decided not to come, fearing her inability to see her off.

The father walked over to his daughter and sat down beside her. He placed his hand on her head, trying to elicit a response. The daughter looked at her father, whose eyes were now turned bloodshot and teary.

"I think this is it. The last resort. Getting institutionalized," the daughter looked at the lined corridors behind her and saw a number of patients with their caretakers tending to them. It was a host of mental health symptoms that erupted and showed up in their physical beings, the hosts, which were otherwise unnoticed in the initial stages. A mental condition symptomized by simple anxiety and depression had worsened and gotten chronic in a man, who now constantly tried to climb onto the ledge of the wall and attempt to bring his tendencies to a guaranteed end. The area lay replete with such conditions, and the caretakers tried their best to constantly talk to them and monitor their movements.

"It's going to be fine," said the father looking at his daughter, whose eyes now turned bloodshot and teary.

"It's only a matter of months, and after much research, we've homed in on this, which they say is the finest institution there is. There are facilities here that will make a targeted approach towards your illness, and all you have to do is participate in whatever they tell you to. "

The father paused for a second to wipe his daughter's ever-flowing tears. It ripped his heart to see his daughter off alone somewhere, much less a mental health institution. But he knew that was the correct thing that had to be done for her.

"Remember, sometimes the only way out is through the fire," the father held back his tears as he hugged his daughter tightly.

She didn't have anything to say, anything at all to save the painful situation, as years and years of mental health symptoms had taken a grip on her and left her inner DNA and fibers in total disarray, thus succumbing to the illness's symptoms.

"I love you both so much, and I'm going to try to come out of this stronger. I promise, Dad. "

And as the two attendants came up to them to escort her daughter into the facility, all emotions were piling inside her as she hugged her father for the last time, and she proceeded to follow them inside the facility. Then, as if by a swift wave of the wand, her emotions torn asunder, and she wept over her dreams unsaid and the unspoken words of assurance, of love. Love for her family and for her life.

"I'm going to make this work," the last thoughts left her head as she entered one of the rooms inside.

"No contacts from the outside world for the first three months," the father went over the advice and order of the doctor over and over in his head as he descended the stairs of the facility. His every step a mix of optimism and heartache. And as he exited the doors of the facility, little did he know that that would be the last time Khyentse Dhzogpa would be seeing his daughter.

Her few months into the facility had been beneficial to her health. Slowly, she started to enjoy and believe in the process. Her activities in the institute and busy regimen of daily life filled with meditational routines and timely dosages of

Serotonin Uptakes saw a spike in her level of active and participating life. Like a revenant, the life of Yang came to its happiest and alive state once again. Slowly and steadily, she fought the odds, and her negative mental energies slowly dissipated. She began an active accomplice of the other caretakers, often lending a helping hand to them. Gradually, a genial disposition of hers started to take place, her positive energy radiated through her and was infectious. The Doctor at the institute also approved of her improvements in their reports.

But fate had other plans for her, and the healing process suddenly took a nasty dark turn. It started with one of the attendants making advances and innuendoes towards her. At first, she laughed it off, thinking about the incident as petulant. But the puerility soon became direct and emboldened by her silence, the actions and advances became serious. Until one day, Yang had the courage to stand up to him in front of everyone and hold him accountable. What followed was a callous treatment of the affair, much to her dismay. But she was relieved that at least she had laid the pervert bare.

Then, on a frosty winter night, about two and a half months into her treatment at the institution, the edge of reason and actions on the attendant's mind no longer existed, and he attacked the victim with more brute force, in the stillness of the night.

Yang felt a chill as she woke up, suffocating and unable to move. She noticed she'd been gagged and tied to her bed, using the bed belts to control violent and aggressive patients. In the night, she tried to make sense of the surroundings around her. She peered hard into the night, and as she feared, a figure stood tall at the edge of her bed. ' *It's him,*' she thought, and then she began the struggle to free herself so that she could defend herself. But the taut belts ate into her limbs with every struggle and chafed her with even greater pain. Before long, the whiskey- and nicotine-laden breath blew all over the hair and face and began the vicious first attempts at forced violation. With no screams to alert everyone and restricted movements, she bit the assailant's ear which led to the perpetrator biting her cheek in impulsive action,resulting in a deep gash...The action stopped the man from robbing her of her dignity further... But she wouldn't take it lying down. The next morning, a huge hue and cry were raised at the institute, but the top decision-makers in cahoots with the attendant and some of his mock supporters had downplayed the incident, considering it a mere *'hoax, a concoction, and behavior symptomatic of delusions.'*

But the incessant recurring act of the perpetrator on other patients hadn't gone unnoticed, and some of the doctors who had seen Yang's progress in the past had actually put a beat on the attendant. Eventually, he was caught and handed over to the police. But not before committing multiple assaults on patients in the institute. Although the attempt on her had failed, the incident however had then scarred her permanently, and she withdrew herself from the murky world of mental conditions with greater adverse effects. Of course, all hadn't been easy for Yang. She had been a fighter, and her initial attempts at bringing the culprit to justice had been met with skepticism.

The upper echelons of the facility, consisting of doctors and other stakeholders, went to any length to protect their institute's reputation, even to the measure of declaring the patient Yang as one whose symptoms had recurred with intense force. 'She is hallucinating and must be given the electric treatment, said one of the doctors, at the behest of the owners of the institute.

What followed was the first unnecessary shock therapy that Yang had been subjected to forcefully.

She was forcefully put on the recliner, strapped from head to toe. She tried to make sense of it as she waited as two big rods were inserted into her ears. Limbs-bound, she studied the environment and pleaded one last time, 'Please do not do this,' her pleas falling on deaf ears.

A switch was turned on, and a wave of charge rushed with force into her cranium, violently destabilizing her with the electronic seismic. A loud noise and a violent tremor suddenly radiated through her senses, and the killer was brought back to the present state of things...

****

A fully loaded truck veered dangerously close to hers, the horns blaring from the oncoming truck. The killer swerved smartly to avoid any collision, with both of the drivers braking in tandem and meeting eye to eye. He cussed and cursed obscenities. *'A convert...from a heathen to a believer...there is no time for small things now...A higher purpose awaits me.'* She gunned the engine and headed forward. *'Unnecessary altercations.'*

She steadied herself, held the wheels, and thought, *I've come a long way from the dark days at the asylum, from those nights of horror and pain.* Yang felt her external vulva twitch, a natural searing memory of pain accompanying the thought as she once again fought the repressed images with great difficulty and force as she tried to forget the harrowing haunt. The recall of the tormenting nights filled her senses with the pungent breaths and the grunts of a bestial beast...

Her troubled state adversely affected her driving, as she skidded to a sudden stop right along the edge of the highway. She looked down to a good 40 feet of height below, opening wide into an ever-flowing Teesta. She heaved a sigh. She took a moment to calm herself down.

'The only help, the source of all my healings, has been my Supreme Teacher, thought the killer as she reflected on those days of advice and learning. For Yang, the Supreme Teacher, had materialized as a beacon of light and hope for her. He had come into her life and intervened. Yang had committed countless attempts at ending herself, and just like a shot across the bow, the Supreme Teacher had come to her rescue.

Countless attempts at trying to reach her by Khyentse by the father had gone futile. The authorities, along with the doctors at the institute, had told the father about her decision not to meet him.

'She is unstable and has relapsed into her previous state, one of the doctors told him.'

"Her volatile nature and her chronic solitude now remain risky, and the only time she talked to any of us in these past many months was just to let us know that she wouldn't be visiting anyone."

"You have to understand her predicament. The events that occurred to her in this facility are regrettable," said one of a close aide to Khyentse one day "...and the effects are still visible in her condition. It has deeply been etched into her system and psyche..."

The father, Khyentse, had come to know about it on one of his routine visits to the institute. He had been devastated upon learning the news and trusted the truth behind her daughter's words and accusations. He had stood by her all the time. And it was he who had vowed to bring the culprit to book and used some backdoor channels in investigating the matter and bringing the pervert to book. It had worked.

'Now, given the critical mental state she is in, we've abided by her decision and let her be, the doctor said before adding something that floored KheyentseDzogpa.

The thought of her daughter trying to sever ties with him surprised and shocked the father.

'I was always with her through this, and even when her accusations fell on deaf ears, I stood by

her. So where is this idea of severance from? Khyentse stood in the lobby of the facility, forlorn and depressed. But he was optimistic that things would come around and that one day there would be a reunion between them.

The father, while exiting the institute, had the final words of the doctor occupying his head and mind in a loop.

'They said that over many months, she had demanded sacred religious books in plenty.' The father had thought about traumatic experiences that forced people to convert to different beliefs and faiths and had even asked, "Has she undergone some conversion faith wise?"

"Nope, sir, all the books and texts she has been demanding are all Buddhist texts. And she is voracious, in that she reads 24/7 and keeps talking and muttering syllables. Whether they're prayer chants or just incoherent babbles, at least she has found her centre; she keeps herself busy, so that's good given her condition. And the exercise has definitely kept her calm. We've been monitoring her."

That had made Khyentse relax as he neared his car in the parking lot. *'Good that she is occupied with something close and natural to our way of life. I hope she beats the odds and comes out stronger.'*

Though they had been away from his daughter for more than a year, Khyentse Dzogpa and his wife didn't leave any stone unturned in trying to hasten the treatment of his daughter.

'If she wants to immerse herself in religion and practice the Dharma, that is great. She is getting an outlet for her conditions, and that's a good sign, 'the husband told his wife.

'And we must ensure that she learns all the scripts and books she's trying to read. That's the least we can do.' The parents had a unanimous, firm belief in their act of helping their daughter, and since Khyentse had a lot of venerated Rimpoches as acquaintances, he knew what to do next.

Khyentse Dzogpa had called on his most trusted and respected Rimpoche. The widely respected leader of the Nyingma sect, the Rimpoche and Khyentse had forged a special relationship over the years. While his life in the new country was still in its infancy, they had always consulted him on any matter before embarking on it. From business ventures to finding a good new residence with all the positive feng shui, and from organizing retreats and prayers at home to even consulting him in naming his newborn daughter, the respected Nyingma leader had been their go-to spiritual advisor.

Over the years, the Rimpoche had monitored the rise of his pupil with much elation. "Rimpoche, I've come to you again with many prayers and great hope. This time, it's not for any material ambitions but something more valuable than all the riches this land has to offer," Khyentse said.

The Rimpoche listened intently to all his prayers and instantly agreed. A meeting was set up with Yang at the institute after much persuasion by her closest doctors. The only reason she had agreed was that she had learned that it wasn't her father, her own flesh and blood, who had abandoned her in that asylum, leaving her isolated to endure those horrific nights of pain and hurt. The long nights spent in immense isolation after the ordeal had generated a mind in heightened fecundity, and the idle, multiplying thoughts had caused her to blame no one but her father for the state she was in. "Who would leave their child in a place like this?" The thought recurred every second in her mind and gave way to much hatred towards Khyentse Dzogpa.

The killer adjusted her robe and fired up the engine. She slowly revved the engine and drove towards her destination. As she did so, she recalled the first time her first visitor in years had entered her chamber.

ENTER THE BARDO.

The crisp autumn leaves crunched beneath the Rimpoche's feet as he walked towards the institute. His walking stick, with its pointed end, playfully poked at the dried and scattered maple leaves strewn across the lawn. A life steeped in the pious practice of philosophy had led him to this new challenge as Kalsang Rimpoche entered the psychiatric ward of Pelham Institution.

As he walked with purpose towards Yang's cell, he soon realized that she had been isolated from the rest of the patients. "A red flag given her condition," the Rimpoche thought. "*This is going to be a bit of a challenge...*"

As the doors to her cell opened, Kalsang found Yang sitting straight on her bed with her legs crossed. She clutched a book. The Rimpoche couldn't identify which book, but he didn't try to pry further.

Kalsang pulled up a chair and sat in front of her. Their eyes met for the first time. A long moment of silence filled the room as the earlier hint of uncertainty and tension started to diffuse gradually.

"I've heard that you've taken the effort to read and understand the Dharma and the scriptures," the Rimpoche said, taking care not to mention her father.

The Rimpoche continued, "It is commendable that you've decided on it. Our reading and comprehension shall be used for the benefit of others. Our twin strengths are compassion and wisdom. "

Yang looked a bit more relaxed. She laid the book on the bed in front of the Rimpoche, and heaved gently.

"The Great Liberation through the Intermediate Stage," the title read. Kalsang Rimpoche was surprised upon learning of the title. "Such heavy Buddhist esoteric literature. "

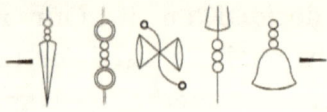

A faint hint of incoherent murmurs from one of the rooms above hit the ever so sharp tympanums of the officer Yangtso Brahma. Stealthily he stole into the monastery closing the big door behind him. Instead of walking straight up towards the room where the noise was coming from, he tried to recce all the four ends of the ground floor first. Armed with his magnum, he tiptoed into the right wing of the monastery and started one full revolution. What he thought would be a short combing exercise soon turned tedious as he felt the distance from one end to the other pretty long. As he walked he could notice all the pantheon of Buddhist Gods and deities from the glass window as he neared into the first end. Vast encompassing murals exhibited the iconography of Boddhisatavvas and Dakinis and the giant Golden Statues of the Gods shone in all its glory amidst the flickering of hundreds of butter lamps.

'The walk won't do, 'thought the officer as he broke into a slight jog. On nearing the third wide extension of the Gompa, Brahma waved at

someone outside the backdoor. The two sentries along with his driver his driver were ready and in position. He signalled them to be vigilant and tight.

The officer now covered the next course of the recce with some speed and in a few minutes he was at the doorstep again. *'Just as I'd imagined, two points of egress and entry,'* Yangtso Brahma slowly ascended the steps with his weapon in perfect balance, armed and ready.

T'mon the first floor now, 'he thought as he made sense of his surroundings. The vastness of space and countless rooms floored him. He wasn't expectingthe monastery to be a labyrinthine maze of hundreds of rooms.

Though the Zurphu monastery as seen in postcards and images threw up a facade of a beautiful temple with the perfect size, it in fact was much bigger in real life. Not counting the area of the monastery that runs into acres of spaces outside, but the confines of the monastery itself was expansive. Add to that some odd hundreds of rooms lodging monks, head monks and other rooms dedicated to meditation and learning, the Zurphu Monastery was truly a gigantic edifice with its exterior resembling crenellations, not for battle purposes but for stationing prayer horns like the traditional Radung, Gyaling etc. heralding the start of a prayer or a new day.

The faint murmurs grew into distinct sounds as Brahma inched closer to the source. A large wooden door. Taking a pause in his stride, he readied himself to barge open the door and enter.

'This could be it, ' thought the officer as he used his shoulders with immense force as a battering ram and the stillness and tranquility of the place was shattered as he broke open the door and as soon as he was inside, he regretted the decision.

His entry and gaze was met with the surprise eyes of hundreds of monks going about their prayer sessions. The interruption was met with terse statement from the presiding monk teaching the other junior entrants.

'Is something wrong, this is a most unusual and inappropriate time for you, 'barked the monk.

The officer Brahma couldn't do anything but feign an apology for his sudden disturbance of the session. *'Wrong room,* ' the apparent mistake dawning on the officer. But still in his regret, he scoured the sea of bodies in front of him. *''I just need the two people I'm looking for,* ' the officer excused himself and exited the room.

As soon as he did that, he realised his mistake and barged into the room again.

The monk presiding over the prayer and recitation sessions walked up to him in total defiance and said, 'What are you trying to do?' his tone direct and his question valid.

'You come barging into the prayer hall and that too with a gun in your hand. Pray tell me, what is this business of yours that requires you to come armed into this hallowed institution of Buddhist faith. '

The officer without further delay told him about the emergent situations.

"You know this is a site of the murder that has been committed here earlier. You of all should know the gravity of the situation. After all if I'm not mistaken, you are one of the teachers here and must be privy to the information at hand."

Saying that Yangtso Brahma produced his credentials and the monk was brought to some amount of respect and fear for the law.

'Pardon me for barging into like this, but I just have a couple of questions for you, 'the officer ushered the senior monk to the side of the room for some brief questioning.

'Yes the Khenpo Lama Tashi is the most senior monk here and oversees everything here. We've been devastated by the events that've taken place in the capital for the past few weeks, but we never fathomed an incident of such barbaric proportions taking place in our own holy temple. '

Brahma could sense the truth in his words and mannerisms, after all if it had been a shocker for the devotees and the general public, he could only sense the heightened stratospheric and palpable tension and shock in the temple dwellers. But being an officer of the law, he couldn't do away with such levels of empathy, but instead had to dig in deep to ascertain the answers.

The officer looked him straight in the eye and asked the most important of all questions using honorifics that were required of him as a Buddhist.

'Lamala, ' the officer started with his interrogation, 'Is your Khenpo Lama Tashi still in this monastery.?'

The officer knew that anything negative would tantamount to the monk's abetment as he had witnessed and been involved in the false chase first hand.

'*Choose your words well,* ' the officer readied himself for a sterner form of questioning.

'Well, officer, 'the monk started, 'we are merely teachers at this monastery with no real clout and power as far as the administrative and executive affairs of the monastery are concerned.'

'Strike one, ' the officer counted. Being a teacher monk meant that the monk in question shared a relationship with the top level Khenpos or Rimpoches that was well established and given their presence in the vicinity of each other in the monastery, the news and decisions, following that chain of command, the top down approach, the absence of it all was all nigh impossible as was being claimed by that monk.

The monk realising the frown on the officer's face was quick to add.

'You see, we were seldom invited to this section of the monastery. Only recently the administrative wing of the monastery presided over by the Khenpo Lama Tashi issued certain points of engagements into the main affairs of the monastery concerning both the groups. ' The officer gave him a surprised look.

'Meaning you... 'he needn't complete his sentence as the monk in charge of the session cut him. 'Yes officer we are from that side of the building, ' the monk said as he pointed towards a building on their right. And I represent and support the other group...

The officer Yangtso Brahma stood mute.

It was true that following many years of row over the real ownership of the monastery and the lineage, a thaw over the relationship between the two groups had miraculously been witnessed. It was as if the masters of both the faith had finally realised the futility of such illogical exercise and aimed at assimilating the warring groups and their ideologies.

The much secret meeting between Thaye Dorjee, the Karmapa recognised by the Shamar and Urgyen Trinley Dorjee from the Dalai Lama's camp wasn't secret at all as every English and local dailies of the nation highlighted the historic meeting, which had taken place in France some time ago and given the nature, their timings had garnered much media attention throughout the world. The coming together of two great claimants to the Kagyu throne was nothing short of a miracle. Where the past years were marred with violent campaigns and protests against each other, the meeting in a bucolic setting south of France was seen as a religious novelty, an inclusive approach, where the two leaders had purportedly tried to iron out differences and talk about ways to take the lineage and millions of its followers worldwide towards the path forward.

Yangtso Brahma being at the helm of affairs of law and order in the state, had to often intervene in the ruckus and fights in the monastery in the past. But as the news of such amicable meetings between the two leaders had been made known, he welcomed the decision and the meeting.

'Well the track of the leaders seem to be on the right one,' Brahma had then mused.

The events that followed at the monastery post that historic meeting was nothing short of an achievement. In that for the first time since the fights over the next successor after the 16th Karmapa broke out between two groups, a healthy albeit restrained co-mingling of monks from both the sides were witnessed. Then the monastery's Khenpo along with the leaders in the administration had laid down rules and timings for both the groups as far as preaching and practicing in the main temple monastery was concerned.

'So how long have you been in this room, ?'asked the officer as he looked directly into the monk's eyes for the truth.

'You must be well aware of the incident over the past weeks and then this one in our own place of worship has shaken us to our core. Our very primal fear has engulfed us all. '

'As soon as we heard about the incident, we were just attending to the Khenpo as he was devastated on learning about the incident. Some of us tried to control the mob of people outside and some were just engaged in discussing the vitriolic nature of the events. '

The monk held out a sigh. The officer wanted to prod further.

'In all this while, do you think any untoward behaviour was shown by the Khenpo or anyone who is second in command here after him?'

'Not that I know of, because he was shocked beyond words and we didn't want to engage him any further. '

'Anyone apart from the police tried to talk to you or get in touch with you about the incident, especially them there?'Yangtso Brahma gestured at the parked media vans outside in the distance.

'Well after your entrance here a little while ago, no one was allowed entry here. '

The final question which was vital here slowly escaped the officer's mouth.

'It's your acid test, choose carefully again,' Brahma pulled up the monk into the far corner of the room. As the officer tensed for a situation that could spiral out of control, even in that emergent predicament of the officer, his psyche kept resonating with the soft chants of the mantras from the junior monks present a few feet away, their chants done with rapt attention and focus.

'After the incident, did you do a full count of the monks here, including all the senior and the junior monks?' The officer readied himself for the obvious.

'Well officer, as the events have cramped the usual schedule of this holy place, we haven't had the time to do a full head count.'

The monk paused for a while, 'Wait, but, there were talks doing the rounds of 2 adolescent monks gunning down a motorcycle down the hill. Some folks who were here pretty early would've sworn by that.'

The officer eased, *'Now lodged and locked up inside the facility and I'll be hearing anytime soon from one of my finer correctional officers in the precinct about their antics.'*

'I never imagined the rooms to be in such huge numbers, Lamla,' Brahma tried an amicable approach towards his strategy.

'Well officer, this is one of the state's biggest monastery and since there are precious relics stored here, the room where the relics are stored itself occupies the major portion of the monastery.'

'The relic room, you mean?' Brahma was surprised. But on my way up, I saw the relics encased behind glass cases and these are the same ones the devotees are allowed near to for worship.'

The monk smiled, 'Yes you are right, but there are far valuable relics belonging to the lineage that needs preservation and protection. And that room is centrally located inside the temple. Three floors up, with surveillance. The keys to the room are always with the Khenpo Lama Tashi. '

The final statement put the officer on edge. 'Remember Lamla, we have full authority over this place now, so we'll be conducting searches all over this place. Do you by any chance have any idea as to where the Khenpo is right now?'

The monk responded negatively, 'we've not heard about him since this morning after he left his chamber. . . . . with. . . , 'silence pervaded the room as the monk went back to the officer's question a few moments earlier.

'Yes with?' the officer prodded.

'A little while ago you asked whether any untoward behaviour was shown by the Khenpo after the incident.'

'Yes, 'a direct answer met the monk's question.

'Well, while I was serving tea to the Khenpo, he repeatedly kept asking me one thing?'

'And that was?' Brahma inched closer for the truth.

'That whether we've been able to contact Karma Wangden or not. The Khenpo just handed us this number and asked us to do the needful.'

The officer rustled through his hair, 'Karma Wangden, so is your name. The guy on the motorcycle. The guy hand in glove with the Khenpo.'

Without much thinking, the officer dialled a quick one. The cell was off. Then he dialled another number.

Samar, the inspector currently making his way to the monastery held onto his wheels as he steered deftly into the ever winding road up into the highway. *'Another 2 kilometers and I'm in, '* As the bolero hurtled upwards towards the monastery, the three Armed personnel inside tried their best not to fall off their seats. Most important of all, they put in extreme effort as they held unto the safety of their rifles with their muzzles pointing randomly at each bump and thump on the road.

The Inspector readied his wireless with one hand on the wheel. The direction and order of his superior still clear on his head. *'Barge into the monastery as soon as you reach,'* Samar recalled as he tightened his grip on the walkie talkie.

****

'Another tiring and trying day begins,' Shusovan Pranj had just inserted his biometrics into the system when a phone from inside of his office began to ring. *'Who could be this early,'*?he fumed under his breath.

The newly appointed Deputy Superintendent of the State's Police by virtue of his background in computers and ethical hacking had earned him a seat here at the State Department's Digital Police Cell of intercepting, tracking cell phones and cryptanalysis of data of suspects. Though he had undergone training of how to use technology to the State's advantage, in a yearlong programme at Virginia State Police Department, well supported by the State, the idea of snooping and infiltrating the private space of millions of users somehow didn't sit right with up. *'It is unethical and the whistleblower was right in blowing the lid off the clandestine spying exercise on its gullible citizens by the United Sates,'* he often muttered to himself... *'Snowden is a hero...'*

Though the surveillance tech had just been introduced in the country . The law and order being a state subject, the State became one of the technology's active proponents with the State declaring that the technology would be used not for snooping or spying, but only for tracking and intercepting suspicious calls and messages. The tech represented a simplified version of the Stingray or the Kleenex, purportedly used by some states in the Developed nations. Where the original version had met with citizen's ire and outcry protesting violently against their nation's rampant snooping of the citizens, the watered down version did meet the support of many with the words like 'influx and mushrooming of more 'outsiders', being words and phrases and easy attributes for a crime of any nature, for the motion, used by true blue denizens.

The officer strode into the room and barely reached the line. 'Just got it...Yes, this is DSP Pranj, 'his light achievement and response co-mingling.

'Yangtso Brahma here, 'a hard tone emanated from the other end.

'Yes Sir, 'the police officer got up instantly.

With information coming in from the other side, the DSP quickly jotted down the number and hung up.

With orders from his superior, he hurriedly got to its execution. A small brief case like object with a metallic exterior sat before the officer on the table.

With some clicks and codes, the case opened up with a slight digital noise. The innards of the case bore a combination of switchboards and a punch pad.

Quickly he punched in the numbers given by the officer and after a few minutes time, he jotted down its location.

The officer also punched in Brahma's cell phone and the GPS on the wall before him bore a combination of lines and map keys and the officer waited as it threw up an address.

The DSP was surprised.

He called his superior. 'Sir is this related to the murders, 'Shusovan Pranj queried, 'because if it is, the locational points on the GPS screen are quite funny. '

'Funny, how, 'the officer barked.

'Because both the cell phones show the same location, i. e. Zurphu Monastery and. . . . , 'the officer paused.

'And what, I need the information fast, 'Brahma lost his cool.

'The distance between the two merely is about less than 50 meters. And if I run the variable parameters and data, then the altitude is 30 meters, the radial circle of the cell number in relation to your position is about. . . 'The officer interrupted the information.

'Stop!. . . the altitude can you repeat it.'

'The altitude is 30 meters Sir.' Brahma hung up.

*'As expected the suspects are here in this building. In fact the cell phone location points upwards at a distance of 30 meters...Brahma slowly walked up to the centre of the room and looked straight up at the ceiling...*The tutelary art of the Yi-dam lay sprawled above him...

'*He is right above me,* ' Yangtso held the gun up into his hands and ushered in the monk inside the room.

'Pray tell me Lamla, what and how many rooms are there above?' Brahma pointed with his gun upwards.

The monk did some thinking and said, 'As you know officer, we've been recently allowed entry into this main shrine and I have but been through the entire monastery just a time or two.'

The officer was getting impatient.

'If my memory serves right then there are about 20-30 rooms for the senior monks, then there is the dormitory allotted for each of them and. . . , 'the monk paused inviting serious expressions of exasperation from the officer.

'And yes, 'the monk finally spoke, 'there is also a huge room where all the holy and valuable relics are lodged. '

That was all that he wanted. Brahma raced up the stairs like a madman onto something. As he neared the new floor, he breathed silently and steadily.

Just then a static went off in the officer's pocket, 'Come in Sir...Come in Sir.'

Brahma quickly answered the walkie talkie, 'Yes, your position, over.'

'Sir we are nearing the gate of the monastery, should we barge in directly inside like you ordered earlier.'

'Yes, the sentry has been ordered to let you guys inside. Come with all guns. . . I think I'm unto the duo. From my position, they should be directly above us. This is our chance to nab them.'

'Officer Samar on hearing his senior's words went full throttle as he embraced for an entry with breakneck speed into the monastery. The vehicle came to a skidding halt outside the monastery, throwing up a good number of pebbly gravels into a slight wave. The inspector along with the armed personnel stormed the premises of the monastery and headed straight up the stairs.

The media van throttled past the army cantonments and the two occupants inside hoped for the truth in the woman's voice…the informer's voice as they drove forward. Aditi tried to position herself upright in her seat as the rough patches on the gammon concrete tipped their balances time and again. She placed her palm firmly on the van's dashboard for support. The listless quest for answers a few minutes before had now turned into a real chase. *'At least a lead is now in place.'*

'But why me, 'the thought kept occurring in her head as Mahesh tried his best to control the capsule vehicle, meandering downwards into the capital.

Given the nature of her work, it demanded journalistic chutzpah or the courage for going into the further to seek and find. Aditi by virtue of her experience in such a short career span had oodles of it packed in her and a story of this magnitude was a novelty for her career.

'The first murder case,' she kept reminding herself.

She took out the paper where she had jotted down the address a few minutes earlier and kept looking at it. Like her journalistic sojourn in the State's borders many moons ago, she hadn't got a chance to explore the land in its entirety, a place known to everyone in the world as the one blessed by the Gods. She had immediately fallen in love with the familiar geographical tracts and contours any hill station had to offer. Her transition from the sweaty confusion of heat and disorder to the cool climes of the hills had been dramatic and episodic to say the least. She had relished in the exotica of the place. From the terraced fields, to lined prayer flags of different hue and colours, from the monks ambling about their business to serenity and contentment writ large on the faces of the Sikkimese denizens, it had been a short visual treat and Aditi had discovered warmth and peace not only in the crowded capital but also in its remote hinterland.

But her work had unplucked her from the place, as she had just about begun to bask in the hospitality and freshness of the terrain and place. And she had made it a point to revisit the place in the future.

'How your wishes get answered?' Aditi kept peering into the hurriedly scrolled address and folded it neatly and safely tucked it away in the confines of her fluffy cardigan.

She quickly took out an IPAD and googled the place. A page popped up and she began reading, immersed in the land's magical histories and myths even as Mahesh gunned the vehicle as they sped away from the capital.

ENTER THE BARDO.

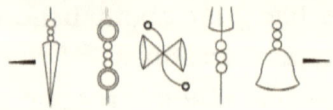

An old man in his late 60s heaved heavily as he tried to trudge upwards on the beaten path towards St. Mary's School, Kurseong. He tried to keep his steps firm as the heavy bundle attached at the end of his slender bamboo stick often kept him off balance. Durga Raj Neupaney, a local resident with a small arable land to his name and six mouths to feed, had been conducting this routine of carrying the bindle without fail for well over 20 years. Every morning and at night, he meticulously prepared food and made it into a bundle, starting the uphill exercise. "To me, it is my humble duty," Durga Raj thought every time he made that uphill climb.

Today morning was no different, but a slight pace in his strides was evident as he panted and labored until he reached St. Mary's School. With his hands resting on the school's wall, he managed to catch a quick breather. "Another 15 minutes, and I'll have reached," he resumed walking upwards with much haste now.

Durga Raj was at a dead end. After walking for almost an hour, battling fatigue and hunger, he had finally made it to the place. The wear and depreciation of his strength over the years showed clearly in his thin, emaciated structure.

What stood before him was a grotto situated on a plateau. The lengthy clingy vines and random growth of the jungle made the cave almost invisible to the naked eye. But Durga had been to this place for many years, and he knew it like the back of his hand.

"I hope he is up and ready now," thought the man as he entered the grotto, a big cavernous place swallowing him up with each forward movement.

With only a portable source of illumination from his 10-rupee lighter to fire his biri, Durga found it enough as he skillfully snaked his frame in the lighter's minimum luminosity.

As he reached further into the belly of the cave, a mild light hit his eyes from the opposite end of the way.

"I was right, he is up," thought Durga Raj as he hastened into the light with the bundle firmly on his shoulders.

"Namaste," he whispered the faint words and immediately regretted doing so as the man in front of him hadn't finished his morning meditational retreat. Durga bowed down before him and as silently as possible, he arranged the food in front of him. He quietly scraped towards the end of one side of the meditating man, so as not to incur the wrath for the intrusion.

The man opened his eyes slowly after a moment's time and looked around him. A familiar thin frame stood at the side of him some few meters away.

"You're up early," the man said, breaking into a slight smile as he said those words.

"Yes, my master, just as you ordered last night," Durga's reverence for the man was sincere and unflinching.

"Yes, I've finished with my ritual ablutions and will have to leave early today," the man said, with some pride coming back into him. The feeling that had been lost in him for many years.

He quickly finished his food and changed into his Chyuba, his traditional attire. After laying down some orders for Durga Raj Neopaney, he walked out of his hermetic chamber and into the openness. The overwhelming blast of fresh air invigorated his system, and he began his walk downhill.

Sister Magdalene, the fiercely respected and strict principal of the school, began her quotidian pedantic exercise of attending to the institution she had been helming for years. Upon her arrival there and taking in the reins, the school that was St. Mary's had witnessed a sharp incline in academic standards. This she attributed to her robust staff and faculty, who were hand in glove with her vision of the development of the school with discipline and innovative pedagogy. After 20 years at the helm, she still devised ways and methods to bring her school and the students more academic glory. As she entered one of the rooms of the institute, she heard a slight rustle in some bushes above the refectory. The sound brought her to a standstill from her daily routine of rationing inventories for the school. A familiar face struck her as the source of noise came into full view.

Upon reaching the school, the man offered his greetings to the Sister in charge.

"So, you're finally out from your retreat, I see," the nun greeted back.

"Yes, some important matters back home need my attention. Sister, I've already ordered Durga Raj some things that need to be done. Here I am leaving a few thousand rupees in your care; please control the payment." The man handed a decent wad in a brown envelope to the nun.

She accepted it readily, as she had been doing all these years.

ENTER THE BARDO.

"Don't let him have it all, else he might squander everything in his twin vices of gambling and alcohol. "

"You know I won't," said the sister as she watched the man fade away into the distant garage the school owned.

He didn't bother to clean the dust off the covers as he positioned himself in his vehicle and fired the ignition.

After an hour of driving the expensive SUV, the man looked out at the spreading greenery below the road swathed with tea plantations... He had always felt humility and pride rush through his system as he starddled between Kurseong and Sikkim with unerring frequency... But today and uncanny pride overwhelmed the man as he rushed towards his home for an important event...

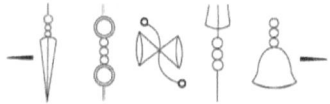

It had been about a year since Kalsang Rimpoche's daily visit to the Pelham psychiatric ward, and he had been happy with the outcome after diligent labor towards his pupil. Though the initial months had been frustrating and filled with failed attempts to reach out to Yang, the patient, the ambitions of the Rimpoche were further set back by the desolate and morose nature of the isolation wing. Yang's disconsolate and forlorn nature added further problems to the rehabilitation process. The sum of all the crestfallen and doleful environmental parts seemed to have stolen the energy from him.

But Kalsang had been strong. "Just one day at a time," the Rimpoche reminded himself and carried out his duty with full optimism. Every day from morning till dusk, the Rimpoche tried to assuage the grief that was deeply lodged in her psyche. Over the course of his involvement with Yang, he had tried to redirect her focus to various instruments of healing, and prime among them were books, huge religious opus that talked about the nature of the mind and how to heal oneself through spiritual and meditative practices. The books served as an icebreaker because Yang had at least given herself to reading and learning in the isolation wing right after the incident. For her, it was the single most cathartic experience. All her repressed emotions and suppressed anger were released in the process, and the Rimpoche had witnessed some hints of proclivity and predisposition towards reading and relishing the Buddhist books and understanding the iconography of the religion. Slowly, she showed signs of gravitation and acceptance, not only towards the idea of lessons derived from reading but also towards her visitor. The shackles of bitter memories from yesterday, which precluded another contact with a human being, much less a male being, gradually saw positivism in the world around her, and Yang once again embraced her life, which she thought had disintegrated and atrophied following the horrifying ordeal. But somewhere in the dark corners of her subconscious, the incidents of abject violence were playing in a loop, and the Rimpoche had often caught her off-guard, mumbling incoherently to the empty space in front of her. She would immediately stop after seeing him and would resume her normal self again.

"She just needs more company and less loneliness," the Rimpoche told himself on countless such encounters. Close to a year and amidst all the healing processes, the Rimpoche and his pupil discovered the spark between the two, a spark that was sincere and true, devoid of the desires of the flesh. Countless sessions of discussing books and religious ideologies kept them busy, and Kelsang was more than happy to oblige her with all her queries and confusions concerning life.

The Rimpoche still remembered the first time he entered Yang's room. She cut a lonely figure in her wing. Kelsang could hear strained echoes of muffled sounds and screams emanating from the other adjacent rooms. As he entered Yang's room, a strange, inexplicable quietness greeted him. He was at ease. And as he had waited to reach out and talk to her, the lama had realized the futility of the exercise. "I must be patient," the Rimpoche thought and eyed the patient carefully, his every move aimed at consoling and earning her trust. "No sudden movements. "

Then Kelsang's eyes caught hold of some of the books she had been reading. A congruent theme ran along those books lined on her small table, including the one she clutched. The book dealing with heavy esotericism was a familiar theme to all the Buddhist practitioners around the world. "I think I better make do with what I have," he thought.

"It is a very heavy book, in terms of understanding it fully," Kalsang Rimpoche tried to break the ice as he mustered enough courage to break into his non-routine assignment. Suddenly his world of prayer halls, retreats, religious lectures, and monastic practices was replaced by the anonymity of this mundane yet challenging exercise. The white-washed rooms of the institution did little to impress him. After all, no artificial beautification guaranteed success when it came to healing the sick, "The mentally sick," the Rimpoche reminded himself every time he stepped into the institution dedicated to healing the mentally ill.

The Rimpoche had gone on for a good 30 minutes about the basic premise and the structure of the book with her non-responsive patient in the solitary wing of the Pelham institute when, out of the blue, Yang opened her mouth for the first time in months.

"What happens to the body when it dies, Kelsang Rimpoche?" Yang had asked the teacher suddenly on the first session.

"The body is just a shell," he thought about blurting out the truth. But Kelsang, being ordered and directed by the authorities, had

taken care to monitor her subtle movements and nuances in speech and thoughts. Any idea or the mention of the word death would've been a red flag. Yet, Kelsang felt obliged to answer her queries as best as he could, for in her question, her words after months, the first sign of healing was witnessed and felt by the Rimpoche. Kelsang had, in the best possible manner, tried to answer her, sidetracking her mind from the imminent conclusion, any chronic mental head wouldn't mind having a stab at. He looked at her, a vacant stare facing him. The Rimpoche quickly doused the uncertainty filling his pupil with a lesson that was at the heart of every faith.

"But I have to tread carefully," he thought. Kelsang Rimpoche readied himself for a lecture that afternoon that dealt primarily with the phenomenon called death and the afterlife...Kalsang Rimpoche had also through years of learning developed a healing practice and had been using them recently on tours and prayer clinics...He called it healing through Regression and Hypnotism...The results so far were promising and he had proofs of tapes that lay secretly in his room at the temple premises...A lot of regression of lives and healing had been completed and achieved...However Kalsang Rimpoche was a bit worried and skeptical about a certain tape marked 23 which he carried with him everywhere he went...He further wanted to inform scientists and researchers at the IRRAB, New Delhi...Death and afterlife were according to the Rimpoche were phenomenons that were inevitable and least understood as far as the billions scattered around the planet were concerned, including his pupil Yang. And as much as the latter part was filled with fear, confusion, and apprehension, yet Kelsang impressed upon her the lessons of the afterlife known as the intermediate stage in the West...but more famously known as the Bardo Thodol to the rest of the Buddhists around the world...

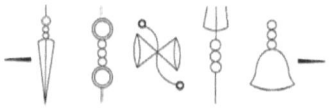

Brahma forced himself up the stairs, puffing and panting, with the gun now holstered on his hip. The monk below was clear in his instructions and directions. "Four doors to the left after the stairs end and an immediate right," he reminded himself as he progressed stealthily forward. Just then, a loud menacing sound of a vehicle being driven at frenetic speed caught the officer's ears. "Samar," the officer guessed, "and in good time."

Brahma reached the end of the flight and stopped for a moment, trying to catch his breath. The nearly vertical climb had taken a toll on his glutes and calf muscles. The depleted air slowly regained its place in his lungs. With respite returning, he then drew out his gun and moved cautiously towards the premeditated destination: The Monastery's Relic Room.

As he moved forward, Brahma could hear faint collective footsteps ascending, the sound growing nearer every second. After the officer moved past the final door, he attempted an immediate right. "What the. . . ," Brahma stood there confounded. A giant mural of a Wrathful deity was emblazoned across the entire section of a wall. He just stood there transfixed as he tried to make sense of the order. "But the instruction was strictly four. . . ," the officer stood flustered.

He didn't even hear the oncoming steps of the reinforcements, which drew clearer with the light of day. "Sir," officer Samar shouted, trying to grab his officer's attention. Startled, Brahma turned to face the sound. He feigned satisfaction at the sight of his backup. However, he was quick to notice an individual out of place. The same monk whom he had met downstairs was standing at the back of his men.

"You better have some explaining to do," the officer thundered towards the monk. "No more niceties and unnecessary obeisance." Brahma walked like a bull towards its matador of prey. Apparently, the inspector had a whiff of a discovery once inside the monastery's premises, akin to his officer's. Samar was quick to work out the probability of his superior's presence inside the room. But much to his dismay and his team's, he had been a witness to prayer sessions inside the room. The monk had signaled them upwards towards their officer's path, but policing instincts had prevailed, and he had dragged the monk alongside him just to prove his words. Facing the glare of the officer and his charge towards the monk now, he then realized that the monk had been telling the truth all along.

"What have you got to say to this?" the bull snarled angrily, his mannerisms ruthless and direct. The monk didn't know what the officer meant, after all, he had instructed him well and correctly.

"I don't see what your problem is, officer," the monk looked at the glaring eyes and stood unfazed.

"What do you mean?" the officer barked, much to everyone's shock and surprise.

"I followed the instructions, your directions, and yet you ask me what seems to be the problem?"

"Look here, do you see this?" the officer signaled to the entire dimensions of the solid concrete.

"Do you think there is a door here? It is just a big slab of cemented wall," Brahma fumed. The monk then let out a sigh. "So that's the problem," he thought and breathed a sigh of relief.

"Well, officer," the monk began, "if you look at it closely, at the painting or the walled mural of this God, you'll be able to mark out distinct divisions and cracks in the walls."

"And what's that supposed to mean?" the officer goaded.

"That means it is a huge door engineered out of a single slab of stone," the monk concluded.

The officer and his team looked amazed. The armed personnel had just discovered a variant of colors filling the figures and other objects surrounding the figure. The idea of a door had never met their prying eyes.

Samar, tried to make sense of the word "God" as he stood there, looking at the menacing figure garlanded with skulls, with fire blazing around it, and adorned with a wrathful and angry smile.

Yangtso Brahma walked up close to the door, looking for a thin vertical crevice, a division any door would have. He eyed the entire slab from all the corners and proceeded to feel them using his hands. His hands ran softly into the cement slab of a canvas, caressing the microscopic ridges and peaks that the vast geography of the mural threw up. And as he bent down and scoped the belly of the painting, he noticed something that seemed straight out of a Tolkien fantasy. "Is that what I think it is?" Brahma felt the crack that was naked to the unobservant human eye and ran his pinky through the elusive lithe slit. "A keyhole," Brahma turned around and looked at the monk as if demanding an answer.

"Officer," the monk called out to him in total reciprocity.

Brahma looked up. "The keys to this door remain with the head monk of this monastery. With him and him only, the power to open and lock this sacred room resides. Now we all know what the incident which he was first witness to has done to him emotionally and psychologically. And the other monks are trying their best to locate and reach out to him as we speak. "

"Really, you expect me to believe that horse-piss," the tone grew harder. "We've been through a steeple chase here, and we have two monks, who in all probability are accomplices from this monastery detained at the precinct and who in all likelihood helped in the escape of your master, your Khenpo here, and. . ." The monk cut in with ferocity now, "You are overstepping your lines of assumptions here. Are you insinuating that the great Khenpo Lama Tashi is related to whatever has happened here at the monastery?" Now it was the monk's turn to grow rabid. "All you've done by coming here is desecrate this holy place, this institutional shrine home to millions of pilgrims and devotees alike. And you come here strapped and packing with these assorted armed possies with your inaccurate inferences and doubts. An act that is sacrilegious coming from a Buddhist like you." The monk stared at the man's nameplate as he spoke the words. The officer thought to rebut the monk's irrelevant assertions, but he wasn't done.

"Remember Officer, Khenpo here is the most revered teacher, and everyone here in this land is deeply attached to his teachings and mere presence. He is a great practitioner of the faith, a noble soul who has dedicated his entire life to the Dharma. Remember your inaccuracies and baseless fabrications cannot go unanswered." The monk stepped back.

The officer looked at the man for a long time and tried to assess the best response for such a situation. "Remember, we are here devoid of passions and prejudices, Lamla. We are operating on our instincts to uphold the law of this land. I know your passions are running high, and I empathize with you." The officer paused and looked into the stony slab again. "But a murder has occurred here in this very holy place, and such a heinous crime demands a strong hand to suppress those responsible. The doubt strictly is out of sound deductions, in that the main head, the Khenpo at this such an important and crucial juncture, is missing from the scene. Now, what does that say about his stand on things here?" The officer looked around and muttered, "Proper Karmic comeuppance is coming your way, whoever you are." The officer slapped on the concrete in front of him and turned around immediately to resume his rebuke.

But as he did so, he met the few eyes of his personnel looking dazed in front of him. *"What's with their gaze?"* the officer thought. But the eyes weren't trained at the officer; they went beyond him. Slowly Brahma followed their inquisitive glance and saw what had ticked them. He focused on the lowest of the slab. A tiny luminous angle had been created with the opposing slab. "It's open," he gasped.

A further push, and the entire assembly of police personnel and a monk were now treading past the portal of a cement door and past it. A wide array and a huge collection of sacred relics swept by them as the officer and his team were hell-bent on a single agenda. The relics faced them from the safety of the bulletproof transparent shields, all stacked and ready to a pilgrim's delight.

Brahma tried to weave into a sea of mazes with his personnel in tow. Officer Samar, tucked in safely behind the officer and made a sudden halt as so did his officer. He looked around for some signs of movement. As he did, he came directly in visual contact that rattled him. A set of a skull and what was once someone's healthy set of teeth, now missing some bicuspids and a few others stared at the two law enforcers. "Someone needs a cosmetic dental procedure," the Inspector Samar was thinking of prophylaxis. The officer felt lucky in a way as the visceral objects that gave him such a fright were safely ensconced inside the glass. The dental deficit clearly shaking the Officer and Samar more than the skull itself.

Brahma listened intently and heard a collective ruffle of retreating steps from the northwest corner of the room and held his ground for further decibel confirmation. He turned around and motioned the officer and his personnel to hold still. "Any moment now," the officer breathed under his neck. The armed personnel slowly clicked off the safety from their semi-automatics and readied themselves for a charge.

The steps became distant with each passing second, and Brahma had no option but to burst into a speed uncannily unfamiliar. His personnel followed suit, and as he dashed toward the direction of the sound, Brahma and his officers knew they had made the right choice. For in front, even as they sprinted across the room, the entire team were witnesses in speed to the two bodies running and retreating away from the noise and away from the law. From afar, the officer could make out a youth and an old monk as the fleeing suspects. "I was right, now I need confirmation," he thought as he rallied his personnel for one final dash.

The officer's brows furrowed in concentration and anticipation as he signaled for a final push, urging his personnel to use all their might and strength to apprehend the fleeing suspects. A deafening bang echoed through the monastery's premises as the officers and personnel raced forward with force and speed, an unsettling sound in such a holy place. Their resounding footsteps in hot pursuit shook the ground beneath them.

As they closed in on the figures in the far west of the room, only the sound of hurried steps reverberated. The officer exhaled with satisfaction at the progress. "We're closing in," was the only thought in his mind. However, as they approached the supposed point of contact, they found nothing. "Are they running in different directions to confuse us?" the officer wondered as each attempt yielded no results. "We must be in the middle of the room," he thought as he slowed down to a jog.

The officer turned his attention to the monk following him. With their focus on the chase, they had failed to notice the decreasing luminosity as they ventured deeper into the relic room. The vastness of the room had left them bewildered and confused. Brahma asked his personnel to slow down, realizing that the echoing footsteps they'd heard for some time had been their own.

"They've stopped, it seems," the officer waited and peered into the almost opaque and dark chambers ahead.

"I know the area has a ready supply of current, especially this room," Brahma waved and signaled to the monk, conveying his thoughts.

The monk was equally surprised by the darkness. The room that should have been brightly illuminated now remained almost pitch-dark, with light only coming from the point of entry.

The monk explained to the officer, "Apart from the entrance, I'm not aware of any other exit in this room. I've been here only once and don't know the room well. "

Brahma scrutinized the monk closely as he spoke, and even in the dim light, he was convinced of the monk's honesty.

After a few moments, as they gathered around the officer, he began to discern some vision as his eyes adjusted to the dark. He noticed two dark figures about 100 feet away; it wasn't just his eyes adjusting, but a faint glow from a digital device that gave their position away. '*A mobile or a laptop, I'll take anything now*,' the officer thought.

The room once again echoed with swift steps as they approached the source of the digital glow. Brahma, with his gun drawn, halted abruptly with a few feet separating him from the fleeing suspects. He yelled, "Your hands where I can see them!"

The other personnel turned toward him and the direction of the suspects, their breathing heavy and panting. Metallic clicks and locks suggested their readiness for action. They surrounded the two individuals in the room.

With their bodies now still, Brahma approached the dark figures. "As I suspected from the beginning," he muttered under his breath, his weapon pointed firmly at them. The dimly lit room provided little room for escape and cover.

Karma Wangden, who had experienced countless similar situations in his past, now found himself on the other side of the law, facing a muzzle of a gun or guns... He stood frozen, his mind in inertia, and his body immobilized, while he and his Gyan-la became silent witnesses to the array of weapons aimed at them.

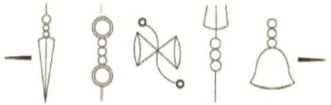

The sacrosanctity of the place had been violated by the intrusion of men and instruments of destruction, and the Khenpo wasn't prepared to accept it passively. He faced this predicament with the same determination that had gripped him in the face of what he and his student, Karma, believed to be an evil force they were trying to avoid. Despite the danger, the old monk maintained a calm demeanor as he approached the group of armed men. Surprised by his unwavering courage, the officer and his men collectively gasped silently.

The scene that unfolded before them was futile; the steel bayonets that usually made even criminals yield had no effect on the monk. Karma Wangden positioned himself protectively beside his teacher. The guns remained pointed at the duo as the Khenpo, in the cavernous room, spoke loudly and clearly, "What is the meaning of this? Do you not know that this is the holy relic room housing valuable religious treasures?"

A collective silence followed, drowning out the clinking of weapons trained on them, if only for a few seconds. "You have entered this holy place without permission or a warrant, bordering on desecration. Your actions are sacrilegious, having blatantly entered with guns. "

While the Khenpo was angered by the presence of armed men inside his temple, he was cautious not to escalate the situation. He still needed to verify the credentials of the men before him. "Carefully," he thought. But before he could inquire further, a tall man stepped forward.

"Are you the head monk of this place?" the man asked authoritatively in the dimly lit room. The Khenpo nodded in confirmation.

"Before you vent your misplaced anger, we have a couple of questions for you. The morning has certainly been eventful, hasn't it?" the officer holstered his weapon and signaled his men. They escorted the duo out of the relic room, with the monk from the study following them.

Once outside, the officer took a deep breath as fresh air revitalized him. Brahma sat in a nearby chair, waiting as the guards brought the men to him. Karma Wangden scrutinized the guards and their tight grip on his arms. He cast a reassuring glance at his teacher.

"You've been quite elusive this morning," Brahma remarked with a hint of frustration.

The old monk and Karma Wangden remained silent, prompting the officer to change his tone. "Why were you running from the police, from us?" he demanded, his tone shifting due to the suspects' silence. "The chase has been quite interesting. "

"Listen, officer," the Khenpo finally spoke. "We did not realize it was the police; we thought it was someone else." He tried to comfort his student by holding his hand. Karma reciprocated the gesture, a touch of defiance toward the armed men in his action.

The officer approached the duo and held up a CD. "Care to explain this?" Karma examined the spherical disc in the officer's hand, ready to go to great lengths to prove his master's innocence. He couldn't bear the thought of his teacher's impending disgrace, knowing deep down that the Khenpo was innocent and far removed from worldly sins.

"We are fully committed to helping you, Gyan La," Karma vowed.

"We've been fortunate that the scene of the crime was cleaned up quite well," Brahma remarked, looking at the composed Khenpo, who still radiated calmness despite his frailty. Karma, though on edge, was eager for confrontation, both verbal and physical, given the chance.

"We found nothing to investigate, except for a lifeless child's body with a distended belly on a gurney. The body had already been sanitized, saving us time and effort," the officer said with a sarcastic tone.

Brahma took out a cigarette, lit it, and took a few puffs, his mind gradually coming to life. He exhaled smoke, creating a smoky barrier between him and his suspects. "No matter the crime or the criminal, they always leave something behind for the police. Such noble souls," he quipped.

He signaled to his driver, who brought a notebook and placed it on the table in front of him. "What you're about to see will clarify the events that occurred this morning." Brahma inserted the disc into the drive, and they all watched as the surveillance footage from a camera placed inside the pedestal, housing the Gods of the faith, played.

The Khenpo sat through the entire playback with one thought in his mind: "Why didn't I think of that camera?"

ENTER THE BARDO.

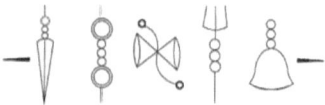

The Nechung oracle, along with three other head monks, all in their 70s, sat up straight and began comparing the unique dates scrolled upon some pages. These writings and images related to the answers regarding the next reincarnated lama.

"The place should be somewhere in the northern part of Sikkim," said one of them. 'One of us is absent from the proceedings today as you all know and the onus of the venerated Nun Ani Yangzey rests with me, 'Kalsang Rimpoche looked for approval after he said that...Everyone nodded their heads in assent as they compared the long list of places, times, and dates in their respective hands.

"Please make sure that the details regarding the new Rimpoche's birth come up correct, and we all agree on it unanimously. We certainly don't want any controversies later on," said the other head monk.

It was true that in the past, Buddhism and its system of appointing and selecting the next reincarnated head of various sects had run into oodles of religious controversies. The very system of selecting and appointing new Tulkus as reincarnated heads by the Nechung Oracle, the body responsible for such processes, had undergone some setbacks. There were instances where a certain head from a particular sect had gone against the selection process and decried a newly instated monk or Rimpoche. With that in the background, he had even gone to great lengths, purporting his own selected child Tulku as the 'genuine' reincarnation, courting controversies that resounded with ignominy to this day. Of course, the controversy and confusion surrounding such selection processes had started when the Chinese Communist Government, after usurping and taking hold of total governance in Tibet, had come up with their own sanctified Panchen Lama, another great Tibetan religious head after His Holiness the 14th Dalai Lama of Tibet. All these things had caused the philosophy of Buddhism to bear the brunt of eroding faiths and doubts, with some religious zealots terming Buddhism as fake and defaming the very institutional practice of selecting a new reincarnation as a massive religious facade.

Kelsang Rimpoche walked into the room where the Nechung oracles were with their discussions and signaled to one of the attendant head monks to get ready. Everyone bowed and obeyed the Rimpoche's directive, beginning to exit the room to join the big religious ritual outside the monastery.

"Just a matter of a few minutes now before they select and present to us the new head of the Nyingma dynasty," said one of the devotees waiting patiently for the exercise to begin, hopeful of receiving the much-needed blessing from the new Tulku.

The killer drew a long breath on hearing this. "Finally, it is about to start, the wait should be over in a matter of minutes before they start with the selection process," said the killer under his breath. "Gyan-la has assured me of the wonderful fruits that await me after all this is done and that my path towards enlightenment is guaranteed through my actions. I must make sure that they take notice of these actions and ruefully try to correct their ways and methods in propagating this beautiful philosophy throughout the world." The killer inched a step closer towards the periphery of the main circle, now lined with tables and stools for the participants and the oracles for the process, waiting impatiently like a deadly predator on the prowl for his hapless prey.

A loud metallic gong went off, capturing the area's attention with its resonance. As the loud musical Raadoongs with their menacing roars waved through the ambience, the giant doors of the Dubdi Monastery swung open. A tall, heavily built monk with closely cropped hair walked slowly towards the circle. His visage maintained the calmness and serenity of that of a learned and erudite man. He was followed by the Nechung oracles, and right after them came the three tiny participants, all decked up in lamaic robes loosely slung on their tiny bodies.

"Alas, it is about to start," said the killer.

ENTER THE BARDO.

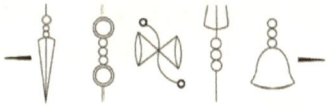

The fresh green juniper trees, slashed and heaped on top of embers on different parts of the Dubdi Monastery, emitted plumes of smoke billowing in every direction and engulfing the entire area in its holy nebulous fold. As the juniper burned, and the smoke crept and occupied any space in its path, the monastery looked awash in the amorphous haze of the smoke.

The loud Raadongs and the Gyalings, Buddhist wind instruments used on religious occasions, roared and screeched, the sounds reverberating everywhere. The instruments were followed by loud growls and chants, enabled by years of practice of manipulation of the vocal cords. The sounds thus created were extraordinary and pleasing to the ears. The loud bass tones and the deep intonations emanating from every single monk hid the real texts and the prayers that were being said, with only a few trained and familiar ears catching them.

ENTER THE BARDO.

The prayers came to an end, and everyone, including the hundreds of devotees, circled around the area where the test would take place. Kelsang Rimpoche, after nearing his seating pedestal adorned and embellished with colorful cloths and scarves, sat down slowly, legs crossed, and looked at the hundreds of people thronging the event. He gave a smile to everyone, and after he sat, the devotees and the tiny tots, the real participants, along with their parents, bowed and sat, waiting for the selection process to begin.

"We welcome you all," announced an elderly monk, the opening words meeting silence from the crowd. "We are all present here for the selection of a highly learned Lama," the words met with collective assents and nods everywhere. "The Late Great Gelug Rimpoche, Rimpoche Ugen Pintso's untimely death 3 years ago had left the sect leaderless, and after months of patience, prayers, and hard work, the Late Rimpoche's Shyapchi, Norden Zamyang, has, after tediously studying, deliberating with the oracles, and following the signs and symbols left behind by the Late Rimpoche before his death, now reaped great fruits in the form of these three tiny individuals, who might be the successor and the next leader of the Gelug sect," the monk said, pointing reverentially towards the three tots perched atop high stools precariously, flanking one side of Kelsang Rimpoche's seat. "The onus and the responsibility now lie with one of these three boys, who after selection and confirmation, shall be identified as the next great leader." Having said that, the elderly monk walked up to Kelsang Rimpoche's seat and after holding his robe and covering his mouth, whispered something to the Rimpoche in utter respect. The Rimpoche nodded and whispered something back. The lama bowed before him and retraced back. "Under the aegis of Kelsang Rimpoche, we the monks and the staff, along with the monastery's trustees, now commence the selection process." Everyone said a tiny prayer with bated breaths and folded hands as the ritual began, of choosing a new leader.

Kelsang Rimpoche took out a long parchment from a duffel bag filled with handwritten words and an assortment of animal images of all hue and color. As he did so, he directed the three little children to sit in the low stools placed directly in front of him. A group of mature monks started with their prayer chants again, heralding the start of the selection process. It had begun indeed. Three years back, the Gelug sect of Buddhism had lost a precious learned/wise man or Rimpoche at the ripe age of 80. The departed, Rimpoche Ugen Pintso, had succumbed to the injuries from an accident after his cavalcade had suffered a head-on collision with a goods-filled lorry on the nearby highway. The sect had indeed lost a great learned man, and it was up to the remaining head monks along with Kelsang Rimpoche to try and locate the next re-incarnated Tulku fast. Thus had begun the arduous task of following the signs and hints that would help them in locating the young monk. The funeral pyre of the late great Rimpoche had drawn up plumes of smoke that had pointed in a certain direction, and the shyapchi or the servant of the late Rimpoche when he was alive, under the aegis of Kelsang Rimpoche, had with great patience and searching zeroed in on those three little tots from similar geographical parts of the State. And the final test of being able to select their various items related to their previous lives would decide the final outcome, of who would be the next reincarnated high lama of the sect in question.

After the prayers, the elderly monk gestured to someone inside the monastery. The young monk standing inside the main temple door bowed and hurried inside. He entered the scene carrying a big table stacked with old clothes and personal items from years gone by. He was helped by three or four other monks in carrying the table. The big table was placed in the circle, in front of Kelsang Rimpoche. The test would be simple: any child from among the three who picked out the items correctly for three rounds would win and be crowned as the next reincarnation. The temple authorities and the oracles had already homed in on the three probable based on the place of birth, gifts, and an uncanny behavior, distinct from what one would normally expect from 2-3-year-olds. . . 'behavioural abnormalities linked to previous births...a potent signal', said the Nechung Oracle...The items placed would be their items from a previous life, ranging from clothes, walking sticks, seals, watches, etc. , and the connection and finally being able to identify those items from previous births wouldn't miss them because they were believed to be the Bodhisattvas, or the reincarnated learned ones, living through Samsara to serve the living...

ENTER THE BARDO.

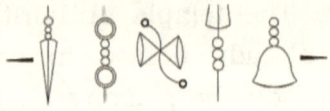

'Let me explain,' Lama Tashi said slowly as he and Karma stood erect, careful with their movements so as not to antagonize the weapons trained at them. Karma Wangden inhaled slowly, eyeing the bunch of trigger-happy police personnel now surrounding them in an arc. He knew that any slow action on their part, after being witness to a surveillance video, had a greater probability for the ruthless killer to succeed. And yet, Karma knew that it was only a question of time, of how long before the authorities doubted them prima facie as prime suspects of a murder inside the monastery. The needle of suspicion, Karma knew, definitely pointed towards them and naturally so in the eyes of the law. He turned and gave his Gyan-la a slight frown. But as soon as he gestured that, Karma suddenly remembered the fallout of a promise of being an accomplice and how he had sworn to protect and help the Khenpo nab this killer. Not that they had committed the murder, but he had utter faith and trust in his teacher's words and deeds. His frown now metamorphosed into an expression of solace, his eyes delivering a comforting glance to the teacher.

'Please, ' Yangtso Brahma retorted, 'Remain where you are and restrict your movements, natural or sudden. ' 'Remember we will not hesitate to shoot you if you do not comply. ' The officer, now sure of their guilt following their earnest willingness to explain after being apprehended, slowly walked towards them, and as he did so, the entire team of personnel homed in on them, closing the arc to a distinct point inwards...

****

Karma Wangden and the old Lama sat crouched in their seats at the back of a police van. They knew that whatever little chances they had of preventing the murders were now on a downhill slide. It wasn't for lack of trying as much it was for getting an opportunity in the first place from the prying eyes of the police. But they couldn't give up, as not only lives but also the faith was at stake. The faith that took years and years of building and which provided solace and comfort to millions around the globe was now facing a threat, and now it was up to the two to prevent such a catastrophic event.

As the IPS himself accompanied the felons on the same vehicle, he ruefully looked at Khenpo Lama Tashi, his eyes evidently displaying despise and contempt. He urgently plonked himself on the driver's seat and then sped down the Rumtek road towards his precinct.

As they neared the cantonment area, Karma adjusted in his seat, ready for an action after a few seconds. After being hesitant for a while, he spoke to the officer in front of him.

"There is going to be some more murders," Karma blurted, his sudden assertion hanging ominously in the air after being said...

The officer in an instant decelerated after hearing that and slowly turned towards the two seated behind and eyed them questionably, his hands blindly controlling the wheel as it reached the army cantonment area in the suburbs. 'This better be real, ' Yangtso Brahma thought and prepared to stop the car...

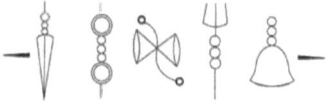

'I don't know how to offer an explanation, Gyan La,' Karma whispered to the Abbot...Lama Tashi and Karma Wangden slowly stood erect, careful with their movements so as not to antagonize the weapons trained at them. They had one chance to prove their innocence, and he knew that he should tread carefully. Their hands and legs bound by chains offered friction to movements, and their restraints at the moment were secured further by two 6-foot constables holding them with a vice-like grip. The officer lit a cigarette and took in a long drag, exhaling plumes of nicotine discharge. His strong jawline and cheekbone muscles pulsed with each pull. He stubbed the last remaining stick and adjusted himself on the bull bar of the vehicle. They were standing at a highway cliff, precariously placed on a boulder with a deep chasm of space underneath.

'It would be a good time for a talk,' chuckled the officer as he turned his steely gaze to the two captives. 'My son, it would do wonders if you listen to what I have to say with an open mind,'

Lama Tashi said, choosing his words carefully. 'My innumerable times spent in the learning and practice of the faith should put me in a position to explain some things about the incident that occurred at the monastery this morning. ' He projected a genial look towards the listening officer, trying to elicit a feeling of trusting faith. There was none. All he encountered was the officer's vacant and piercing gaze, free from fear or favor.

"The events that've occurred in the past few hours will put a dent in the faith, lose millions of worshippers who've reposed their trust in the dharma." Lama Tashi exhaled as he chose his words. "I have no time for melodrama and lies," shot back the officer, immediately lighting another stick. "I'm going on a limb here and hearing your pleas; you can do better than to waste my time with your slow approach." With that, the officer signaled the old monk to continue. . . fast.

The old monk, weighted and burdened by the events, looked forlorn and weary. His fingers clinging to Karma Wangden's jacket loosened time and again, a frailty of age. A hint of a smile broke on the old monk's face, and he asked, "What is the one thought that scares us in this life, my son?"

'Something that is bigger than all the fears put together. It makes us cower and cringe. The mere thought of it creeps up your spine, rendering you powerless—an inevitable phenomenon that covers you in its deathly talons and tears your peace asunder. '

'And yet, 'Lama Tashi resumed, 'nothing is as beautiful and promising as death itself. '

'Death. . . ?! Beautiful and promising, you say?' retorted the officer, who along with the other police personnel, was confounded by the monk's words.

"Yes, my son, it is beautiful as death ends one cycle. . ." Lama Tashi continued, "and all the things connected to the body in the present life come to a close. And it is hopeful because it heralds the start of a consciousness in the next body, a fresh start to a new beginning. . ."

"Stop it," replied the officer. He rose from the vehicle to stand in front of the monk, eyeing him angrily. "You promised me an explanation, and this is what you give me?" He threw away the last remaining cigarette and resumed, "I give you a chance at redemption, thinking that you've got a sound and plausible explanation for the murder. But all this abstract and esoteric religious talk doesn't hold much water. The stories and theories are best left to books and monasteries. Here in the real world, no one will buy it. . ." With that, he turned around and exhaled deeply and said, "Now if you have something better, then say it, or else..." The officer motioned for others to start to the capital.

"Wait,"said Karma. "All the Khenpo is saying is the murders have a motive, and it's clear that the killer won't stop anytime soon..."

"...And the reason he is talking about death is that the murder has been attributed to and has links to Buddhism and the esoteric Buddhist texts which describe in detail about death and the journey beyond..."

The officer, shell-shocked, didn't know how to react. . . For a while he was transported to a hospital's emergency ward in the distant past...He snapped out of it however...He just stood there mute...Karma Wangden continued trying to find words and phrases that would convince the officer...

"Ever heard of terms like 9 levels of Hell, Purgatory, NDEs, Astral Projections, Mental Projections in the Afterlife, The Bright white Light or The Collective Force/Records also called the Akashic Records?" Karma asked the personnel around them. A blurting of words more than a question...After meeting silence for a few seconds, Karma mustered a measure of confidence...He shrugged a bit and commenced, "I can spend an entire session talking about it, or we can try to nab the killer responsible and prevent further murders."

The officer shook his head. That made sense. If he is so convinced that he can prevent the 'other' murders and help catch the killer, he mounted the vehicle, and the others followed. *'Let's see how far he takes us...'*

Yangtso Brahma was all ears...

www.ingramcontent.com/pod-product-compliance
Lightning Source LLC
LaVergne TN
LVHW091703070526
838199LV00050B/2264